MW00834396

GUILTY
UNTIL PROVEN
INNOCENT

Cylinda Mathews

Copyright © 2021 Cylinda Mathews
All rights reserved
First Edition

Fulton Books
Meadville, PA

Published by Fulton Books 2021

This is a work of fiction. Names, characters, places and incidents are products of the author's imagination or are used fictitiously and are not to be construed as real. Any resemblance to actual events, locales, organizations, or persons, living or dead, is entirely coincidental.

All rights reserved. No part of this book may be used or reproduced in any manner whatsoever without written permission, except in the case of brief quotations embodied in critical articles and reviews.

ISBN 978-1-63985-267-3 (paperback)
ISBN 978-1-63985-271-0 (digital)

Printed in the United States of America

PROLOGUE

He who walks with wise men will be wise, but the companion of fools will suffer harm.

—Proverbs 13:20

Five years earlier…

Brad woke suddenly with heart pounding and sweat beading his forehead. The nightmare had to be worse than reality. Throwing off the covers from his lean frame, he swung his legs over the side of the bed, planting his feet firmly on the floor. He sat tensed, running a shaky hand through sleep-mussed hair; his gut clenched knowing *the* day was at hand. The day he'd turn over evidence he collected. Peering over at the bedside clock, it read 4:45 a.m. He reached over and turned off the alarm. The last thing he wanted or needed was to wake Michaela.

He rubbed his forehead, trying to alleviate the headache that threatened; procrastinating wouldn't do any good, not today, not tomorrow, or even the day after.

Slowly rising, he crept around the bedroom in the grays of early morning dawn, gathering his clothes to slip into the bathroom to dress. Zipping his jeans, he placed his hands on either side of the sink and peered at his reflection in the mirror. He flinched seeing red-rimmed eyes, pallid skin, a five-o-clock shadow, and dishwater-blond hair that needed trimmed. He splashed cold water on his face and grabbed the hand towel next to the sink and briskly dried off. He needed something stronger than coffee.

Cracking the bathroom door, he peered out; Michaela was still asleep. Closing the door softly, he lifted the lid from the toilet tank and grabbed the plastic ziplock bag he hid there. Pulling a couple pills from the bag, he downed them without water and then replaced the bag in its hiding spot.

God, what would Michaela think if she knew how far down the rabbit hole he'd gone? This wasn't who he was, but it was who he'd become.

Turning off the light and opening the door, he made his way across the bedroom. Leaning over the bed, he peered at the form of his sleeping wife and stilled. She slept soundly despite the argument they had the night before. With soft hair splayed across the pillow and long lashes resting gently upon fair cheeks, she lay peacefully, breathing deeply in slumber.

The argument had gotten heated. He found himself laying down alternatives, and he shook his head recalling what he'd said. He knew how much the bed-and-breakfast meant to her. And having it dropped in her lap as an inheritance from her late aunt had touched her deeply. She practically grew up there thriving under the care and tutelage of her aunt. And then like an ass, he was telling her to sell it or else. He knew deep in his heart he wouldn't make her sell, but he also knew if push comes to shove, she'd give it up for him.

In truth, he disliked the amount of time she spent there helping her aunt. And as her aunt had grown weaker, the amount of time Michaela spent at the bed-and-breakfast grew longer. And the more hours she worked to maintain the business, the more it bothered him. He never shared her enthusiasm for the place.

He rubbed his eyes in frustration. He had a considerable drive ahead of him to turn over evidence that might seal his fate. But for all he knew, no one was the wiser to his deception or that he wanted out. Dealing in fine arts and antiquities, he stumbled into a black-market ring accidentally and was now in over his head.

What started out as a small operation in accepting and selling black-market goods turned out to be so lucrative that he was drawn in. His greed got the best of him—all with good intentions, of course. He hated the small rental they had lived in and wanted to provide Michaela with a nice home and a future they could all depend on. That was his reasoning at first. He should have stopped when they had plenty of money saved up and a new home and cars. He shook his head realizing where his thoughts led; he shouldn't have gotten involved, period! Though he wanted financial independence for his family, they were happy. Now, they had everything he hoped to provide materially, but the long hours at work put a strain on their marriage. If he was honest with himself, he was away from home most nights to receive stolen goods.

He sighed deeply. He was in too deep which had him fearing for his life. Trying to make amends for the error of his way was at best risky, if not downright foolhardy. With shady characters whose god was the almighty dollar, one just didn't turn state evidence against them without consequences. He rubbed his chin sporting blondish whiskers as he recalled the nightmare that woke him.

Michaela stirred in her sleep and threw the covers off her upper body; Brad's eyes followed her movement, and his breath caught in his throat as he peered down at her slender form which was barely concealed under the light nightgown.

The evening before last was in such sharp contrast to the fight they had the previous night. Michaela put Chase to bed, and when she walked into the bedroom, he tossed the covers back for her.

"The TV isn't on!" she exclaimed. "Are we going to bed already?"

He pulled the covers down further to reveal his erection, and her eyes widened before mouthing "Oh!" She smiled and asked him to wait a moment as she disappeared into the bathroom.

Opening the door, Michaela stepped into the pool of light cast from the bathroom doorway. She purchased a negligee that revealed far more than it hid. Outlined by the light that haloed her, she stood hesitantly. Her breasts, fuller after giving birth to Chase, were begging to be kissed as they teased the sheer fabric. Rounded hips flared from a tiny waist that he appreciatively admired. She smiled again and turned the bathroom light off, leaving just the light on from the small bedside lamp. The bedroom was cast in shadows, and the flickering light cast from the fire in the fireplace danced around the room, adding to the ambience as it crackled and popped in the hearth.

Bending over the bed, her soft hair brushed his chest as she stretched to kiss him. "Do you like it?" she breathlessly asked.

"Mmmm, I do!"

"I bought it a few weeks ago, waiting for the right time to surprise you."

He reached out and circled her areola through the sheer fabric with his finger. Then he leaned down and kissed her through the negligee. She moaned softly, letting her head fall back, enjoying his attention.

"Sweetheart, I have a surprise too," he said, lifting his head from her breast.

"What?"

"Here…" He reached into his nightstand drawer and pulled out a small box.

She looked up at him with shimmering eyes. "Is this for me?"

He nodded. "Do you like them?" he asked, opening the lid to reveal diamond earrings.

She laughed and threw her arms around his shoulders.

"Let me show you just how much I like them," she said, smiling.

Lifting the hem of the negligee over her head, she inched it over her naked body and dropped it, letting it pool on the floor beside the bed. Slowly easing the clasps that held the satin stockings, she teased them off each leg and let them feather down to land beside the negligee. And then using her fingertips, she slowly pushed the matching lace panties down over her buttocks, revealing a firm backside that had Brad's undivided attention. Pulling them off slowly, she let these, too, fall to the floor. Brad guessed she had no idea she was performing a strip tease of sorts that fueled his need for her. Now fully naked, she sat on the bed, tucking her legs beneath her; she donned the earrings. Lifting her hair off her shoulders, she turned her head from side to side so Brad could admire the diamonds.

He had eyes only for her.

Straddling his lap, she kissed him while he reached up to cup her breasts, and then holding her hips, he guided her onto his erection, slipping his fullness inside. She arched, enjoying their lovemaking as he nibbled at her breasts, neck, and ears.

Their passion continued into the night, and he almost reached out now to awaken her then hesitated.

He couldn't. He had to set things right before she ever found out.

CHAPTER 1

But the Lord said unto Samuel, "Look not on his countenance or on the height of his stature because I have refused him."

—1 Samuel 16:7a

Present day

Dropping the cup, it shattered, and coffee splattered everywhere. Michaela was vaguely aware of the brown stain dampening the hem of her jeans and slowly spreading or that her cloth slippers were now wet. Snickers yelped, jumped up from where he was lying beside the desk and ran for the dog door. Only when she stepped forward and flinched was she completely aware of the shards of glass that penetrated the flimsy slippers covering her feet.

"Ouch!" She grabbed the desk chair and rolled it forward so she could sit.

Continuing to stare at the TV screen, she couldn't get over the shock of hearing that an acquaintance was found dead in his home. This man, though, had been more than an acquaintance. He was an ex-boyfriend, if one could really call him a boyfriend at all. It wasn't really serious but merely a few dates that ended badly. Michaela pushed back the tendrils of hair that escaped the clip on her head that held the reddish-brown mass of curls off her neck.

"Foul play is suspected in Mr. Collins's death, but for now, the police are not saying much as this will be an ongoing investigation."

CHAPTER 1

The reporter stood in front of James's estate where crowds gathered standing behind yellow crime-scene tape. "As more information comes forth, I'll keep you updated. Now back to Rod in the studio."

No, no…what happened! Michaela shook her head as she sat back in the desk chair. James was good-looking; one could even say he was too handsome. But where he excelled in looks, he lacked in character.

They met when James booked a room at the bed-and-breakfast while having his home fumigated. Michaela recalled the bright-red convertible sports car that pulled up out front of the B&B. A handsome, dark-headed man exited the car, slamming the door behind him. Leaning over the car into the back seat, he pulled out a briefcase and laptop before turning and heading toward the door.

"Hi! I need a room for a couple of nights…" he said without looking up as he laid his stuff on the counter and proceeded to pull out his wallet.

"Would you like a room with a view of the ocean or of the gardens?" she asked, standing up from behind the desk.

Looking up, he slowly smiled as his eyes assessed her from top to bottom and then back up again as she walked toward the counter. "What do you recommend?"

Michaela couldn't help but be drawn to this handsome stranger with deep-blue eyes. Pushing her hair back behind an ear, she said, "The gardens are nice, but the view of the ocean is stunning. Right now, you can have your pick of either."

"I'd probably be distracted by the ocean, so I guess it's the garden view. I need to work…" he said with a lift of his brow, and leaning into the counter, he sighed in resignation, waving a hand over the briefcase and laptop to emphasize his point.

"Ah, then I shall give you the room at the end so you won't be disturbed by other guests," she replied.

Once he was checked in, Michaela walked him to his room when she could have easily given him directions. She unlocked the door to his room and opened it before stepping back, allowing him to enter.

"Nice," he said, taking a quick glance around the room. Turning back to her, he continued, "Even without the ocean view, I might be distracted by the beauty I see before me."

Michaela blushed and dipped her head. His laughter snapped her eyes back to his face, and he reached out, cupping her cheek. "You're refreshing. I haven't seen a girl blush in I don't know when. I'm afraid I didn't catch your name."

"It's Michaela!"

"It's nice to meet you, Michaela," he said, dropping his hand back to his side. "Will you be around tomorrow?"

She smiled revealing dimples. "Yes, I actually own this place," she replied and feeling a need to elaborate, "It was left to me by my late aunt."

"Well then, I hope to see you often."

Later, she remembered thinking that it'd been way too long since she was interested in other men. Brad was her world, had been their world. She needed to get on with life not just for her sake but Chase's as well. Chase would be excited over a red convertible parked out front, and he'd be pestering her with questions over its owner.

Walking toward the front office, Michaela appreciatively admired the bed-and-breakfast, trying to see it as a guest would. The six guest rooms were located at the back of the B&B with three on the west overlooking the ocean with a balcony to better enjoy the view while the opposite three rooms backed up to gardens with a small patio so guests could enjoy the outdoors.

The dining area, situated between the hallway leading to the guest rooms and the common area, held a few small tables for those wishing to breakfast alone and one larger table for guests who preferred to mingle. Both the dining area and common room had French doors leading to a long balcony overlooking the ocean with seating arrangements for guests to linger and enjoy the view.

The common area was for guests to meet others, relax, and gather for the social hour or simply sit idle to work a jigsaw puzzle, read a book, or play a game. Both the main areas boasted large beautiful rock fireplaces, making the rooms, though large, feel cozy. On cold days, guests seemed to enjoy sitting on the sofa or recliners that were placed around the hearth where a fire crackled and popped with a glass of wine in hand while they conversed about their day.

She smiled to herself and nodded her head; Aunt Jane would be so pleased with what she'd done with the bed-and-breakfast!

At first, while James was booked at the B&B, he flirted with her outrageously, and she enjoyed their bantering. But after a few days of outright flirting, staying longer than the original two nights he requested, he asked her out, taking her to an expensive restaurant.

She was nervous to be dating again after so many years. Indecisive over what to wear, she discarded several dresses before choosing one she thought appropriate but yet sexy.

Later that evening, they sat out under the stars on her private patio to have a glass of wine. He leaned in and, putting a finger under her chin, lifted her head, and warm lips brushed hers. The mixture of his heady aftershave, the smell of gardenias blooming in the garden, coupled with jasmine had her head spinning. The wine also helped to relax her, and she found herself enjoying the kiss. As the kiss lingered, his hands wandered, and he brushed her breast before placing his hand around her nape to pull her closer. Her senses stirred as the kiss became heady, and she found herself leaning in for more.

He moved his hand from her nape to her shoulder, and she moaned softly as his fingers grazed the swell of her breasts. She tilted her head back as he nibbled on her neck and kissed her earlobes. She sighed contentedly, enjoying the moment.

His hand splayed across her breast, and Michaela wanted to go limp as heat flooded, but she couldn't allow him to take further liberties. She reached for his hand, holding it softly in hers.

"You're beautiful..." he murmured while continuing to feather soft kisses on her neck and earlobes. Then his head lowered further, and he was feathering kisses over the swell of her breasts, and she wanted to give in to the feelings he stirred. But she couldn't consciously allow this to continue for several reasons; one of which she felt it a betrayal to Brad, and she was no longer taking birth control.

James raised his hand and pulled the fabric of her dress away from her breasts, and she inhaled sharply. "Please, stop. I'm not into casual sex," she said while pushing him away.

After he checked out of the B&B, he stopped by one evening after Chase had gone to bed. She hadn't expected him to drop by, much less to knock on the door to their private quarters at nine in the evening. She had already dressed for bed and told him she wasn't prepared for company, but he seemed to brush off her protests, saying he didn't plan to stay long. He just needed to see her.

"I missed you;" he declared. One thing led to the next, and he had Michaela moaning softly as she let him take things a step further in their lovemaking. He gently nudged aside her robe, and lowering his head, he suckled a budded nipple into his mouth through her thin nightgown.

She gasped, and placing her hands on his shoulders, she tried pushing him away. He lifted his head and looked at her with confusion, which quickly shifted to anger. "You want this as much as I do!" he rasped out.

"Please, don't…stop…" she whispered.

He chuckled. "Don't stop…"

"We can't. I can't!"

He left the bed-and-breakfast that evening, clearly angered over her refusal to have sex with him.

Michaela jumped when the phone rang, bringing her back to the present. She needed to clean up this mess before any of the guests came by the office. Using the rollers on the desk chair, she rolled herself back far enough to where she could reach the phone and picked up the receiver.

"Good afternoon, this is Bayside Bed-and-Breakfast. this is Michaela speaking, how may I help you?"

"Michaela, it's Heather. Do you have the news on?"

"Yes, and I just heard. I can't believe that James is dead. They're saying it's foul play. While we ended on bad terms, I would never wish this on him. Do you think the police might question me since we dated not long ago?"

"It's hard to believe he's dead, but at the same time, maybe he went too far if you know what I mean. And I doubt the police will talk to you. He was a playboy and had plenty of females falling for him. And between you and me, I think there were quite a few women who were more than happy to fall in bed with him, hoping for a marriage proposal from one of the richest men in this town."

"I know. I can't help but think back to the last time when he tried to…force me." Michaela shuddered at the memory. "He was furious when I refused…"

"You should have reported it to the police."

"Maybe…"

"No maybe to it! Do you want me to stop by?"

"No, actually I need to clean up this broken mug and the coffee that splattered everywhere."

"What happened?"

"When I heard about James on the news, I dropped my coffee cup. It's not a big deal really."

Hanging up the phone, she recalled the last time she saw James. She reached up and tentatively laid a hand on her cheek, recalling how hard James had slapped her, causing her head to whip to the side. She'd been stunned. He immediately apologized and cupped her face, kissing her cheek with tenderness.

"I want more, Michaela. I need you! Let's go to your bedroom so I can make this up to you…"

The bell above the door to the front office rang, alerting them that someone had come in. She welcomed the intrusion and the safety that a newcomer brought.

James let his hand fall away and then ran it through his dark hair, mussing it. Stepping back, he stared at the cupboards above her head. Dropping his eyes to hers, he whispered another apology and then turned, exiting the back door.

She never saw James after that though she feared he may show up unexpectedly during the day or, worse, late at night. She felt her resolve to abstain slipping and was afraid she might have gone to bed with him. He awakened feelings she thought long dead. It had been exciting to share the warm, passionate kisses, and when he touched her, she responded.

She pulled her slippers off and threw them in the trash, noting that no fragments remained in her flesh. As Michaela worked to clean up the mess and pick up shards of glass, she recalled how

Heather, not trusting James from the very beginning, had inquired around about him. James liked to play the field. That still hurt. She had come to think that he was actually falling for her, so to find out that while he was seeing her he also was seeing other women at the same time was a literal slap in the face. She stopped momentarily and closed her eyes against the sudden pain she felt. Yet she was glad to have found out his dark side knowing all along; he would never take Brad's place.

CHAPTER 2

The heart is deceitful above all things and desperately wicked. Who can know it?

—Jeremiah 17:9

Tom and Sean sat in the squad room behind their respective desks writing up reports when a folder landed on Tom's desk. "Got a new case for you two. James Collins…" their sergeant stalked off before either could respond.

Tom opened the folder. "I was hoping we'd dodge this one. I know the guy was wealthy and high up in the corporate ladder, but we've had our hands full lately," he complained. Scooting his desk chair back making a screeching sound across the old hardwood floors that long since were aged and scarred from use, Tom signaled Sergeant Ricks over to his desk.

"What's up?" Ricks asked, chewing nicotine gum like there was no tomorrow.

"You still need that to stop smoking?" Tom asked, pointing to his mouth.

Ricks was in his early fifties, hair that was more gray than dark, built wiry and compact, with eyes that were small and beady. It was rumored that in his youth, he had a temper and nobody wanted to cross him. The years hadn't smoothed out the wrinkles, and Sean judged the man to be cockier than mean-spirited. That and the fact he always seemed to have a chip on his shoulder.

"What the hell is it to you?" he asked, spittle shooting from his mouth. A blob landed on Tom's desk.

"Why isn't Conners and Peters on this? They were the first ones on the scene," Tom said, grabbing a tissue to wipe up the spittle in disgust.

Listening to their verbal sparring, Sean shook his head. Everyone in the squad room knew they had a dislike for one another, and it was the light annoyances they inflicted on each other that kept their dislike fueled.

"Conners was called back to Colorado for a family funeral, and Peters is out sick. Word has it he may have appendicitis. They're both off the case, so you, lucky assholes, got it."

"Well, shit! You know that we haven't had any time off, and it's only a little over three weeks 'til Labor Day weekend!"

"Suck it up, Hanson." Ricks stalked off, snapping the gum with even more disdain than before.

Tom turned back to face his desk with a scowl. In his late forties, he was partially bald and sported a paunch from many years of eating fast food on the run while chasing down leads. He was good at his job.

Sean spoke up, "Word has it that Collins was murdered by blunt force trauma to the head. He was no doubt dirty if you ask me. Have you seen that little mansion of his?"

Tom looked up and frowned. "Meaning the suspect pool will be large. Where do you want to start, work or relatives?" he asked in resignation.

They could probably forget having any time off soon with a case like this. And unlike his younger partner, he couldn't keep the pace. Sean was in his midthirties and in great shape. Tall, dark, and handsome was what came to mind in describing him, and it wouldn't be the first time that he managed to turn a girl's head.

"Work. If he was high up the chain as I'm told, it's possible he didn't rise to that position without some backstabbing."

Tom called his wife, Mimi, telling her he'd be late in getting home while Sean stood and holstered his service weapon in his shoulder harness. Tom hung up and grabbed the case file and cell. It was going to be a long day trying to shake something loose. But cases like this needed viable information on which to build an investigation. If luck was on their side, they'd get some leads today to follow up on.

Their first stop was corporate headquarters where James Collins worked. Henderson, Rose, and Collins Law Offices were located in one of the busiest sections of downtown with more corporate buildings on either side. The building itself was several stories high with a sleek and modern interior. Steel and glass were everywhere. It was obvious they catered to the powerful and elite in this town.

Stopping at the front desk, a polished receptionist looked up from her monitor when they asked for the law office. "Eighteenth floor," she told them brusquely.

Stepping onto the eighteenth floor, they were met by another receptionist. "We'd like to see Mr. Henderson or Mr. Rose," Tom said.

"Do you have an appointment, gentlemen?" she asked, looking up.

"No, we're here in regard to Mr. Collins."

"I'm sorry, but you'll need to make an appointment."

Tom pulled out his badge. "We'd like to speak with one or the other, police business."

Her eyes widened ever so slightly. She rose from behind her desk and told them she'd be right back. Stepping to a closed door, she knocked lightly and entered. It was just a few seconds later she emerged from the room and told them that Mr. Henderson would see them shortly. She indicated they be seated until he was ready for them. She didn't offer refreshments and returned to her desk without giving them another glance.

The twenty-or-so minutes they sat waiting, secretaries and attorneys whizzed by with papers, folders, or cells in hand. The suits, mostly younger men, passed briskly with heads held high and cells plastered to their ears. Tom shook his head in disgust, wondering aloud who their stylists were. Sean ignored him. He nodded once again as a young secretary passed, wearing a short skirt to show off her shapely legs. She smiled in return and kept walking. The waiting game tested their patience, but even given the delay, Sean enjoyed the show.

They were finally shown to Mr. Henderson's office just as Tom was ready to stampede the receptionist's desk.

Standing up behind his desk, Mr. Henderson extended a hand. "Detectives, we are sorry to hear of Mr. Collins's passing. How can we help?" Henderson was probably in his sixties with a mass of gray hair that was artfully cut and styled. Of a tall, lean build, he wore his Armani suit well, but he looked tired with shadowed light-blue eyes.

Both detectives took proffered seats that faced Mr. Henderson's massive cherrywood desk.

The room itself contained cherrywood bookshelves that displayed law books. On one side of the room, a bar was positioned with a decanter full of amber liquid, presumably Scotch, and an ice bucket with silver tongs.

Sean spoke, "Mr. Collins's passing was more than that. He was murdered. What can you tell us about him?"

Clearing his throat, the attorney added, "We did hear he was murdered and it's under investigation. We have been busy with all the paperwork and referring his clients to other attorneys within our law firm. I'm not sure what I can tell you other than he worked hard becoming a partner of the firm. His name is on the door and documents, all of which need changed now." He sighed deeply before continuing, "He seemed to have many satisfied clients, most of whom have taken this news hard."

"Did he get along with the other attorneys working here?" Tom asked.

Shifting his gaze to Tom, Henderson replied, "He got along great with everyone!"

"So no enemies, no one he screwed over to get his name on the door?" Sean asked.

"Don't get me wrong, everyone employed here wants to make partner at some point. And we always try to be fair, but only the best make it. Mr. Collins was good at what he did, and he earned partnership on his own cognizance."

"Are you sure everyone was on board with that?"

"I'm quite sure. Regardless how they felt, they knew he earned it."

"What about clients. Anyone have a beef with him over how their case went?" Sean asked.

"As far as I know, all his clients were happy. They all had the outcomes they desired. Like I say, he was good at what he did."

"Then possible defendants? Any who lost their case that might have threatened him?"

"If there was, I never heard about it. I could ask his secretary if she knew of any threats."

"Please, do that…" Tom spoke up.

Mr. Henderson hit the intercom button and asked his secretary to summon Ms. Atkins to his office. Glancing at the detectives, he said, "She'll be here shortly. Would either of you like coffee or a bottle of water?" he offered.

Both declined, and a few moments later, Ms. Atkins was shown into the office by Mr. Henderson's secretary. Ms. Atkins, as it turned out, was an older woman with graying hair and in need of shedding a few pounds.

"Mr. Henderson, how can I be of service?" she asked.

"Ms. Atkins, meet Detectives Hanson and Ryan. They're here to find out if Mr. Collins had enemies, anyone who might have threatened him over losing a case."

"Detectives," with hands clasped in front of her, she inclined her head. "There were a couple of people who lost their cases in recent history who threatened him, but he took none of it seriously."

"We'll need their names and any information you can garner."

"Of course, I'll be happy to gather all the information I have available. Will that be all, Mr. Henderson?" she asked, turning her attention back to the man behind the desk.

"Thank you, Ms. Atkins, that should do it."

After Ms. Atkins left the room, Sean spoke up, "From what we've seen of other secretaries around here, it seems Ms. Atkins isn't your run of the mill…"

Mr. Henderson paled slightly. "Mr. Collins was a playboy." He shrugged his shoulders and added, "The guy was good-looking, and many would say he was handsome. But he had an eye for the ladies. Ms. Atkins was hired to keep him in check while at the office."

"Was he having an affair with anyone who works here?" Tom asked.

"If he was, they kept it under lock and key."

The detectives exchanged glances, and Tom asked if he planned on making one of the other lawyers a partner to take Collins's place. He sat back and regarded both detectives for a moment before answering. "We have someone from outside the firm we're looking at. He comes with credentials and recommendations that make it hard to turn down."

"How will those within the firm take the news they've been selected over once again?" Sean asked.

"They'll be disappointed, but that's just the way it is."

Ms. Atkins returned with a folder in hand. The detectives thanked her and then shook hands with Mr. Henderson, stepping out behind Collins's secretary. All three stepped into the elevator at the same time, and it was then they took advantage of questioning her further.

"Thank you for gathering this information so quickly," Tom stated.

"I already had a list somewhat compiled since I knew the police would be here inquiring about all of Mr. Collins's associations."

"Was Mr. Collins having an affair with anyone that works here?" Sean asked.

She raised her eyes to Sean and smiled. "He liked women, and he played the field. If any of the women who work here knew he was having an affair with another, there was no gossip, or I would have heard something."

Ms. Atkins got off at another floor, and a man joined them in the elevator. After the doors closed, he turned to the detectives. "In spite of what you hear about how well everyone gets along in this firm, it's not true. James Collins did what he could to get partnership. There were others, including myself, who should have gotten that position ahead of him."

The elevator stopped at another floor, and the man exited before they could ask further questions.

CHAPTER 2

"I wonder who that leaves that didn't hate him?" Sean asked turning to Tom.

"His secretary…"

Back in the car, Sean pulled up a map on his cell to chart the best course to investigate the leads handed to them by Collins's secretary. Unfolding the paper, Sean whistled.

Tom leaned over. "What?"

"Bless Ms. Atkins's heart! She included all the women working here that had sex with Collins but also the other attorneys' names and addresses that were cheated out of partnership." Looking at Tom, he continued, "She also put down names of other people who work here that Collins treated shabbily. And she also included a note about a Trina Myerson. Apparently, she was Collins's latest girlfriend at the firm. She says that she never saw any credentials to earn her the right to work as a top-executive secretary. But what was odd is that she was transferred around among top executives and associates throughout the company."

Taking a deep breath, Tom muttered something under his breath.

CHAPTER 3

"Vanity of vanities," saith the preacher, "vanity of vanities; all is vanity."

—Ecclesiastes 1:2

Two months earlier...

James straightened his tie and ran his hands through his hair. Looking at his reflection in the gilded mirror, he turned his head from side to side and liked what he saw. With semi-wavy dark hair that was styled and highlighted gave him the look he sought. But it was his charismatic blue eyes that attracted women and gave everyone pause. It didn't hurt that he worked out at the gym, giving him an athletic appearance with broad shoulders and a trim waist. Add being wealthy, it was just icing on the cake, and it usually meant he could have any woman he wanted.

The mirror reflected movement from the bed behind him. Trina awoke and stretched beneath the covers. He turned as she opened her eyes, and upon seeing him, she smiled lazily. Her hair was a wild mass of shoulder-length blond hair, and her petulant mouth now beckoned him to come closer as she pursed her lips together.

Rolling onto her side, she propped her head on her arm, and James leaned over to kiss her. She moaned softly under the slight pressure, and when he raised his head, she pulled the sheet down, smiling encouragingly.

CHAPTER 3

"To work so soon," she purred. "I was hoping for more of what we had last night..."

Trina enjoyed sex. And if the truth be told, even he had a difficult time keeping up with her needs. While no one at the firm spoke about what went on, it was still common knowledge that Trina was passed around between the associates and partners. She was terrible at her job and lacked needed skills, but she made up for all that in the bedroom or on the corporate couch. There'd been more than one incident where someone walked in catching her lying on her back, splayed on a desk, with an associate's head buried between her legs.

James reached out and cupped a bare breast, bringing another soft moan. He felt himself harden and more than willing to indulge her. Running his fingers down her torso, his hand plunged under the covers, coming up between her legs. She was swollen and damp. He slipped his fingers into the wetness, and she rolled onto her back moaning and raising her hips to meet his demand. She slid one hand under the covers to aid him. And with her other hand, she reached out to run a finger over his hardened erection through the fabric of his trousers. He groaned. Ah, hell, he might as well get undressed; they'll just have to start the meeting without him.

A couple of hours later found James rolling into his parking space with a smile plastered on his face. A tumble under the sheets was nothing compared to the time spent with Trina. His smile faded though; while Trina was great for casual sex when he wanted it, his thoughts wandered to Michaela. He just knew she'd be great in bed. The fact that she had a kid didn't bother him in the least. Developing feelings for her, there was more to this relationship than just wanting to get her into bed. The way she blushed, the way her eyes sparkled, the dimples when she smiled had him thinking about her at the most inconvenient times. He reflected on how Trina awakened this morning and then pictured Michaela in her place, with her long, reddish-brown tresses mussed from a night's lovemaking. How her green eyes would be dazed and linger on him, silently pleading for more. He felt himself stiffen again. He needed a fresh start with her, to make amends for going too fast, and slowly romance her until he could have her, all of her!

With determination, he cut the engine and got out of the convertible with new purpose and a plan forming.

CHAPTER 4

Now the works of the flesh are manifest, which are these: adultery, fornication, uncleanness, lasciviousness.

—Galatians 5:19

Tom popped the lid on the antacid and shoved a couple into his mouth before taking a swig of water from the bottle sitting in the cup holder of his Nissan Sentra. The car was a disaster as always, and it had Sean thinking how Tom's wife kept an immaculate home. They say opposites attract, and in Tom's case, that seemed to be true.

Sitting across the street from Trina Myerson's home, they watched as she came out and opened the back end of her SUV. They admired the view as she leaned into the interior to grab shopping bags. When she turned, Tom's intake of breath caused Sean's head to swivel in his direction.

"Whoa!" Tom sighed, ogling her from afar.

Sean glanced back at the blond. "You're married. Put your eyes back in your head." Sean laughed, turning back to Tom. "I'll tell Mimi…"

"Right, and get me in trouble! Besides, I'm not dead…yet!"

Sean only laughed as he turned his attention back to the pretty blond.

One of the bags started to slip from Trina's hand, and she stooped, setting it on the ground to get a better grasp.

"Maybe, we should help her…" Sean offered.

They exited the car, and as the doors slammed shut, Trina looked up. Walking across the street toward her, she admired the younger one with dark hair and smiled. The other one was older, heavier, and slightly balding.

"Can we help?" Sean asked as they neared.

"I'd like help, but I also like to know whose offering?" she teased with a smile.

Sean pulled out his badge and introduced them. "I'm Detective Ryan and this is Detective Hanson of the Los Pinos Police Department. We're here to ask you a few questions about James Collins."

Trina eyed his badge and then Tom's. "James?" she asked.

"You are aware he was recently found dead in his home."

"Yeah, I know. I heard it on the news."

Sean held out his hand. "May I? We should go inside."

"Of course." Trina handed him a couple of bags and turned toward the house. Over her shoulder, she asked, "What do you want to know?"

After putting the bags down in the entry, Trina offered them a seat in the great room. The room was centralized to the kitchen and dining with an open-floor plan. To one side was a door leading to a hall and what Sean guessed were bedrooms and bathrooms. The place was clean, and her decor was contemporary but stopped short of being personal. It was like walking into a staged house rather than a home.

Trina sat down on one end of the sofa and motioned them to sit wherever. Sean sat down on the opposite end of the sofa from Trina while Tom elected to sit in a chair angled toward the sofa.

Sean looked over as Tom pulled out his notepad. Turning back to Trina, he couldn't help but notice she wasn't wearing a bra.

Lifting his eyes to hers, he began, "We'd like to know more about your relationship with Mr. Collins."

Trina sat back and crossed her legs. "We had sex." She lifted a brow and smiled, fluffing her blond hair. "We had an arrangement if you will. Neither of us was in it for a relationship, just the sex…"

"So there were no commitments then?" Tom spoke up.

CHAPTER 4

Trina turned to him. "No commitments in that I was expecting him to marry me if that's what you mean. Or that I expected him to be monogamous. I knew he was interested in someone else and…"

"So you both had a polygamous relationship while seeing each other?" Tom asked, cutting her off midsentence.

"Yes."

"And?" Sean asked.

"And…" Trina turned back to Sean and leaned toward him. "We were free to see whoever we wanted. It was an open relationship." She sat straighter, pulling her shoulders back, stretching the fabric taut across her breasts. "But James was into another woman. He met her while staying at the B&B over on Bayside Drive which is run by a Michaela McCrea. They started dating, and when she found out he was also seeing me, she got mad. Really mad!" she emphasized with a lift of her brows.

"James told me that she wasn't into polygamy and even has a kid. Of course, James wanted to play the field. He was seeing me after all. When Michaela found out, she even called and threatened me! I was upset and told James about the call." She held her hand up to her heart and instinctively, Sean's eyes followed her motion. She smiled when he made eye contact, and then she continued, "James told her in no uncertain terms that he would see whoever he wanted, whenever he wanted. She threw a tantrum and told him they were done. It was then that he started receiving calls, and when he'd answer, she'd hang up."

"How do you know it was her?" Tom asked.

Trina glanced over and raised her shoulders. "I don't, I'm assuming, but anyway, I recorded one call where she threatened me."

"Do you still have the recording?" Sean asked.

"No, I deleted it after I let James listen to it. He was as upset as much as I was. Anyway, someone that hostile and jealous," she lifted her shoulders and uncrossed her legs, "I wouldn't put it past her to try and harm James. Or me either for that matter!" She sat back again, crossing her legs.

"And what about you, did you end up falling for the guy and want to change this open relationship?" Tom spoke up.

She looked down at the notepad he held in his hands and then glanced back up at him. "I told you, we had an agreement that made us both happy. We were in a relationship solely for the sex." Flipping her hair over her shoulder. she looked over at Detective Ryan. "He knew how to satisfy a girl. How about either of you two, know how to please your woman?"

She tossed a quick glance over at Tom and then turned her head, looking him square in the eye with a raised brow.

Tom cleared his throat and wrote something down in the notepad.

Sean almost laughed. Standing up, he said, "Ms. Myerson, thank you for your time. If you think of anything else, be sure to reach out."

Trina stood too and smiled up at Sean. "By all means…if I think of anything, I'll be in touch." She took the card Sean handed her.

Tom cleared his throat and dropped his card on the nearby table as they left the room. Both men moved toward the door; Sean turned back to Trina from the doorway. "Call if you have any other information. We'll see ourselves out. Thank you."

As they made their way across the street back to the car, Tom let out a whistle. Climbing in behind the wheel, he looked over at Sean. "Can you believe that? I think she was coming on to you. It could help in our investigation. Get close to a possible suspect, and she may tell you more than we got out of her today."

Sean laughed. "Yeah, maybe, I can contract some venereal disease for the cause for that matter. She's hot, but you couldn't pay me to sleep with her."

This time, Tom laughed. "What a way to go…" And raised his brows at Sean before turning the key in the ignition and firing up the engine.

"You think there's something behind this Michaela person? I can check her background once we're back at the department to see if there are any priors. That should give us a bit more information to go on when we question her."

"Perhaps, but I also think Ms. Myerson might be holding a grudge. She says they were in it for the sex, but you know women.

They may think that at first, but it's not long before the M word pops up in their minds. If Collins started seeing someone else, her chances might have blown up in her face. Jealousy has led to murder before…"

"Yeah, but usually the one that ends up dead is the competition."

Back at the office, Tom did more research on Myerson while Sean got to work looking up who owned the bed-and-breakfast in public records in the county's tax assessors' database.

"Tom," he said, looking across his desk. "Michaela McCrea does own the bed-and-breakfast. The previous owner was Jane Holton. Apparently, this McCrea has owned the place for the past five years. And I couldn't find any priors whatsoever. With further research, it appears that she's widowed, and her deceased husband was in a mysterious car accident that was ruled as a homicide. After a few months, the case went cold. Pretty damn interesting, wouldn't you say?"

"Was she the benefactor of any wills?" Tom asked, sitting up straighter.

"I'll have to investigate further, but this looks promising. We need to question her."

Tom nodded in agreement.

CHAPTER 5

But as for the pure, his conduct is upright.

—Proverbs 21:8b

Pulling into the small graveled parking area of the Bayside Bed-and-Breakfast, Tom cut the engine and reached for the antacids. Picking up the bottle, he hesitated and then put it back. "This is becoming a habit more than a need," he grumbled to himself.

As they entered the B&B, a bell chimed that was located over the door. On the left, shelves lined a couple walls with jams on one and ceramic mugs with the name of the bed-and-breakfast on another. To the right, a counter separated the office from the entry where guests checked in.

Tom started to ring the bell on the counter when a woman, who looked to be in her thirties, stepped through a doorway into the office. She was quite attractive with long, straight, dark hair that reached down to the top of her waist. Considering her catlike blue eyes and slender build, she was more exotic in looks rather than gothic.

She now flipped her long hair over her shoulder and asked, "How can I help you, gentlemen?"

Sean pulled his badge out and held it up for her inspection. "Mrs. McCrea, we're here to ask you a few questions about James Collins."

"Me? Why would you want to question me?" she asked, pausing in the middle of folding a towel to look at the men.

"You are aware that Mr. Collins was found dead in his home."

CHAPTER 5

"Well, yes, but I don't know why you'd want to question me about it!" She tossed the dishtowel on the counter in front of her.

"We're here to learn more about your relationship with Mr. Collins." Sean took out his notepad and pen, ready to take notes.

"Wait…" She held up a hand. "Exactly what do you mean by 'my relationship'?"

"You did date Mr. Collins, correct?"

"No…"

"We heard from another source that you had a relationship with Mr. Collins," Sean spoke up.

"Perhaps, we should find a more convenient place where we can ask questions," Tom said, looking around.

"I mean…" she tried again, turning her attention to Tom.

"Ma'am, let's settle someplace where we have privacy," he interrupted.

"Look, I'm not Mrs. McCrea," Marissa spoke up.

Tom sharply turned his head back to her and was about to say something when Sean spoke up. "But you said …" he began.

"I am Mrs. McCrea, but you want Michaela. I'm her sister-in-law, Marissa, she's the one who dated James. Let me get her."

She opened a small gate next to the counter and led the detectives through the office to the kitchen. To the left, a large kitchen island separated the stove and refrigerator that was against the wall. Cabinets lined the wall on the right side of the kitchen, and beyond was a small kitchen table.

"Please, have a seat, and I'll get her." She gestured toward the table and left through another door, leaving them to pull out chairs and seat themselves.

A few moments later, Michaela opened a door that was on the far side of what appeared to be a butler pantry. Stepping into the room, she warily eyed both men.

Two pairs of eyes followed her across the room, and bright-green eyes met theirs. Her hair was caught up in a clip at the back of her head, but a few tendrils of the soft curly mass had escaped. Void of makeup, she was still striking.

"Good afternoon," she said. "My sister-in-law tells me you're here to ask about James. How can I help?" Standing a few feet away, she crossed her arms over her chest in a protective gesture.

"We understand that you were dating Mr. Collins. How long had you been dating?" Sean asked, with pen poised above the notepad.

"Not long. We only dated a couple of times, maybe three at the most."

Tom leaned forward. "Can you account for your whereabouts on August 5?"

Michaela brushed the soft curls from her face with shaky hands. Both detectives noticed and exchanged looks before turning their attention back to her.

"That was last Wednesday, so I was here at the bed-and-breakfast."

"Do you have anyone who can alibi for you?" Tom continued.

"There were guests staying here…"

"And these guests can attest that you were here on the premises between 2:00 a.m. and 4:00 a.m.?" Tom leaned back in his chair with brows raised.

"No, I was in bed and assume they were all tucked in for the night too."

"So the answer is no." Tom stopped talking and just stared at Michaela in what was his intimidating mode, hoping to get the person to talk. Most often it worked. Talking to fill the void was a defense mechanism to break the silence.

After a few moments, Tom began, "So you don't have an alibi. For all we know, you could have snuck out and taken the time to murder Mr. Collins and get back before anyone missed you."

"That's absurd! I wouldn't have left my son alone. Besides, why would I want to murder the man to begin with?" Michaela's raised voice brought Snickers to the doorway where Marissa stood. She put a foot out to stop his progress and snapped her fingers for him to return to his bed.

"From our understanding, you expressed concerns over Mr. Collins's other affairs," Sean stated, resting an ankle over his knee in a relaxed pose.

Michaela nodded, and both detectives again exchanged glances. Sean wrote something down in the notepad.

"We understand that you called one of his other girlfriends and threatened her."

"What? No! I didn't know he was seeing anyone else until after we stopped dating."

"You're telling us that you didn't know about the other girlfriends but yet voiced your concern to him while still dating?" Tom asked.

"What was the exact relationship you shared with Mr. Collins?" Sean cut in.

Shoving her hair back off her face again, Michaela turned and got a cup from the cupboard behind her and poured coffee. With her back still turned, she asked if either detective would like coffee.

Both declined.

Turning around, she started to sip her coffee but felt she might spill it and hurriedly set it back down. "We didn't have sex if that's what you're asking. I didn't know James was seeing other women while we were still dating until after the fact. I expressed my concern to Marissa and Heather, a friend of mine."

"We are told that's not the case and that you were not only upset but you called and threatened the other girlfriend."

"I don't know who told you that, but it's not true!"

"How did you meet?" Sean questioned.

Michaela once again picked up the coffee cup and managed a sip before replying, "He booked a room here at the bed-and-breakfast. He was nice, and we were attracted to one another. We dated a couple of times after that, and that's about all there is to it. In fact, I was the one who ended it."

Marissa spoke up, "Look, Detectives, Michaela broke off the relationship after James tried to rape her."

"Rape, care to expound?"

Michaela looked over at Detective Ryan with big, round eyes. He couldn't help but notice the heartbeat at the base of her throat.

Marissa spoke up again, entering the room to stand beside Michaela. "He tried to force her, and when she wouldn't succumb, he pushed her against the wall and took unwanted advances. When she started to scream, he slapped her hard enough that it left a clear handprint on her cheek. The only thing that saved her was a guest entering the office."

Michaela stared at her feet as a blush crept across her cheeks.

Tom spoke up, "We understand that your late husband left you a considerable life insurance policy that you collected on when he was in an accident." He lifted his hands and air quoted his doubt to the accident. "Care to explain?"

Michaela was stunned by the turn in questions. They were here to ask about James, and now they were questioning her about her late husband? "I don't understand," she faltered. "Why are you asking about Brad?" Her face had gone from red to white, and as the last word came out, she threw back her arms with her hand hitting the coffee cup she'd sat on the counter moments before. Knocking the cup over, the coffee spilled onto the counter and started to drip off the edge onto the floor.

Flustered, she grabbed a towel and immediately started to wipe up the mess. Marissa set the cup upright and then turned her attention to the detectives.

"Look, Officers…" Marissa began.

"Detectives," Tom corrected.

"Detectives, if you think for one lousy minute that Michaela had anything to do with James's death, then think again. And as far as Brad goes, when that accident happened, I was with Michaela and Chase. Brad was miles away. I have no idea why you're even asking about him!"

"And who's Chase?" Sean asked.

"Her son and my nephew!" she snapped. "Look, Michaela is upset, and this line of questioning has gotten out of hand. It's time for the both of you to leave."

"We're not through with our questions, but we will be back. Until then, it's best to stay close. You not only have cause but motive and no alibi." Tom held up a card and slapped it on the table. "Here's our number should you think of anything."

CHAPTER 5

Exiting the room ahead of Sean, Sean reached for his card and extended his hand out to Michaela. "We'll be in contact again. Here's my card in case you need to call."

Michaela was flushed again and reached for his card. He noted her slender hands, and when he looked up, pain etched across her brows. He had a lot more research to do on her and was more than curious to know more about this woman. He felt a strong attraction to her. She was in complete contrast to her sister-in-law who was tall, slender, and shapely. He found himself hoping Mrs. McCrea was innocent.

CHAPTER 6

Be not forgetful to entertain strangers for thereby some have entertained angels unawares.

—Hebrews 13:2

Sean took a sip of coffee only to grimace since it had long since grown cold. Nothing like office coffee notoriously bad but now stone-cold! He'd been working steadily on the list of suspects in the James Collins's murder. It was official now that he'd been murdered by a blunt force trauma to the head. Something heavy had been used, but they were still trying to identify the type of object. The list of suspects had grown exponentially. The guy had plenty of enemies. Having stabbed many in the back to climb the corporate ladder, coworkers had plenty to say, and none of it good.

On the other hand, most of the women he dated had nothing but praise for him. He prided himself on not only how to wine and dine them, but showering them with gifts. And Trina, she was a secretary to one of the top execs. And apparently, she'd slept her way to the position she now held.

Her boss gave her high praises as being adept at her work and always on time and often working late. Sean shook his head. More likely the two of them were working late horizontally.

The only piece of the puzzle so far that didn't fit was Michaela McCrea. Though she was quite pretty, she wasn't the type of woman that Collins would have normally dated. So what was up with that? And having looked further into her late husband's death, it seemed the accident was ruled as a homicide but never solved. That was over five years ago. Coincidental or suspicious that at the same time she inherited her aunt's bed-and-breakfast. It was at the very least suspicious in that both would die within a couple months of each other.

Brad McCrea was a fine arts dealer. And he was doing quite well. The house they owned prior to his death was evidence of the money he made. There were way too many unanswered questions.

Shoving the papers into a folder, he placed it in the holder on his desk and then stretched. It was getting late, and he was hungry. But he wanted answers more than filling his belly. He decided it might prove useful to drop by the bed-and-breakfast without notice. Catch her off guard and most likely alone.

As the idea formed, he shoved back his desk chair and holstered his weapon before donning an overcoat. Grabbing his keys, he was out the door.

*****

Chase was playing a game on his device at the kitchen table while Michaela cooked supper. This was their time together without interruptions since most guests would either be out having dinner or gathered in the common room to read or play games. Though summer was coming to an end and school would be starting soon, the bed-and-breakfast only had two guests for the evening. An older couple, having checked in earlier that day, seemed quite content reading in the common room after eating an early dinner out. The other couple, honeymooners, were having dinner at one of the nicest restaurants in town, one that she would love to try. Michaela reflected on how happy the couple appeared and completely smitten with each other. Did people still use that word, she wondered. Somehow, it just felt like the most accurate word to describe them.

When the bell above the office door rang, she sighed heavily; this was her time to be uninterrupted so that she and Chase could have dinner together. Soon, she'd be setting out cookies and milk or taking glasses of port or sherry to rooms where guests desired it. And then paperwork; it left her little time to get Chase settled and into bed for the night.

"Chase, watch the chicken, someone just came in…"

"Sure, Mom," Chase muttered without looking up.

As she stepped through the kitchen door into the office, she saw Detective Ryan and paled instantly. What did he want now?

"Hi," he said, turning to her. "I'm sorry to be dropping by this late, but I have more questions that I hope you can answer for me." He smiled apologetically and tilted his head to the side, looking slightly chagrinned.

"This is a bad time, Detective. I'm cooking supper and need to get back to the chicken before it burns."

"No problem. We can go in the kitchen so you can continue cooking," he replied easily and swung toward the gate.

Michaela hesitated. She didn't want him asking more questions; she didn't want him here, period!

He smiled again and stopped short looking down at her upturned face. Her eyes reflected far more than she realized. With hair loose about her shoulders, soft curls framed her face. The small lamp on the office counter put out enough light to bring out the reddish hues in her chestnut-brown hair. She finally turned and walked toward the kitchen.

He entered and stopped abruptly, realizing that her son was sitting at the kitchen table. He didn't want to ask her personal questions about either Collins or her late husband in front of the boy. He realized his mistake in coming at this hour. He wouldn't get many answers, especially those he wanted most.

Chase looked up and nodded toward Sean and then went back to playing a video game.

"Hi, you must be Chase. What game are you playing?" he asked, pulling out a chair.

The game Chase mentioned was lost on Sean. He hadn't heard it before. The boy had light-brown hair, a spattering of freckles across his nose, and bright-green eyes. One could definitely see traits of his mother in him. But other aspects, like the shape of his nose and the squared chin, must have come from his dad's side. According to information garnered, he would be about nine years old now.

CHAPTER 6

Michaela turned her back to them and worked at the stove. The smell of chicken frying was enough to undo him. His stomach growled loudly. His eyes riveted to Michaela, and she hesitated in turning the chicken.

Chase laughed. "I'm hungry too! Mom's chicken is the best! Are you here for dinner?"

Michaela turned suddenly, and Sean hesitated. "Uh, no, I just stopped by to ask your mom a few questions. By the way, I'm Det. Sean Ryan." Sean held out his hand in a manner they could touch fists in camaraderie.

Chase extended his fist to match and then asked, "About Mr. Collins, you mean?"

Looking over at Michaela uneasily, he nodded. "Yeah, he stayed here for a bit and seemed quite fond of your mom," he said, turning back to Chase.

"Yeah, he dated her a little. I liked him well enough but thought he was too full of himself." Chase went back to messing with the device he was playing games on.

Sean liked this boy a lot! And then the unthinkable happened, his stomach growled again.

"Maybe, you should eat so your stomach stops growling," Chase said. "Mom always fixes plenty, don't you, Mom!"

Keeping her back to the table, Michaela closed her eyes…turning slowly, she said, "Sure, you're welcome to eat with us, Detective. There's plenty. Unless, of course, you have somewhere else to be…"

Sean smiled inwardly. She was damn cute with an apron on. Even his own mom never wore an apron while cooking or, for that matter, his grandmother. "I would love to stay if that's alright…" He knew he should decline, but he couldn't help himself. It was so obvious she didn't want him to stay.

Pushing her hair behind an ear, she reached into the cupboard and pulled out three plates. Sean stood up and took them from her. "Here, let me. It's the least I can do, set the table."

"Chase, it's time to put things away so we can eat. Food will be ready in another five minutes. Wash your hands…"

"Okay, okay, Mom. It's not like you have to remind me every single night to wash my hands before I eat," he grumbled, slowly getting up.

"And don't forget to feed Snickers. His bowl needs filling;" she called over her shoulder as Chase swept through the doorway.

Sean set the table after Michaela showed him where the silverware was. Pulling chicken from the hot skillet to drain on paper towel, she started making gravy. When she pulled out a masher for the potatoes, Sean offered to mash them for her while she continued to make gravy. She accepted his offer in silence.

"The chicken smells delicious. KFC is the only chicken I eat these days."

She merely nodded and knifed soft butter into the mashed potatoes and poured in warm milk. Sean mixed them in and looked around for salt and pepper. Seeing them on top of the stove on the other side, he reached for them.

Her sharp intake of breath brought his attention back to the petite woman at his side. She stepped back quickly, allowing him to grab the seasonings.

"Sorry for the reach," he apologized.

Chase came back into the room, and Michaela asked him to get the salad and dressing out of the fridge while she pulled corn on the cob from the steamer and poured gravy into a boat to set on the table. Sean brought over the chicken and placed it in the center of the table.

"I think we're ready," she said hesitantly.

Sean removed his overcoat to sit down, and Chase exclaimed, "Wow, is that for real?" He pointed at the shoulder harness Sean wore.

Michaela paled seeing the harness and gun. Sean apologized, stating it was police gear they were required to wear.

"Can I see it?" Chase asked excitedly.

"No, you may not!" Michaela piped up immediately, then turning to Sean, she asked if he could please put it away, somewhere out of sight. He complied.

CHAPTER 6

After sitting, she bowed her head to say grace, catching Sean by surprise. Holding Chase's hand, she extended her other to Sean while Chase extended his to him from the other side. He took their proffered hands, liking the feel of Michaela's small hand that was placed inside his much larger palm. And though it was a short prayer offering up thanks for the food, Sean guessed the last part of the prayer was not so honest when she thanked the Lord for his presence at their table.

Michaela slowly raised her eyes to his and blushed, knowing that he could tell she was anything but thankful.

As food was passed around the table, Sean piled his plate with chicken and all the sides. He dug in without preamble and groaned. "This is really good." Looking up, he found two sets of eyes peering at him, which almost had him blushing with the amount of food he plated.

"I told you Mom was a good cook!" Chase said.

"No, you said she made the best fried chicken, which she does, but she also makes great mashed potatoes and corn on the cob. If you ever want to be a detective, you must learn to pay attention to what is said and what's not said." He winked before turning to Michaela.

She froze with her fork halfway to her mouth.

Sean wanted to kick himself. And for some unknown reason, he wanted to reach out and comfort her!

Chase seemed to take a liking to Detective Ryan, and they both conversed easily throughout the meal with Chase asking plenty of questions about being a detective, which Sean easily answered. When supper was over, Michaela stood to take dishes to the sink and told Chase he could watch TV if he liked.

Sean also stood helping to clear dishes. The silence between them was uncomfortable once Chase left the kitchen. Sitting plates in the sink and running water over them, Michaela turned to Sean. "Look, let's get this over with, shall we? You have questions, and I'd just as soon get on with my evening before I tend to guests and Chase goes to bed."

Sean nodded and sat back down at the kitchen table. Michaela followed suit and clasped her hands together on the tabletop.

"You have to understand, I need to ask questions," he began and halted. "It could help eliminate you as a suspect. And having a complete picture will help us find the murderer."

Michaela peered up at him through long lashes. "I don't understand why you need to question me about my late husband. He has nothing to do with James's murder."

"True, but the one common denominator…is you."

"Oh!" She slid her hands off the table and onto her lap, looking uncomfortable. "You don't really think I murdered both my late husband and James?" she asked almost incredulously.

"I don't, but part of my job is asking questions to make sense of all the information out there. One of which is why your husband's death was labeled a homicide that was never solved. And your aunt died around the same time. You inherent a bed-and-breakfast and gain money from a life insurance policy. One, I might add, that said policy was taken out about a month before your husband was murdered."

Michaela flinched. "Brad said he thought it was time we took out a policy. Chase was four at the time, and he said if anything happened to him, he wanted Chase to have a home and a future. He was earning a good income by then, and after a few years of scraping money together just to pay the bills, it was a welcome relief. Brad's car was found at the bottom of a ravine." Michaela inhaled deeply and then went on, "The investigation led to the fact his brake lines were cut. He left earlier that morning for a business meeting down south. Driving the scenic route, the police determined that the lines had to have been cut after he started the trip, which ruled me out as a possible suspect."

With a shuddering breath, she continued, "They never could find out much more in their investigation, and after months with no fresh leads, it became a cold case. And my aunt, she was much older than my mother, almost like my grandparents had a second family. She owned this place, and when her husband passed, my uncle, she was in no shape to keep it up. Being a favorite aunt, I spent most every summer here helping. I love this place." She shrugged her shoulders, looking around appreciatively. "She taught me to cook and taught me a lot during those summers." Smiling, she fell silent.

"Do you have other aunts, cousins?" he asked.

She lifted her eyes to his and shook her head. "No cousins, unfortunately. My aunt Jane was never blessed with children, which is why I think she sort of adopted me. My other aunt is my mom's twin, and while she just lives a couple hours away, we never see each other and rarely talk."

Sean remained silent, letting her speak.

"Those were good years, great summers that I spent with Aunt Jane…" Her smile broadened into a laugh, revealing dimples on either side. He was captivated.

"When she fell ill, she refused to see a doctor. But as time elapsed, her health grew worse, and finally, we discovered that she had cancer. Once they opened her up, they just sewed her up again and said there was no hope. She was eaten up. A week later, she passed. I thought I'd die, and then come to find out she left this place to me since I was the only one who showed any interest. Brad wanted to sell and we fought over it. We fought the night before he left." Her head dropped, and a tear slipped down her cheek.

Without thinking, Sean reached over and placed his hand on her forearm. "I'm sorry," he said.

She looked up with shimmering eyes. "Thank you. My last words to him will haunt me for the rest of my life. He'll never know how much I really loved him and just how sorry I was, still am. If only life could give us a second chance."

After a moment of silence, she continued, "I was forced to either sell our home or this place, but I just couldn't live there. A place we hoped to build a future on. Have more children…so I used the insurance money to restore this place and refurbish it."

The bell on the office counter rang, startling them both. "Excuse me," she said, standing. "A guest must need something."

Sean said he needed to be going. What he really needed was time to mull over the information she'd given. Stepping on the front porch, Sean stood catching the evening breeze as he thought about their conversation. Looking up at the clear night sky, stars twinkled above, and he sighed heavily. His gut instinct told him that Michaela was not guilty of murdering either her late husband or Collins. But with her husband's unresolved homicide, an aunt who left her a big investment, albeit in need of repair, and now Collins made her look guilty as hell.

He sighed again and stepped off the porch heading to his car. Once inside, he peered back at the bed-and-breakfast. A shadow appeared across one of the windows that according to floor plans downloaded from records was Michaela's private living quarters. He wondered now if she might be peeking out through the curtains.

Starting up the car, he headed home for the evening, but this time with a full belly and a woman with light reddish-brown hair and green eyes who would linger in his mind.

CHAPTER 7

Let us not become weary in doing good for at the proper time, we will reap a harvest if we do not give up.

—1 Corinthians 9:24

After tending to guests and evening tasks, Michaela settled at her desk to do paperwork, but her mind wandered to some of the questions Detective Ryan asked. She reached for a photo of her and Brad that sat on the corner of her desk. Lovingly tracing a finger across Brad's cheek, she reflected how happy they were when this picture was taken.

They'd gone to the mountains to camp with friends. They spent the evening sitting around a fire toasting marshmallows and sipping coffee with Baileys. It was romantic, and as the conversation lulled, Brad slipped his warmed hand underneath her jacket and sweater. He gently rubbed her back before slipping his hand around to the front and gently cupping the underside of her breast. Leaning in, he kissed her, and as the kiss ended, she looked across the fire to see their friends also fondling one another.

Brad whispered in her ear "It's time for bed..." and then announced to their friends they were tired and heading off to their tent. Michaela smiled, recalling that their friends didn't even respond as they continued to kiss passionately.

Once inside their tent, Brad proceeded to undress her. The air was frigid without the warmth of the fire, and they both quickly settled into their sleeping bag. Brad couldn't keep his hands off her, and his kisses were warm with a trace of coffee and Baileys. She instinctively knew that was the night Chase was conceived.

The next morning while making breakfast, their friends teased them about how noisy it was the night before, and Michaela's cheeks flushed. She looked over at Brad, and he smiled, lowering his head.

Her thoughts turned to Detective Ryan, and she compared the two men. Brad was of medium height, slim, and muscular. Detective Ryan was big and tall with a muscular build. She pictured his dark hair that was a little too long like he hadn't had time to get a trim. His penetrating gray eyes fringed with dark lashes and how he seemed to look into her very soul. She almost laughed; wasn't that what they said in movies, and yet for the very first time in her life, she understood the meaning. She closed her eyes in frustration. She had no business dreaming of another man.

Jumping from her seat, she switched off the desk lamp and turned the picture on her antique desk face down. Enough! She was so confused. Yes, she loved Brad and still did, but five years was a long time to mourn someone, especially if one didn't move on with their life.

The next morning after serving breakfast to her guests, Michaela took time to work in the vegetable garden. She wanted to pick some tomatoes and bell peppers for the afternoon social hour, which included more than just appetizers and wine. For those guests who enjoyed something sweet, she always served cookies or quick breads with hot tea. And guests seemed to like the little extras. Hopefully, one day, the place would be constantly booked so she could hire the help needed to keep the bed-and-breakfast running smoothly.

With hair piled on her head held by a large clip, she knelt beside the tomatoes to pull weeds that had long since sprouted and put down some fresh mulch. Picking a bright-red tomato, she held it to her nose and inhaled deeply, appreciating the fragrance. She closed her eyes, thinking about the bruschetta she'd serve guests that afternoon. She dropped it in the basket she brought with her and set to work clipping and weeding.

As she worked, she reflected on Detective Ryan's visit the night before. She would need to talk with Chase about extending invitations for dinner without first consulting her. She did not want the detective there to begin with, but sharing a meal…she'd been distracted, afraid of saying the wrong thing. But more than that, Detective Ryan was attractive.

She loved the dark stubble, his five-o'clock shadow, his gray eyes that really held a person, and his strong arms and shoulders. And the way his muscles bulged under his shirt sleeve in doing something as simple as passing potatoes across the table. Her eyes popped open; the last thing she should be thinking about was how attractive this man was. He was merely doing a job, and last night's visit was solely another expedition searching for more answers to whether she was guilty. She shook her head, recalling just how much she revealed.

But as her thoughts returned to the man himself, what she found truly attractive was the way he interacted with Chase. And it was obvious Chase liked the detective too. This morning at breakfast, he couldn't stop talking about him.

She paused in her thoughts and sat back on her heels. Resting her hands on her thighs, she closed her eyes and enjoyed the sun's rays across her upturned face. It was times like this she loved the solitude, feeling closer to God and marveling at his handiwork in the beauty of something as simple as a vegetable garden.

A small cloud passed, temporarily blocking out the sun's rays, and Michaela's world darkened for a moment. And with the darkness, a chill crept up her spine. Her eyes popped open, and she instinctively looked around her. But the feeling that someone was watching was palpable.

Standing, she surveyed the area. Not that she could see much from the garden, but looking over the fence, she could see her neighbors' homes easily enough. Craning her neck to the right, toward the ocean and peering through the rose bushes that lined the fence to the garden, there was nothing to see except the graveled parking lot for guests. It was void of cars, and what few guests that checked in were out and about. And beyond the parking lot, the ground dropped off to a cliff overlooking the ocean.

Her cell rang, and she looked at the number, not recognizing it. It rang a few more times before stopping. The phone calls started a few months ago, and at first, she thought it was just kids, bored. But that changed when the calls continued, whether she answered or not. If she answered, they'd simply hang up, but occasionally, she could hear deep breathing on the other end and that bothered her.

Something was off, she could feel it. It was like thinking of something and then losing that thought; it bothered you until you could recall it. Kneeling once again in the garden, she resumed weeding, thinking maybe it was her imagination working overtime.

She heard a car's engine close by, and standing once again, she saw a small car pull up in front of her neighbor's. And then she saw Detective Hanson getting out of the car. He was alone.

Looking toward the bed-and-breakfast, he turned his attention back to the house in front of him. As he made his way up the sidewalk, Michaela spied on him through the fence of the vegetable garden. She knew she shouldn't, but her curiosity got the best of her. Why would he be stopping by her neighbor's?

Standing on the stoop, he rang the doorbell, and it wasn't long before Mrs. Hensley opened the door. Michaela saw Detective Hanson pulling out his badge, and a few words were exchanged. She could hear their voices but nothing distinguishable.

Mrs. Hensley opened the door further, and he disappeared inside. Michaela squatted down in front of the fence and wondered what was happening. Maybe, he was the one who'd been spying on her earlier…

*****

"Mrs. Hensley, thank you for agreeing to speak with me for a few moments. Reiterating our earlier conversation on the phone, this is about the James Collins's murder. And the reason I'm here is because Mr. Collins stayed at the bed-and-breakfast located next door. That was approximately three months before he was found murdered. I'm not sure if you are aware, but Mrs. McCrea and Mr. Collins dated for a while. She's the owner of the bed-and-breakfast."

"Please, be seated, and can I get you anything, coffee or tea?" she asked, indicating a chair.

CHAPTER 7

Mrs. Hensley was seventy-five years old and, according to records, had lost her mate almost four years earlier.

"Actually, I would love a cup of coffee if it's not too much trouble," Tom replied, taking a seat on the sofa instead of the chair which was covered with cat fur.

"No problem at all, Detective, I have some made in fact. I'll be right back."

While Mrs. Hensley was in the kitchen, Tom took the time to look around her living room. The house was old with a living room in front and a bedroom located off the living room on the right. He peered in to see that it was a small bedroom with a double-wide bed properly made up. A bathroom was off to the left, which he presumed was shared with another bedroom. The back part of the living room housed a small table and hutch with a door to the right that led to the kitchen which was in the back of the house. Nothing grand by any means but with exception for the cat fur seemed to be clean and neat. As he circled the room, he took in photos on a side table, knickknacks on an end table, and eventually stood in front of a tall, narrow window that faced the bed-and-breakfast.

That's when he saw Mrs. McCrea leaving her garden. Closing the gate behind her, she looked toward her neighbors and they made eye contact through the window. Her eyes widened, and then she immediately turned away, and Tom stepped back from the window somewhat embarrassed, but he couldn't fathom why he'd feel that way.

He could see the entire parking lot from Mrs. Hensley's living room window and some of the side yard. Hearing Mrs. Hensley, he resumed his seat on the sofa to wait for her.

"Here we go. I didn't know if you like sugar or cream, so I grabbed both." She sat the tray down on the coffee table and took a seat in the recliner that was angled toward the couch.

"Thank you so much. It's been quite a morning, and I haven't had nearly enough coffee," he said, picking up the cup.

"Now, what did you come to see me about?" she asked, perplexed.

"Your neighbor, do you like Mrs. McCrea?"

"Oh, heavens yes! She's such a sweet neighbor and was widowed at a young age. I've known Michaela since she was a child. She helped her aunt for many years while her aunt was still alive. Her aunt and uncle originally owned the place, but her uncle got sick and passed not too many years after they opened. Her aunt, Jane, who was a good friend of mine, simply couldn't keep up with the business without Hubert as she aged. But during that time, I saw Michaela over there quite often and up to her neck in work. But as Jane grew weaker with cancer, Michaela was spending much of her time there. The poor girl worked herself silly trying to help. After Jane passed, Michaela moved in and has done a wonderful job in rebuilding the place. She still works way too hard if you ask me."

"I see, so you like her?"

"Michaela, good heaven's yes! She's got her hands full, and yet from time to time, she brings cakes and cookies over for me to enjoy. In fact, she's even asked me over for dinner too. She's a sweetie. We even go to the same church. And when my John passed, she brought over casseroles and offered to help me in any way she could."

After leaving Mrs. Hensley's, Tom got in his car thinking about their conversation. The woman had nothing but praise for Mrs. McCrea. He feared Sean was getting in too deep which skewed his investigation. After leaving Mrs. McCrea's place the other night, Sean sat quietly in the car on the way back to the precinct, and when Tom peered over at him, he could tell Sean was deep in thought. But oddly, he didn't broach the subject of the interrogation. It hadn't gone as planned, and the sister-in-law basically threw them out on their ear. If only she hadn't been there…

No, it was imperative he interview others without Sean's presence. He could see why Sean was attracted to her; she was pretty, but things weren't adding up.

He made a U-turn and parked on the other side of the street. Mr. Owens who was eighty years old lived here. Maybe, he disliked the bed-and-breakfast being practically across the street and would give a true account on how he felt about the young proprietress.

Stepping up to the front veranda, Tom rang the bell, hoping he'd find Mr. Owens home. The only person in the neighborhood he contacted was Mrs. Hensley asking if it was okay to drop by. He still had a list of other people he wanted to speak with including an aunt that lived in a nearby town and a few people from her church, specifically, her pastor.

A few moments later, the door cracked open a margin, and an elderly gentleman poked his head out. "What do you want?" he barked.

Tom showed his badge. "I would like to speak with you about your neighbor, the bed-and-breakfast." He pointed across the street where the B&B sat caddy corner from his home.

"What about it?"

"Do you know the owner?"

"Yes, I know the owner, what about her?"

"May I come in, sir, so we can speak?" Tom asked having replaced his badge.

"I'm busy. My favorite shows are on…"

"Can you tell me more about the owner of the bed-and-breakfast?"

"Like what?"

"Are you upset that there is traffic with people coming and going all the time?"

The door opened wider, and Mr. Owens stepped back. Tom entered before the crotchety old man changed his mind. Mr. Owens walked away with the aid of a cane and almost tumbled into a big recliner. He was tall and spindly with thinning gray hair. The TV was blaring, causing Tom to wonder how the old man even heard the doorbell in the first place.

The house was a mess with newspapers scattered around the base of the recliner, dishes with dried food littered the coffee table, and the TV tray beside the recliner indicated Mr. Owens had been eating a snack when he was interrupted. Moving the tray closer to the recliner now, Mr. Owens picked up the sandwich he'd been eating and took a bite.

Tom, after moving papers that were stacked on the couch, sat on the edge. "Mr. Owens, would you mind turning the sound down on the TV?" he asked.

The old man looked at him and then grabbed the remote to turn it down.

"How do you feel about the bed-and-breakfast being so close?"

"I don't have any problems with it," he said, taking another bite of the sandwich.

"And what about the owner, Mrs. McCrea, is she a pleasant neighbor?"

"She bugs me!" he muttered around a mouthful of food.

Tom sat up straighter. Now he was getting somewhere. "Why is that?" he asked, pulling out his notepad.

"Because she's always asking if I need anything, and if it's not that, she's bringing food over. Sometimes, she asks me if I need anything from the store. I just want her to leave me the hell alone!"

Tom put away the notepad and sighed. "Did you know one of the guests was murdered, a man Mrs. McCrea dated?"

The old man shifted his gaze to Tom and frowned. "Someone was murdered at the bed-and-breakfast?"

"Not at the bed-and-breakfast, but I'm sure you probably heard on the news that Mr. Collins was found murdered in his home."

"I heard about that, but what does it have to do with Mrs. McCrea and the bed-and-breakfast?"

"Mrs. McCrea dated Mr. Collins."

"News to me… I probably should have offered my condolences to her," he said gruffly.

Tom let out his breath. He didn't want to explain that there was no need to offer condolences, so he thanked Mr. Owens for his time and left.

CHAPTER 8

As we have therefore opportunity, let us do good unto all men, especially unto them who are of the household of faith.

—Galatians 6:10

Over the course of the next few days, both detectives stayed busy questioning attorneys at the firm as well as a few secretaries who dated Collins at one time or another. The days slipped by quickly with no new fresh leads. Everyone had an alibi for the time of Collins's murder. Alibis the detectives intended to verify.

Sean took the time to research the files he checked out from storage to go through Mrs. McCrea's late husband's homicide. Opening the file, Brad McCrea's photo was paperclipped to the inside, and he pulled it out to get a better look. The man was handsome with blond hair and a rakish sort of look. Returning the photo to inside of the folder, he read on and noted the detectives assigned the case, both of whom retired a few years back. He remembered Detective Owens though the other escaped his memory. He decided to give Owens a call, hoping to get some inside information that wouldn't normally go into a report, a gut hunch more than anything else.

He hoped the number listed in the files was still active. On the third ring, the phone picked up. "Hello…"

"Detective Owens, this is Detective Ryan…"

"I'm no longer a detective, I'm retired." His voice was clipped and to the point, almost harsh.

"I know, sir. I was hoping I could pick your brain on an old unresolved case."

"What case?"

Sean frowned. As far as he knew, there weren't many cold cases on file at the precinct or were there? He'd have to check it out.

"It's the Brad McCrea file. According to the data, it appears his brake lines were cut, but there were no leads..."

"I remember that case. We thought it was the missus, but after the mechanics checked the brake lines, they determined it had to have been cut after he left. The line was partially cut, and it wouldn't have taken long, on the road he was driving, for the brakes to go completely out. The little woman couldn't have done it unless she had help."

"Do you think she had help?" Sean asked.

"If she did, we couldn't prove it even though she was the benefactor of a large insurance policy. Everything is in the file," he concluded.

"I've read through the file several times. But I didn't see anything about setting up surveillance on her. I was thinking that if she was in cahoots with another person, that possibly..."

"The department didn't have the resources available to approve for surveillance. But if you must know, my curiosity got the best of me. There were many nights I watched the place on my own time. The only thing I was rewarded with was my wife threatening to leave me."

"I see, so nothing out of the ordinary then."

"Nope!"

"Thank you, sir, can I call you if I think of anything else?"

"There's nothing else to tell. The case went cold. Not quite the bright spot I wanted on my record prior to retiring. If that's all, I need to go."

"Again, thanks for your time."

Peering over the desk, he found Tom staring at him. "Did you hear?"

"I did. I think setting up surveillance is smart. Should I put in a chit?"

CHAPTER 8

"First, I'd like to do this on my own time just to get a feel. If I find anything off, then I want to pursue it legally with department funds."

*****

The next morning, Sean pulled up across from the bed-and-breakfast with intentions of setting up surveillance, but he no sooner cut the engine when he spotted Michaela struggling to bring a large piece of furniture through the office door. It just didn't feel right to watch her struggle while he simply sat in the car and did nothing!

Grimacing as he exited the car, he slammed the door behind him. At the sound, Michaela looked up, spotting him.

"Hi," he said, approaching the porch.

Michaela stood erect with arms akimbo. Wearing shorts and a T-shirt with her hair pulled into a ponytail, she looked more like a teen. And as he neared, he could see she was once again void of makeup. With the exertion of trying to move the piece of furniture, her face was flushed, causing the spattering of freckles across her petite nose to stand out in contrast. Damn, if she wasn't cute as hell.

"Detective," she said. "To what do I owe the honor..."

Sean smiled as the last word spoken came out clipped. "Can I help you with this?" he said, pointing at the piece of furniture, ignoring her question.

"I'm fine, thank you."

Sean belly laughed and peered up at her. Folding his arms across his chest, he tilted his head. "What is this anyway?"

She was clearly annoyed. "It's a Hoosier cabinet."

"A what?"

"An antique," she stated.

"Okay, so what's it used for?"

"It doesn't matter. If you don't mind, I'd like to get it inside." Once again, she started struggling with moving the piece of furniture across the threshold while trying to ignore him.

"Stop, you'll hurt yourself. Let me...stand back." He cautioned having stepped up on the porch.

When Michaela stood back, Sean stretched his arms finding purchase and started sliding the furniture through the door, lifting it to clear the threshold. After lifting the piece, he slid furniture sliders under the feet to protect the hardwood floors. Thankfully, she'd already had the sliders ready to go.

As aggravated as she was with the detective showing up again so soon, she couldn't help but admire his strength. He easily pushed the antique through the space, not even breaking a sweat! And when he peered up at her with those gray eyes etched in dark lashes, she was almost spellbound. And she didn't want to be attracted to this man. Not one bit!

"Where do you want it?" he asked, peering at her intently with those luscious eyes.

"Thank you, Detective, but I can take it from here," she said rather too quickly.

The phone on the desk rang, and she scowled. "I need to get that…"

"Okay, where do you want this?"

Flustered, she pointed to the opposite wall where there was an empty space. "Over there." She gestured with her hands.

While she answered the phone, Sean pushed the cabinet across the floor to the opposite wall centering it in the space provided between other shelving loaded with candles, mugs, and what looked like homemade potpourri. He stood back and looked the piece over, clearly puzzled.

Michaela came up behind him. "It was used in the kitchen, and flour was stored in this bin…" She pulled out a drawer that was on hinges to show him the metal interior.

"Interesting…"

"I'm going to use it to display items that are sold at the B&B. It fits perfectly in this spot, and it's a great accompaniment to the bed-and-breakfast. Just the look I was going for." She smiled. Reaching up, she pulled her ponytail, tightening the band that held it in place though strays had already escaped their confines, framing her face. "And I got it at a bargain price too, so I couldn't say no!" she exclaimed.

CHAPTER 8

Turning to him, her smile faltered. "Why did you stop by again?"

"I was thinking you might be privy to any enemies Collins had."

"James…? Detective, I really didn't know him that well. Like I said before, we only dated a few times."

"But it was your sister-in-law who told us that he tried to rape you. Did you report it to the police?" Peering down at her, it angered him that any man would try to manhandle her. Michaela was petite, and guessing her to be about 5 feet 3 inches tall, she wouldn't have been able to protect herself.

"No."

"Why not…" he said, resting his hands on the top of his hips and jutting one foot out in front of the other in a nonchalant stance she'd seen men do often.

"It's not important." She turned away.

"I think it was important, and I'd like to know the reason why you didn't report it."

"Look, he didn't rape me. There was nothing to report!" she exclaimed with hands raised in the air as she turned to face him again.

"I didn't come over to anger you, just try to get more questions answered." He started to leave, heading toward the office door when she stopped him.

"I'm sorry, Detective. Thank you for helping me with the cabinet. The least I can do is offer a glass of iced tea."

Sean stopped and turned in the doorway and then nodded. "Thanks."

He followed her to the kitchen and sank down in one of the kitchen chairs as she grabbed a glass from the cupboard, filled it with ice and then sweet tea from the fridge. She handed the glass to him, and when he reached to take it, their fingers brushed. It was like the moment stood still as their eyes locked, held, and then shifted away. He grasped the glass, and she let go only to sink into the chair on the opposite side of the table.

They sat in awkward silence for a few minutes before Snickers came running in. "Hey, there, little guy." Sean reached down, and Snickers came to him for petting. Michaela watched transfixed by his strong, tanned hands as they ran across Snicker's back. Heaven, help her! Why was she so attracted to this man? He was the enemy, wasn't he?

Sean put the glass of iced tea to his mouth and gulped hardily, draining the glass in one full sweep. She could see his Adam's apple bob with each swallow. He sat the glass down on the table and looked over at her. She sat transfixed, staring at him.

"Heaven to earth?" he said with a smile, waving his hand in front of her. "Do I have something on my face?"

She blinked and then blushed, having been caught staring rudely. "I'm sorry, it's just been a long while since I've seen a man guzzle a drink down so fast." She placed her hands on the tabletop and clasped them together tightly. "It reminded me of Brad."

But the truth of it was Brad might have guzzled down a drink in his time, but he was never quite as sexy as Detective Ryan. The thought flitted through her mind, and immediately, she felt guilty.

Sean was clearly uncomfortable and mumbled an apology. "I need to go, thanks for the tea," he said, rising from the chair. As he rose, his eyes slid across the room to the counter where muffins were cooling; lingering for just a moment, he inhaled deeply of their scent, and then he looked away.

"Let me pack a couple of muffins for the road," Michaela said.

Crossing the room, she placed muffins in a brown paper bag, but when she turned to hand them to Detective Ryan, he was closer than she realized, having come up behind her. When she turned, his arm grazed her breasts, and both took a sharp intake of breath. The room was filled with tension as their eyes met, shifted away, and then met again. Neither spoke. Michaela's lips parted, and her tongue darted out, licking her bottom lip, and Sean could see the heartbeat at the base of her throat.

Then in unison, they apologized. Sean took the paper bag, thanked her again, and quickly exited toward the office. He stepped out on the porch; his heartbeat had accelerated with the mere brush of her breasts. And that wasn't the only thing on the rise, so making a hasty retreat was the most appropriate thing given the circumstances.

CHAPTER 8

Michaela normally would have walked a person out, but she stayed in the kitchen, feeling the heat across her face. She closed her eyes and replayed the scene. Reaching up, she brushed her hand across the tips of her breasts and thought she couldn't be more embarrassed than she already was. How could she ever face the man again!

CHAPTER 9

But examine everything carefully, hold fast to that which is good.

—1 Thessalonians 5:21

After further research on Mrs. McCrea's relatives, Tom discovered that her mother had remarried and lived somewhere over in Europe. The next closest living relative was an aunt named Hilda Montgomery.

Dialing the number, he sat back in his desk chair and waited. "Hello?"

"Mrs. Montgomery, I'm Det. Tom Hanson of the Los Pinos Police Department. I'm inquiring about your niece, Michaela McCrea. When was the last time you saw or spoke with her?"

"Who is this?" she asked.

"Det. Tom Hanson. I'm investigating a recent homicide in which your niece is a person of interest in the case."

"A murder case, why is Michaela a person of interest?"

"Right now, I'm not at liberty to say, but any information you can provide will help us." Tom cleared his throat and sat forward in his chair, resting both forearms on the edge of the desk.

"I haven't spoken with Michaela in some time, so I'm afraid I can't tell you much."

"What *do* you remember about her then?"

"I never saw much of her while she was growing up either. Her mother, Heidi, and I are twins and both went our separate ways once we left home. It wasn't long after leaving home that Heidi found herself pregnant, and after giving birth, the baby, Michaela, went to live with our mother. Our family was never close, and I think the last time I spoke with Michaela is when I found out that my older sister had passed and Michaela's late husband was killed in a car accident. I only called to offer my condolences, and that's about it."

"Most people know more than they think they know. For instance, while speaking with your sister, did she complain about Michaela? What type of person is she? Is she prone to violence, or do anything contrary to the law? Does she have any homicidal tendencies, etc.? Her late husband's demise was labeled as an unsolved murder case. His brake lines were cut." He added, hoping she'd open up.

He heard an intake of breath on the other end of the line. "I-I didn't know that. And you think it was Michaela who murdered her late husband?"

"We're not investigating that case. This is a new one."

"I really don't know my niece that well. Like I say, none of the family were close. My sister and I rarely spoke to each other back then. But what few times we did speak, she never mentioned Michaela at all. You have to understand, our parents had two separate families with Jane, our older sister, who was born eighteen years before Heidi and I were born. After raising an only child, our parents weren't ready for another family, much less twins. As soon as Heidi and I could, we left home and went our separate ways. A few months later, Heidi married and had Michaela almost right away. Then the next thing I know, our mother is raising Michaela, and Heidi is off somewhere. We were wild, but as far as I can tell, Heidi never really settled until she remarried and moved to Europe."

"Thank you for your time. Background information like this helps a great deal." Tom hung up and mulled over the chain of events. Mrs. McCrea didn't have much of a family life.

Going through the files Ryan had pulled from storage on Brad McCrea's homicide, he found information on the brother living in Alaska by the name of Brent. Were he and Marissa still married and simply separated?

He dialed Brent McCrea; it was possible that having his brother murdered and Michaela getting off scot-free, that he'd be willing to talk.

The line answered. "McCrea Trucking."

"Yes, I'm looking for Brent McCrea." Once again, Tom settled back in his desk chair. The precinct noise grew louder as more people were brought in and reports were being typed up. The hum of activity was one thing he'd grown accustomed to.

"May I ask who's calling?" the receptionist asked.

"Det. Tom Hanson of the Los Pinos Police Department."

"One moment, sir." At first, he thought they were disconnected since there was no music or recording indicating that he was put on hold.

Shuffling was finally heard on the end of the line and then a voice. "Brent McCrea."

"Yes, this is Det. Tom Hanson. I'm calling in regard to your sister-in-law, Michaela McCrea. I need some information on her as I'm investigating a recent homicide."

"Recent. My brother was murdered over five years ago, and as far as I know, the case went cold. Michaela was declared innocent." His voice hardened.

"I'm investigating another homicide that took place just a couple of weeks ago. Mrs. McCrea was dating the man who was murdered. Can you tell me more about your sister-in-law?"

"Another homicide? I didn't think Michaela was guilty of murdering my brother, and it was proved the brake lines were cut while she was at home. I never knew Michaela well since I left for Alaska shortly after she and Brad started dating. But what's this about a boyfriend?"

"I really can't provide details since it's an ongoing case. Mrs. McCrea is a person of interest, and I'm trying to get background information on her that will help with the investigation." Tom rubbed his eyes. He was tired.

"Like I say, I didn't know her well though she invited me several times to visit saying she thought Brad would be excited to see me. They both seemed quite happy and very much in love, which is why I didn't think she had any involvement in Brad's death. But finding out another man she's dated is murdered, it makes me wonder. I wished I could provide you with more information."

CHAPTER 9

"Thank you for your time. If you should think of anything else, please don't hesitate to call me at this number. Oh, I have one other question. Are you and the Mrs. still married?"

"We're separated. Have you spoken with Marissa?"

"We have."

"I haven't spoken with her in a few months. I don't know why we haven't signed the divorce papers and gotten on with our lives," Brent sighed.

After hanging up, Tom sat back in frustration. Either those who knew Mrs. McCrea liked her very well or they simply didn't know her at all. It was particularly odd; those who should be closest didn't have a clue about her. He would try church members next.

Sean was out surveilling Mrs. McCrea's activities to see what went on at the bed-and-breakfast. She may have been in cahoots with someone else, and watching the place may provide more information.

On the off chance that Collins had spoken with his secretary, Ms. Atkins, about Mrs. McCrea, Tom decided he'd give her a quick call.

The phone only rang once before it was picked up. "Mr. Collins's office, this is Ms. Atkins. How may I help you?"

"Ms. Atkins, this is Det. Tom Hanson of the Los Pinos Police Department. If you recall, my partner and I were there not long ago investigating Mr. Collins's murder. I was wondering if he ever spoke about a Mrs. McCrea?"

"Yes, Detective, I do recall your visit to the firm. And I remember Mr. Collins asking me to order flowers for a Mrs. McCrea over at the Bayside Bed-and-Breakfast. He said that she ran a great B&B and wanted to personally thank her for her hospitality."

"Did he mention anything else about her?"

"I don't believe so."

"Did he act differently after meeting Mrs. McCrea?" Tom scooted back in his chair and opened the desk drawer to pull out some aspirin, a headache was forming.

"Now that you mention it, he seemed more distracted after staying at the bed-and-breakfast. I really didn't think much of it at the time, but he, well, changed. He seemed to have more purpose, and as far as I could tell, the only one he was seeing at the time was Trina Myerson. He usually was dating several women at the same time, but that ceased."

"And how do you know all this?" Tom asked.

"Easy! Mr. Collins loved to boast about his love life to me. I was the one who often made reservations for him at fancy restaurants and the like. But it was later that he changed. He no longer was asking me to make reservations or to buy expensive gifts to send."

"Thank you, Ms. Atkins, for your time." Tom hung up and jotted down notes. Mrs. McCrea it seemed had some kind of hold over Collins, and maybe, he fancied himself in love with her.

Sitting back in his desk chair, he stretched his legs out and crossed his ankles. With his fingers entwined across his stomach, he leaned his head back and closed his eyes. His eyes popped open, the parents, her in-laws. Looking through the files, he didn't see parents listed, which meant more research. It didn't take long to find the information he was after. Brad McCrea's parents were Bryan and Jean McCrea who were residents of New York for twenty years before moving to Florida.

He called the number listed, and the phone was answered after the first ring. "Hello."

"Mrs. McCrea? I'm Det. Tom Hanson of the Los Pinos Police Department, and I was calling hoping you could provide some information on your daughter-in-law, Michaela McCrea."

"Did you say Los Pinos?"

"Yes…"

"About Michaela? Can I ask why?" she hesitated.

"It's in regard to an ongoing investigation in which your daughter-in-law is a person of interest. Can you tell us a bit about her?" With his elbow on the desk, Tom rested his forehead in his upturned palm.

"Are you still trying to find out who murdered our son…"

"Actually no, there has been a more recent homicide."

"I see, well actually, no I don't see. Are you saying you suspect Michaela?"

Tom exhaled. "She's a person of interest."

CHAPTER 9

"You should still be trying to find our son's murderer before you try to solve a more recent homicide, Detective." She sighed loudly into the phone. "Both our sons moved to California to attend college and loved it there so much they stayed. Both married. While we attended both weddings, we never knew either Michaela or Marissa well. Although we understand that Marissa was, well, I'm not sure how to put it, but she wasn't the right girl for Brent, or any man for that matter. Anyway, we didn't know either very well. A year later, Michaela had Chase, our grandson, and we flew out after she'd given birth and stayed for a couple of weeks. She was very nice and gracious while we visited, and we loved being able to hold our grandson.

"Bryan, my husband, and I were tired of the cold winters in New York and decided to move to Florida where I have some relatives. After moving here, Bryan had an accident and is now homebound. It wasn't long after Bryan's accident that Brad was murdered. I'm afraid we haven't seen Michaela since the funeral. She was pretty torn up, but then so were we. There's really nothing more to tell you."

"Do you think your daughter-in-law might have had a hand in your son's murder?"

Mrs. McCrea gasped on the other end of the line and finally said, "No. Do you think she did?"

"We're not investigating your son's murder but trying to establish ground if she might be involved in the current homicide investigation."

She exhaled heavily. "If she's guilty, I want my son's case reopened!"

"Yes, ma'am. Thank you for your time." He hung up more exasperated than ever. Why didn't any of Michaela's relatives know her?

With a new thought forming, Tom put in a call to Trina Myerson. She just may have more to say about Mrs. McCrea. He called her work number, but it went to voice mail. Sighing, he tried her home number, and it was answered after the fifth ring.

"Hello…" a soft moan could be heard and then some other background noise.

"Ms. Myerson, this is Det. Tom Hanson. I would like to stop by and ask a few more questions."

"Questions, oh, you mean about James. I'm actually busy right now, can this wait until another time?" A giggle erupted, and Tom pulled his cell away from his ear. It was apparent she had company, and they weren't just chatting.

"I need to speak with you right away. I'll be over to your home in about ten minutes." He hung up before she had a chance to protest. He sure hoped to hell that she wouldn't bail.

Pulling up to her house, her SUV was parked in the driveway but also a black BMW was parked behind it. Yep, she had company, and Tom wondered who she was entertaining.

He started to ring the doorbell, but the door was opened with Trina wearing a robe. She looked past Tom and then back up at him. "Where's your partner?"

"He's working."

"Oh, I was hoping he'd be with you. What is it you want to know?" She hugged her robe a little tighter to her body, and as Tom was about to speak, he caught movement behind her and glanced past her.

Trina looked over her shoulder. "I have company," she said.

"I know, I saw the BMW in your drive. I wanted to know if you thought that Mr. Collins changed much after meeting Mrs. McCrea."

Trina stepped back into the foyer and motioned for Tom to come in. "Please, have a seat. Can I get you anything, coffee or water, perhaps?"

"No, thank you."

Both of them took a seat, and Tom took his notepad out, ready to take notes. "Yes, James changed considerably after meeting Mrs. McCrea."

"Can you be specific?" Tom asked, leaning forward.

"He was distracted more than anything. He was here, but yet not here. I would have thought it was a particularly difficult case he was working on, but there were a couple of times while having sex that he called me by her name." Trina sighed deeply. "I was hurt, and we even fought. He tried to reassure me everything was okay and that he didn't have feelings for her, but I know that he did..." She looked off in the distance.

Again, movement caught Tom's eye, and this time, he saw a man dart across the hallway entrance completely nude. He turned back to Trina, and she merely smiled.

"I need to get busy," she said and rose from her chair.

Staying seated, Tom asked, "Were you upset enough to kill Collins?"

"Of course not, if I had wanted to murder anyone, it would have been that woman!" she said vehemently, placing her arms on her hips.

Tom stood and thanked her for her time. Getting in behind the wheel of the car, he reached over and grabbed a stick of gum, his attempt to stop reaching for antacids. He shoved the gum into his mouth, and the burst of flavor was satisfying.

Outside of church members, there was still others at the law firm they needed to interview. So far, those they had called in for questioning turned up nothing new.

CHAPTER 10

The heart is deceitful above all things and beyond cure. Who can understand it?

—Jeremiah 17:9

Later that same evening, Sean parked on a side street that allowed him to see the front of the bed-and-breakfast. There were three cars in the parking lot, and over on the side sat Michaela's car. For well over an hour, there was no obvious activity, but he was rewarded when he saw her come out a side door from their private entrance. She had a trash bag in her hand, and walking across to the barrels, she threw it in. Turning, she looked in his direction and paused.

For a minute, Sean thought he was caught given that even with dusk, the days were still long, and he hoped she didn't recognize his car and come over to question him.

She changed into pants and an oversized sweater from the shorts and T-shirt she wore that morning. His eyes slid down, stopping at her breasts and replayed the morning's scene. He swallowed hard. She stood for a moment longer and then went back inside.

He was becoming fascinated with this woman, and each time he saw her, the sexual tension was building. And he could tell that she was as affected by this as much as he. The problem was he was investigating her for possible murder. The two simply didn't mix.

He sat in the car for another hour. Nothing! He finally turned the key in the ignition and fired up the engine. It was time to leave.

He silently hoped for another glimpse of her before leaving, but it didn't happen.

*****

On Saturday morning, Sean stopped by the farmer's market, knowing one of the vendors sold fresh baked pastries. He was hungry after pulling in a late night, and the delicate pastries with fresh brewed coffee sounded good.

After purchasing a couple apple fritters and a cup of coffee, he headed over to one of the nearby tables to enjoy his meal. He no sooner taken a bite when he heard a familiar voice. Looking up, he saw Chase. He knew Michaela had to be near, and then he spotted her picking through the vegetables. She picked up several zucchinis, and looking them over, she felt for soft spots. He almost groaned watching her examine the vegetables. God, what was happening to him?

She looked up to ensure Chase was close by and then looking beyond spotted Detective Ryan. He was staring transfixed at the zucchinis she held. Dropping the vegetables into a small tote, she turned to the cashier to pay for her purchase. Losing his appetite, Sean put the pastry down and then rolled it up in the paper bag and tossed the works into the nearest receptacle.

After tossing his breakfast, he turned and almost bumped into Michaela who was standing right in front of him.

"Detective, are you following me?" she asked.

He shook his head, wondering if she was referring to last night. Maybe, she did recognize his vehicle. This morning, her reddish-brown curls framed her face, and soft strands were picked up in the morning breeze. Bright-green eyes were fixed on him. She wore shorts and a T-shirt with a V-neck with a hint of cleavage that had his imagination running rampant.

"I sometimes stop by the market to pick up Henry's fresh pastries for breakfast," he explained.

Michaela peered at him through squinted eyes, clearly not believing him. She brushed hair from her eyes and then said awkwardly, "It's nice running into you. We have to go." She turned on unsteady feet and seeing Chase held up a hand, indicating it was time to leave. But Chase, upon seeing Detective Ryan, had other ideas.

"Hey, Detective Ryan…" He ran up, and they high-fived, slapping palms in the air. "What are you doing here?" he asked.

"Having breakfast, and you?"

"We're picking up food for the bed-and-breakfast. Mom likes to get here early so we can get the best stuff." He looked up at Detective Ryan with adoration.

Michaela wanted to tell him not to trust this man, but that went against everything she'd taught him about respecting the police.

Chase continued talking to the detective about something which Michaela totally missed as she watched Detective Ryan interact with her son once again. He was good with kids, and that pleased her for some odd reason.

When his eyes shifted to hers, she blushed, realizing she'd been watching him intently once again. She blinked hard and looked away only for her eyes to rotate back to his.

"Mom, can we get some pastries?" Chase cut in. "Mom…"

Michaela forced herself to look away and asked, "What?"

"Pastries, can we get some? Please! I really want a jelly doughnut…"

Her eyes riveted back to Sean's, and he still held her gaze. It was like everything else faded in the background, and she found herself leaning toward him. She licked her lips, and Sean's eyes dipped down to the luscious full lips that glimmered in the sunlight. Her eyes widened.

"Mom!" She was snatched back to reality as her son tugged on her arm. Looking down, she nodded but couldn't remember to what she was giving ascent to.

Chase ran over to the vendor and pointed to one of the jelly doughnuts. Thankfully, he only wanted a pastry, and as she turned to walk that way, she found Detective Ryan's hand on her arm, guiding her toward the vendor. It felt good, and she didn't try to extricate herself from his grasp. It felt endearing somehow, even safe.

Sean took the liberty of steering her toward her son. He wanted to kiss her badly, and seeing her lean in only confirmed that she was developing feelings for him as he was for her. While he only had about an hour before work, he wanted to spend that time with her.

"Can I get you a coffee?" he asked, his own appetite returning. "And maybe a pastry, I'm buying!" He smiled.

Michaela looked up at him with wide eyes.

"Let me guess," he continued. "You probably would like a fancy coffee drink, and I'm guessing chocolate-covered doughnuts?"

She laughed. "How'd you guess?"

"It's easy, I'm a detec—" he stopped short and then finished, "Most women like chocolate!"

She didn't flinch or look away this time but instead replied, "Caramel latte and, yes, to the doughnut."

As they ate at the table Sean recently vacated, they talked about a myriad of things, and she found Detective Ryan quite interesting. Wearing tight jeans and a T-shirt, he appeared so casual, friendlier than he did when he wore a shirt and service weapon. She admired his strong arms, the girth of his neck, and wanted to reach up and run a hand through his hair that was a little too long. The ends curled slightly, resting on the back of his neck. When he rose to toss the trash into the receptacle, she enjoyed watching him.

"It's almost time for me to get to work," he said. "I really enjoyed your company."

"I enjoyed this time too, Detective Ryan," she said.

"Please, call me Sean…"

Michaela cleared her throat and looked down. Should she ask him to call her by her given name or keep everything formal? She was after all under investigation.

When he placed his hand over hers that were clasped together on the tabletop, she inhaled sharply but didn't attempt to remove her hands. Looking up at him, he smiled. "If it makes you uncomfortable…"

"No, I like the name Sean."

"Can I call you Michaela?" he asked.

She nodded; she loved how her name rolled off his tongue.

After parting ways, she realized just how much she'd come to like this man. And if she were being honest, it was more than like, she was very much attracted to him, and though it was awkward considering the circumstances, she was sexually attracted to him and enjoyed his company. Her heartbeat notched up whenever she saw him.

CHAPTER 11

Now the works of the flesh are evident, which are: adultery, fornication, uncleanness, lewdness.

—Galatians 5:19

"You can't be seen here!" she said, looking beyond him.

"I know that…but you haven't been taking my calls." He brushed past her, stepping toward the makeshift bar and poured himself a glass of Scotch. "You want some?"

"Why the visit…?"

"Like I said, you weren't returning my calls."

"I didn't have reason to return them, nothing new has unfolded."

"Then since I'm here, maybe you should make my visit worthwhile." He smiled and set his drink down.

"Really now?" She smiled despite that she was upset with him for showing up unannounced.

He stepped over to her and pulled her face toward his and planted a kiss that was rough. Having just swallowed Scotch, he tasted good, and she parted her lips for him.

"Hmmm, you taste wonderful?" he said.

They started fumbling to remove each other's clothing. He removed the T-shirt she wore over her head and admired the lacy bra she wore underneath. He rubbed his thumbs over her nipples through the bra before tweaking them with this thumb and index. She inhaled sharply.

She unbuttoned his shirt and pulled it off his shoulders, running her hands across his pecks. He in turn unclasped her bra, freeing her breasts. He cupped the mounds and enjoyed the feel of their softness against his calloused hands.

"Come..." he pulled away and grabbed her hands to lead her to the bedroom. Pulling her close, he pushed her shorts and panties off in one full sweep. Cupping his hand between her legs, she almost collapsed against him. He started kneading her clitoris and then pushed his fingers deep inside. She spread her legs further apart, and he took full advantage. Pushing her onto the bed behind, her eyes widened as she landed softly. He pulled his pants off, revealing his erection and need for her.

"Come here!" he demanded, holding his penis outward for her to take. She complied, and he almost ejaculated right then and there. But wanting to prolong their lovemaking, he stopped her short of coming.

Pushing her back on the bed, he lowered himself and spreading her legs; he thrust his hardened shaft inside, causing her to rise to meet each of his thrusts. Again and again, he pushed deep inside only to pull his shaft partly out. He enjoyed driving her wild with need, and it drove him almost to the brink. Together, they climaxed, crying out in delight before settling back to earth, lying spent in each other's arms.

Resting her head on his shoulders, she could feel his heart beating as fast as hers. "That was heavenly," she said, circling his nipple with her finger.

"That is one thing. You're good for a fuck..."

Stiffening beside him, she heard him chuckle. "You take everything so seriously. You make it nigh to impossible to want to have sex with any other woman."

"And do you want to?" she asked, lifting her chin to better see him.

"Want to what?"

"Fuck someone else other than me!"

"No, but if I did, she would fall short, very short in coming up to your standards, love!"

Rolling over on his side, he reached for her nipple, but she pulled away. “Come here, sweet, I want to make love to you again before I leave.”

“You’re using me!”

He once again chuckled. This time, he pulled her into his embrace with force.

“Ouch, you’re hurting me!”

“I’m not hurting you, and you know it.” He chuckled.

And under his deft fingers, she once again was ready…

CHAPTER 12

Go thy way, eat thy bread with joy, and drink thy wine with a merry heart for God now accepteth thy works.

—Ecclesiastes 9:7

Michaela was tempted to warn Chase about running up and down the stairs, but she didn't want to take away his enthusiasm. He was excited they were going out for pizza but more specifically where they were going. Marcella's Pizza Hub had great pizza, but the arcade area at the back of the restaurant was a favorite for families. With several pinball machines, kids flocked to the back with parents pulling out bills in exchange for coins to keep their kids entertained. Chase ran up the stairs now to pull coins from his bank, a football that Marissa had given him a few years earlier for his birthday, prefilled with coins to get him started.

Running back down the stairs, Chase's pockets jingled with the coins he managed to pack in, anticipating the games he'd play at the arcade.

Marissa laughed, and Michaela turned to her to thank her again for watching the B&B while they went out for pizza.

"Go have fun, you two. Don't worry about the B&B. There's not much to do in the evening as it is. Go…" She urged, steering Michaela toward the door.

As they entered the restaurant, Chase immediately ran to the back with coins he'd pulled earlier ready to play the coveted games he loved. Michaela smiled at his enthusiasm and settled for a booth relatively close to the arcade so she could keep a close eye on her son.

Michaela loved the little Italian restaurant. Tall wood dividers separated the booths with latticework at the top where faux grape clusters were woven into the lattice. A red tablecloth was spread across the table with a lit candle. The walls were decorated with faux brick with stenciled Italian scenery. The booth she occupied was of an arched window looking out to a landscape with vineyards and cypress trees.

Sean heard the bell ring over the door, but it wasn't until slender legs and a well-shaped posterior passed his booth that he looked up from his meal. He almost choked when he saw it was Michaela. He was glad Tom declined his offer to stop for pizza. As it was, Tom needled him about being too involved. Tom was worked up over the fact that Sean had eaten supper with them. No self-respecting detective got involved with a suspect.

Sean debated whether to let her know he was here. She'd opened to him and told him far more than Tom could have gotten from her. Tom was old-school. No point beating around the bush, and he often came out as the bad cop even if that wasn't their game play.

As she settled into a back booth, a waiter came over with a menu, and it bothered Sean that the kid hung off to the side, making small talk with her. He laughed far too much at whatever she said.

When she got up and walked over to the salad bar, the same kid came over to refill some of the bins with fresh produce while he continued to chat with her. She smiled politely and nodded a lot, indicating to Sean she was just being nice to the kid. It wasn't until she started to return to her booth that she looked up and made eye contact with him. He smiled and held up a hand. She smiled in return and then headed for her table.

He debated with himself if he should walk over to say hi. It wasn't like they were friends. On the other hand, while he was attracted to her, his gut told him she wasn't guilty. After wrestling with the idea, he finally got up.

"Hi," he said, walking up to her booth.

Michaela looked up and returned his greeting.

"I was working late and decided to stop for pizza on my way home. Fancy running into you here..." *Lame,* he thought, *lame!*

She slowly smiled. "It's a great place to eat, and Chase hasn't been out for pizza in long time. He's in the back playing games."

"This is a great place for pizza, and the arcade is a big draw for kids, so I'm not surprised he's back there playing," he said with his hands in his pockets.

"Would you like to sit?" she asked.

"Thanks, but I have pizza back at my table."

"Chase happens to like you a lot," she confessed, looking toward the back. "The other night, he couldn't stop talking about you and how you helped him understand things about being a detective and what it takes to become one. And he enjoyed running into you the other morning at the farmer's market. He'd be disappointed if you didn't join us." She looked down at the book she brought and slowly closed it.

Sean didn't know if she truly wanted him to stay, and he was about ready to leave when Chase walked up. Seeing Detective Ryan, he greeted him enthusiastically.

"Are you going to join us?" he asked expectantly.

Sean smiled and explained he had pizza at his table.

"Go get it, I'll slide over so you can sit next to me," Chase encouraged.

Sean looked over at Michaela, and she nodded. That was all he needed.

Once everyone was settled, he gave Chase a piece of his pizza while they waited for the one Michaela ordered to be brought out.

Sean asked Chase if he was into sports and what he liked. It didn't take much for Chase to start telling him all about soccer and that he was in a team that played every Saturday. As they continued the topic of sports, Michaela watched Detective Ryan. He seemed to read her too well, and she felt raw and vulnerable around him. He glanced over at her and smiled when he caught her staring. She blushed and looked down at her salad.

Sean liked that she blushed so easily. Tonight, she wore a simple tank top and jeans that hugged her well. He couldn't take his eyes off her when she walked past his booth. Her shapely backside was way too pleasing, and with each step, the slight sway of her ass stopped him with a pizza slice halfway to his mouth!

When their pizza was delivered, Sean's was already long gone, so they shared the second pizza between the three of them. Sean ordered another beer and told the kid waiter that Michaela would like another glass of wine.

Michaela held up a slice of the pizza and sunk her teeth into the crisp crust with lots of rich, red pizza sauce and cheesy goodness. The olives, pepperoni, bell pepper, and pineapple toppings were liberally sprinkled on top.

"This pizza is so good," she muttered, and Detective Ryan nodded in agreement.

"It's the best pizza in town if you ask me," Chase spoke up, chewing with his mouth full.

Michaela didn't have the heart to remind him of his manners.

As the meal was consumed, Michaela observed Detective Ryan speaking easily with Chase; she had to admire the man. Anyone who showed genuine interest in a mother's child could easily worm their way into her heart. And though he might not believe it, Chase raved about Detective Ryan for at least a couple of days after the dinner which was only reinforced at the farmer's market. He was turned toward Chase now, catching every word with interest. He was big and strong with capable hands. Her turn of thoughts had her blushing.

"Mom can't attend many of my games or practices because of the B&B," Chase was saying. This turn in the conversation caught Michaela's attention.

"I imagine running a B&B can be time-consuming." Looking over at Michaela, he asked, "Do you have part-time help?"

She nodded. "From time to time, my sister-in-law, whom you met, and my friend, Heather, helps out. It's nice when they can be there on Saturday morning or afternoon so I can attend Chase's games."

"She usually can't go to any of the practices because she has to serve wine and cheese and stuff. Everyone is boring, and all they talk about is what they've been doing. Occasionally, we have guests that stick to themselves. Once I heard a lot of noise from one of the rooms like the lady was crying for help. I told Mom that I thought the guy might be hurting his wife. Mom said she'd check on them but not to worry."

With a glass of wine halfway to her mouth, Michaela quickly set it back down on the table. Embarrassed, she glanced at Detective Ryan.

Sean laughed and winked at Michaela before replying. "I'm sure your mom was able to reassure you nothing was wrong."

A wink, and yet it was so much more. Michaela's heart softened even further.

"Hey! My birthday is next weekend, and Mom is throwing me a party. She's fixing one of my favorites, lasagna! You want to come?"

"How old will you be?" Sean hedged.

"Ten."

"It sounds like you're going to have a lot of fun."

"I'd really like it if you came," Chase insisted.

Sean looked over at Michaela trying to figure an easy way to decline when she spoke up. "We'd both like it if you could come. I always make more food than I should, and actually, I could use some help with supervision." She smiled, revealing those dimples that Sean adored. He wondered if her late husband tried to make her laugh often just to see them. But it was more than that; it was the way her eyes sparkled and the spattering of freckles across her petite nose.

"In that case, I'd love to come. Can I bring anything?"

"Just you and a lot of energy!" she exclaimed.

*****

Sean was told to come around to the side entrance of the bed-and-breakfast, the main door to their private living quarters. After asking his sister what a ten-year-old might want for a birthday gift, he was able to pick up a Lego set, hoping Chase didn't already own one. He thought of a baseball mitt but quickly discarded the idea since Chase was into soccer.

CHAPTER 12

He knocked on the door, and it was opened by none other than Chase himself. His eyes got big when he saw the huge gift in Sean's arms.

"Is that for me?" he asked.

"Of course, big guy, it's your birthday after all!" Sean laughed.

"Wow, thanks!" He grabbed the box, opening the door wider for Sean to enter. "Mom's in the kitchen."

Leaving Sean to find his way to the kitchen, Chase ran out through the French doors to the small patio where other kids had gathered, showing them the big gift he just received.

Sean entered, and seeing the small dining area was set up with balloons and other gifts, he turned left into the hallway that led to the kitchen on the right and the B&B office to the left. Peering through the doorway, he saw Michaela bending over to push a casserole into the oven. He hesitated, enjoying the view. When she straightened, he noticed she was wearing an apron again.

"Hi," he said.

She turned around quickly and smiled. "Hey, glad you could make it!"

"My pleasure. What can I do to help?" he offered.

"I think the food is underway, and I'm just waiting for a few stragglers before we start the games!" She laughed.

Marissa slipped up behind him holding a bakery box that held the birthday cake. "Hope I'm not too late, traffic was a bear!" she said before glancing at Detective Ryan in surprise when she realized it was him.

Michaela took the box from her and set it on the counter to open it. "Oh, I love it!" she exclaimed. "Chase will be so excited to see it's a soccer-themed cake and chocolate, one of his favorites."

Sean inclined his head to Marissa. Michaela, unaware of the sudden tension, closed the lid on the box. "Marissa, you remember Detective Ryan..."

"Of course, where's your partner on this bright afternoon?" she asked.

"I assume he's probably home with his family," Sean replied easily. "I think I'll see how the boys are faring on the patio."

As soon as he left the room, Marissa shot Michaela a look. “What were you thinking in inviting him to the party?”

Michaela glanced up from the tray where she was arranging food. “Chase has taken a keen liking to him and invited him to the party when we ran into him at the pizza place.”

“Just be careful…he is after all investigating you. I don’t want you thinking he’s Mr. Nice Guy!”

“Don’t worry, let’s just have fun, okay?” Michaela went back to arranging food on the tray.

Marissa stepped out of the kitchen to check on the boys and to see what Detective Ryan was up to. Much to her surprise, he was teaching the boys to shoot baskets, and they all seemed to be entranced. *Smooth*, she thought.

Sean was so busy with the boys showing them how to dribble and shoot baskets that it took him by surprise when a woman jumped in front of him and spiked the ball right out of his arms and then shot it into the basket. She belly laughed and then held out her right hand.

“Hi; I’m Heather!” She was petite with short wavy blond hair and friendly blue eyes.

“Sean Ryan.” They shook hands.

“You mean Detective Ryan, right?” Her friendly smile held no grudge.

He smiled. “Yeah, that detective.”

“Well, I hope you’ve discovered that our Michaela is innocent.”

Sean simply smiled.

“Okay, ask?” She held up her hands in front of her.

The boys had started playing another game, sitting around the patio table.

“Ask what?” Sean hedged.

She laughed again. “You’re the detective, don’t you know? Okay, I’ll give you a huge break. Michaela and I have been friends since grade school. She was married to Brad McCrea, and after he was killed, she’s remained a widow. Her social life is practically nonexistent. Running a B&B is pretty time-consuming, and she has little help. James Collins booked a room here, and for a very short time they dated, but it wasn't serious. Shall I go on?"

"You're doing fine."

Sean crossed his arms in front of his chest and waited for her to go on. But she could tell from his slight smile that he was enjoying their friendly banter.

"Okay. Shall we find a quieter place to continue?"

She reached up and grabbed Sean by the elbow and led him out of the patio area to the gardens. A lone bench stood empty amidst the foliage, providing a bit of privacy. A small water feature was running, and the spot was cozy and inviting.

Sitting, Heather turned to Sean. "Let me be completely truthful with you. Brad was murdered. It nearly killed Michaela. She went into a state of depression and had a hard time handling the fact that he was murdered. The police never found out why, and it became a cold case. It still haunts her to this day, no closure, no answers.

"Her aunt passed not long before Brad was murdered, leaving her the bed-and-breakfast which has become her lifeline but also her chain and anchor. When James booked a room here, he showed interest, and it opened a new chapter for Michaela. She thought she would never have a passionate thought toward another man ever! But then it turns out that James was a playboy, and while he may have held some feelings for Michaela, he basically just wanted sex. They broke it off when he came on to her a little strong as in manhandling her in a way no gentleman ever should.

"Then, of course, this is where you come into the picture. James is murdered, and now she's under investigation once again for something she never did or ever could do! And I'll add that police investigations don't include eating with the suspects or attending birthday parties. If you want my advice…" She held up her hand when Sean started to speak. "If you have feelings for her, you better solve this case."

Sean's head shot up.

"From what Michaela's told me, and reading between the lines, I think you like her. Don't let her get away. She's one in a thousand and has a good heart. She's already got a soft spot for you, mister.

You've taken a shine to Chase, and everyone knows a way to a mother's heart is through her children. Take it or leave it for what it's worth," she finished.

"I would say that Michaela isn't the only one who is one in a thousand. Good friends like you don't come along every day." Sean leaned back against the bench.

"So do you have feelings for her?"

"As you so eloquently pointed out, I must!" He smiled and got up. "We should head back to the party."

Sean stopped on the patio to talk with the boys, and Heather went inside. Marissa was arranging the cake and paper plates on the dining table, so Heather took the opportunity to speak with Michaela.

"Wow, is Detective Ryan good-looking or what?" she asked.

Michaela blushed. "I hadn't noticed."

"Sure, you can say that till the cows come home, but you noticed." She laughed. "What can I do?"

As the party unfolded, they placed food on the outside table with paper plates and drinks. The boys went first leaving the adults to go last. Sean's mouth was watering when he slid a slice of lasagna onto his plate. It smelled heavenly. Piling on salad, he almost didn't have room for a huge slice of garlic toast. He looked up apologetically when he noticed that the women's plates held small quantities of food while his was piled high.

Michaela poured soda for the boys while Heather poured each of the adults a liberal amount of red wine. Sean was in heaven! The day was perfect, not too hot, and for a short while, the crowd grew quiet as they started eating.

He looked across the table and found Michaela watching him. She smiled.

"This is really delicious. I don't think I've ever had lasagna this good," he complimented.

"Thank you," she said.

"I think Michaela has got to be one of the best cooks in this county. You should try her breakfasts, or for that matter, happy hour around here. The appetizers and the sweets are heaven!" Heather spoke up, and when Sean glanced her way, she winked. "And this day is perfect, but by next weekend, a storm is headed our way, and it's not even officially fall yet!"

Sean liked this woman and was glad that she seemed an ally and not an enemy. On the other hand, Marissa wasn't nearly as cordial and seemed overly protective of Michaela.

Presents were next, and Chase went into ripping off wrapping paper like there was no tomorrow. When he got to the gift that Sean brought, he was exuberant. The smile he slid to Sean after opening the gift was gratifying. He did well, or rather his sister did a great job of telling him what a ten-year-old would like.

After cake, most of the boys were picked up by parents, and eventually, even Heather and Marissa left, saying their goodbyes. He knew he should have left long ago, but he couldn't seem to tear himself away. He liked watching Michaela. She was deft at putting people at ease around her and making sure everyone was well taken care of. But more than anything, he liked the fact that she easily smiled, and those dimples, he wanted to keep her smiling just to see them. His feelings for her were growing stronger by the day, and Heather was right; he better solve the case as quickly as possible.

He offered to help with the cleanup, and though Michaela declined his offer, he picked up a few dishes anyway and placed them on the kitchen counter.

"So you use the bed-and-breakfast kitchen for both personal and business use?" he asked, setting some glasses in the sink.

"I do. There are pros and cons to the idea. First, I only have one kitchen to clean instead of two, but I have to keep the foods separated, business and all." She turned on the water and started rinsing the dishes.

Chase came up to Sean and held out his right hand. Sean shook hands with him, and Chase thanked him for the gift. "I wanted a Lego set for the longest time. Thank you again for such a great gift!"

"You're welcome." Sean reached out and started to ruffle his hair and then thought better of it. "I better take my leave and want to thank both of you for inviting me to a great party!"

Standing at the kitchen sink, Michaela looked over at him and ran her eyes down his frame. His biceps bulged under his sleeves, and he looked so strong and capable. She wondered what it would feel like to be in his embrace. She shook herself mentally as her eyes shot back to his face. He smiled warmly, and she blushed.

"You make the best lasagna," he said, noticing her blushed face.

"Th-thank you," she stammered.

"I'll let myself out." He reached out and brushed his knuckles against her cheek. "Thanks again for inviting me."

Michaela stood stock still; his touch was warm, and she wanted to lean her face into his hand. She wanted more. Acknowledging where her thoughts led, her blush deepened. She closed her eyes and then opened them, searching Sean's eyes. He smiled warmly and let his hand drop before pulling out his car keys. Jiggling them, he inclined his head and turned toward the door.

When the door closed behind him, Michaela felt bereft of his presence and wondered if he felt the same way and how this would play into his investigation.

CHAPTER 13

But I tell you that anyone who looks at a woman lustfully has already committed adultery with her in his heart.

—Matthew 5:28

Sean sat at the bar sipping a bourbon deep in thought when he felt something soft pressed against his back.

"Hey, stranger…"

Sean looked over his shoulder right into the eyes of Trina Myerson. She stepped from behind him and sat on the empty stool that had just been vacated.

Her hair was mussed, either by design or she was just with someone, he wasn't sure. The black dress she wore, if one could call it that, barely covered her. One spaghetti strap fell off her shoulder, revealing as much of the creamy flesh as possible. She crossed her legs, and her dress hiked up.

"Imagine running into you here…" Sean said before taking another sip of his bourbon.

She smiled seductively. "I come here from time to time. I haven't seen you since you and your partner stopped by my home."

"We're still investigating Collins's murder."

"You haven't found the murderer yet? What about that owner of the B&B?" she asked.

"While the investigation is ongoing, I'm not at liberty to discuss it."

"Buy me a drink?"

As the bartender walked by, Sean asked for another drink for the lady.

Looking over at Trina, his eyes dipped to her cleavage, and she leaned forward. "If we find someplace private, they can come out to play…"

Sean's eyes darted back up to hers. He had a hell of a day, and he entertained thoughts of fucking her.

She placed her hand on his upper arm. "We can go to my place or yours if you like."

Sean was sorely tempted. He threw down the rest of his drink and grabbed her by the elbow. "Lead the way."

Walking out the door, a woman bumped into them entering the bar. When she turned to apologize, she stopped short. "Sean?"

Sean turned his head at the familiar voice. "Heather, what are you doing here?"

"I'm meeting a client for a drink." She pointedly looked at Trina and then back at him with an arched brow. "It looks like I interrupted something." Her voice had gone from surprise to acid in a heartbeat.

Sean looked away and bid her goodbye as he continued up the street, guiding Trina with his hand on the small of her back. When they arrived at her car, he took the keys from her and used the fob to unlock the door. After Trina got in behind the steering wheel, Sean shut the door firmly. "Go home, Trina."

She looked up at him with an open mouth. "I thought you were coming home with me. Don't you want to have sex, mind-blowing sex?" She smiled.

"Not tonight…"

He turned and headed back to his own vehicle then decided to go back into the bar to see if he could find Heather. He found her seated at the bar with a glass of wine in hand. He took the seat next to hers which was thankfully empty. Her eyes widened upon seeing him.

"I thought you were headed out with that blond."

"I won't pretend to be an angel," he said ordering bourbon.

"Look, it's really none of my business, but it sure looked to me like you were about ready to find a place to fuck that bimbo."

Sean chuckled. "I'm actually glad I ran into you. I had one hell of a day, and here I am sitting at the bar all alone when Trina Myerson, who is also a suspect in this case, practically attacks me. I walked her to her car. Granted, the thought crossed my mind to fuck her as you so eloquently put it, but that's not what I really want."

Heather took a sip of wine.

Sean continued, "You're right, it's none of your business."

She turned sharply. "Sean Ryan, it is *none* of my business, but I'm making it my business because Michaela is a good friend of mine. If you plan on seeing other women, then break off this thing you both feel for each other. Don't lead her on because she's been through enough!"

"I don't take orders from anyone but my sergeant, but I will take your advice under consideration," he said sharply, wishing he hadn't bothered to come back inside. His intentions were not to spar with Heather but reassure her that he had honorable intentions toward Michaela. He had enough of women telling him what to do while he was married. Hell, this was coming out all wrong.

He turned to Heather. "Look, I really don't want to pick a fight with you. My intentions toward Michaela are nothing but honorable. I care about her, and I am developing feelings for her."

She took a long sip from her wine glass but didn't say anything. Looking up at the mirror, she turned, "My client's here…"

As she was getting up, Sean grabbed her elbow. "I'm serious. I'm not a saint, but I wouldn't do anything to hurt Michaela. I do have feelings for her."

Heather looked pointedly down at his hand on her elbow and then back up at him. "I'll take that under consideration…"

Sean dropped his hand, and Heather walked away.

CHAPTER 14

The heart is more deceitful than all else and is desperately sick. Who can understand it?

—Jeremiah 17:9

On Sunday morning, Marissa said she'd watch the bed-and-breakfast so Michaela and Chase could attend church. As Michaela finished dabbing on lipstick, she surveyed herself in the mirror and frowned when her thoughts turned to Detective Ryan. If she were honest with herself, she was hoping to run into him because deep down, she wanted him to see her dressed up for once. Each time he came by the bed-and-breakfast, she was wearing jeans. She shook her head. "Get real..." she said to herself.

"What?"

Turning swiftly at Chase's voice, she smiled. "Just talking to myself, sweetie. Are you ready?"

"Sure, Mom. And before you ask, I fed Snickers and made sure his water bowl is filled."

"Thanks, sweetie. Are you ready!" She placed an arm about his shoulders and gently squeezed.

On the way to church, Chase asked, "Mom, do you like Detective Ryan?"

Surprised at the turn in conversation, Michaela looked over at her son and smiled. "Why do you ask?"

"Because I really like him. He's nice, and he talks to me instead of above me like most adults do. It's really cool that he wears a gun too!"

"Then why is it important if I like him or not? You already do!"

"But do you like him?" he looked up at his mom expectantly.

Michaela nodded. "I do."

"Are you going to date him?"

"I doubt it, but why?"

"Well, if you did start dating him, will you have sex?"

Michaela sucked in her breath. "Where did you get that idea?"

"I have friends whose moms date, and I overheard talk at school and over at Brian's."

"I'm not sure where to begin, sweetie. First, if I should date, I wouldn't have sex. There is far more to sex than just the act. It's a gift from God meant to be enjoyed within the confines of marriage. It's a form of intimacy between the couple and can be very gratifying for both the man and the woman."

"You mean you can't enjoy it otherwise?"

Michaela took another deep breath before replying, "I can see that Detective Ryan has taught you to pay attention to what's said and not said." She laughed. Turning serious, she continued, "A sex drive is something all humans are born with. And it's an act that can be enjoyed outside of marriage, but the couple should refrain until they are married in the eyes of God."

Chase turned to look out the car window. "Who do you think killed Mr. Collins?"

Frowning, Michaela laid her hand on Chase's shoulder. "I have no idea sweetie. What made you think of that?"

"Because of Detective Ryan…"

"Did he say something to you?" Michaela looked over at her son, but his face was still turned away.

"No, but he's been investigating you, and I'm worried." He finally turned his head, and tears shimmered in his eyes.

"Oh, sweetie, nothing's going to happen to me. It's Detective Ryan's job to dot all the *I*s and cross all the *T*s. And by questioning those who knew James is part of the job. It'll be fine, I promise!"

Chase sat back in his seat and rubbed his eyes, trying to remove all traces of tears as they pulled into the church parking lot.

Before getting out of the car, he leaned over and gave his mom a quick hug. "I like Detective Ryan, Mom, but I would hate him if he took you away."

Smiling down at her son, she said, "I love you so much, and I wouldn't want either of us to hate Detective Ryan."

One of Chase's friends shouted from the church steps, and Chase got out, slamming the car door behind him and ran to meet his friend.

"Hey…"

Michaela jumped at the sound of Heather's voice. Turning, Heather was stooped over, peering in at her through the driver's side window. "You gonna get out or do you plan to try and hear the sermon from out here?" She laughed.

Michaela laughed, feeling lighthearted, and unfastened her seatbelt to get out. Looking over at Heather, her brows furrowed. "You look tired. Is everything okay?"

Heather's smile waned a little, but she shook her head. "I'm fine. Just a late night since I met a client at Lerner's Bar last night. I happened to run into Detective Ryan while I was there." She glanced sideways at Michaela to gauge her reaction.

Michaela's smile broadened. "Really? Did you get a chance to say hi?"

"Oh yeah, small chitchat, and then my client came in, so we parted ways." Heather decided to not say anything about what happened at the bar. First, she wanted Detective Ryan to come clean, and secondly, she didn't want to hurt Michaela. She couldn't bear the thought of another heartbreak for her best friend if Detective Ryan was playing the field, but she felt deep down that he wasn't, and what he'd told her the night before, was the truth. She had a hunch he was falling fast for Michaela.

As Michaela got out of the car, she saw Gavin on the front steps of the church, and she cringed. "I hate to say this," she confessed to Heather. "I was hoping Gavin was busy with his sporting goods store today and wouldn't make church. He's been hedging for the past year to date, but I've managed to dissuade him. Over the past few months, he's, well, getting more demanding."

CHAPTER 14

Gavin was handsome with sandy-brown hair that was always cut short, showing off his chiseled chin. With an aquiline nose, deep, brown eyes that were set far apart, he was distinguished. In his mid-forties, he was graying at the temples, which made him even more handsome. From the time Michaela started attending the Good Samaritan Church, he'd taken notice of her. But what started out as an attraction quickly turned to acid. He was far too domineering for Michaela's taste.

"I'm sorry I didn't warn you." Heather sighed. "He was here early and asked me if you'd be attending church today..." Heather grimaced and looked over at Michaela apologetically.

Before she could say anything, Gavin had walked up to them. "It's so nice to see you this morning, Michaela," he all but gushed. He held out his arm for Michaela to take, but instead, she switched her purse to her other hand to avoid taking his arm and greeted him with a smile.

"I have a pew staked out for the three of us," he said. "I'm afraid it's near the back of the church though. I wasn't able to snag one closer."

Michaela's smile waned. He took her elbow and steered her toward the entrance where Pastor Hodges greeted them. "It's great to see you, Michaela. I know you aren't able to get away from the bed-and-breakfast often."

"Hi, Pastor Hodges, it's nice to be here this Sunday. You haven't by chance seen Chase, have you?"

"I believe he's already in church sitting with his friend."

"Just as long as he's behaving." Michaela laughed.

"Pastor Hodges." Gavin inclined his head and then led Michaela forward with slightly more pressure to her elbow. Heather followed helplessly, wondering what she could say to extricate Michaela from his grasp.

Stepping to the side of the pew he reserved for them, Gavin blocked the women from advancing further into the church unless they went around him. Having little choice without causing a ruckus, Michaela settled into the pew. Heather settled next to her, and for a moment, she thought that Gavin intended to sit next to Heather, but she should have known better. He sat next to her after pushing through trying not to step on toes.

As the sermon began, Gavin placed his arm around Michaela's shoulders, allowing his hand to drop over her shoulder grazing the swell of her breast. She took her purse and leaned forward to set it on the floor, but settling back against the pew, he placed his arm once again around her shoulders. She pushed his hand away, and he removed his arm. And for about five minutes, she had some peace, but then his hand crept up to her thigh to give her a slight squeeze when the pastor said something funny that had the congregation laughing. She removed his hand. He replaced it after just a bit. She removed it again, and so the morning went with a tug-of-war. As the sermon ended and everyone rose, Gavin placed his hands on her shoulders and leaned in for a brotherly kiss as he called it. It took all her willpower not to wipe the wet kiss from her lips.

"Let's have lunch together, shall we, and go over the sermon. I know a wonderful little place."

Michaela's head snapped up. "I have to get back to the bed-and-breakfast, but thank you for the offer, Gavin."

"Well, if you need to get back, perhaps I can come by and bring lunch to you," he offered.

"That sounds nice, but honestly, I have way too much work for a sit-down lunch."

"Nonsense, everyone has to eat, and I want you to keep up your strength. I'll be by in about half an hour." He let his hands fall from her shoulders after giving her a slight squeeze.

"Can I come?" Heather spoke up, hoping that might do the trick to dissuade him.

"Sure, why not! The more the merrier, am I right?" He laughed easily.

Michaela stopped to thank Pastor Hodges for the wonderful sermon on the way out but made a hasty retreat when Clara, his wife, joined him. A tad bit shorter than Michaela, the woman was almost anorexic but still pretty enough. With short brown hair that was cut into a late style of shaggy, chic, she almost looked like an imp with her upturned nose and pixie eyes. Her thin lips that always held a perpetual sneer ruined the effect however. And for the past couple of years, the woman had turned a cold shoulder to Michaela.

Even Heather noticed Clara's attitude toward Michaela having mentioned how odd it was. But what hurt most was when they had a women's gathering at their pastor's home over the summer, Michaela had been excluded from that invitation. And before that, it was a May tea party.

"Hello, Mrs. Hodges. What a lovely sermon the pastor delivered this morning."

"Yes, he always has wonderful sermons. I noticed that Marissa wasn't here this morning. Is she with her boyfriend?"

Michaela frowned. "Boyfriend?" Turning her head, she looked at Pastor Hodges. "Does she have a boyfriend I don't know anything about?"

Pastor Hodges shrugged his shoulders. "If she does, she hasn't said anything."

Clara harrumphed and turned away without saying another word.

*****

"I thought for sure that if I asked to join the party that Gavin would find an excuse to not make lunch after all," Heather stated once they were back at the bed-and-breakfast.

"He's gotten so demanding over the past few months. Did you see what he was doing in church today?"

"How could I not. You were doing everything to keep his mitts off you, but he was persistent, I'll give him that!"

The bell above the office door rang. "Are you all in the kitchen?" Gavin yelled.

"We're in here…"

He came through the office to the kitchen holding up two large bags. "I have lunch, and it smells divine!"

Heather's cell chimed, and looking at it, she sighed heavily. "Oh, dear, I have to run. I have a client who is insisting I meet with them over what they've deemed 'not their style.'" She looked over at Michaela apologetically again. "I'm sorry."

Heather worked at a design firm downtown and was quite the interior decorator. Michaela sought her advice when renovating the bed-and-breakfast and was more than pleased with the outcome. Although Heather told her that if she ever decided to close the bed-and-breakfast, she should be an interior decorator herself. Michaela knew her friend was being overgenerous with the compliment.

"Not to worry, we'll miss your company though."

"Of course, but the customer always comes first," Gavin spoke up. "That's been my motto since starting my sporting goods store, and I will do almost anything to appease the customer." He spoke so smugly that it was plain to both the women he was happy that Heather was leaving.

After Heather left and the food eaten, Chase excused himself, leaving Michaela alone with Gavin. The moment she dreaded.

"That was a wonderful meal, Gavin but I'm afraid I must get busy and ready for guests."

"Let me help with the cleanup then."

He jumped up and grabbed the bags to toss in the trash while Michaela cleared the table of dishes. She sat the dishes in the sink when Gavin walked up from behind and wrapped his arms about her waist.

"I enjoyed our meal together, but I wished you'd have let Chase go home with Marissa and Heather hadn't invited herself over. I like spending time with you alone."

Michaela removed his arms and turned to finally give him a piece of her mind.

"I like this dress, but you should wear your hair down," he continued, and then reaching up he removed the clip that held up her curls, letting the mass fall about her shoulders. "Ah, much better!"

"Gavin..."

"Shhh." He leaned in, pushing her back against the counter and kissed her.

Michaela pushed against him, but he wouldn't budge. She turned her head, and he savagely turned her face back to his and kissed her, forcing her mouth to open for him. He plundered with his tongue, and Michaela thought she'd vomit.

When he finally pulled away, he spoke with a clip, "I love you, Michaela, and you don't know to what lengths I'll go to have you as mine."

Startled, she stopped struggling. "What?"

"You heard me. I love you. Now it's your turn to say you love me too."

She frowned. "I don't love you, Gavin, and to be completely honest, I don't think of you romantically at all."

He stepped back, his eyes narrowing. "Didn't you hear me? I'll stop at no lengths to have you as mine!"

"What does that mean, Gavin?"

"It means just that." He hung his head, looking disapprovingly at her. "I will do anything to win your favor and your hand."

"Would you kill for me?" she asked quietly, dreading the answer.

His head snapped up. "That would be a sin, of course not."

Michaela visibly relaxed. "I need to get busy, Gavin. You need to leave. Thank you for lunch!"

Gavin leaned in for another kiss, and Michaela reared back. "I mean it, Gavin, you need to leave."

His eyes narrowed once again. "I will have you, you do know that, don't you? I've loved you for years but from afar, but the hour grows close, and I will not be dissuaded from my pursuit," he warned.

Michaela's eyes widened, and with his finger, he traced her chin from ear to ear. She swallowed hard. Their eyes locked. And then he smiled abruptly. Placing his palm to the side of her cheek, he let his thumb play with the corner of her mouth.

"You're so beautiful, and we'll make a handsome couple, and our children will be as beautiful as we."

"I already have a child."

"Yes, that's something we'll need to discuss…" He let his hand fall away. "Tuesday evening is open for me. We'll have dinner."

"I can't, I have guests," Michaela's voice hardened.

And once again, his eyes narrowed, and out of the corner of her eye, she saw his hand fist. For a moment, she thought he might hit her.

"Mom…" Gavin stepped back, and Michaela turned at the sound of her son's voice.

"What's going on?" Chase asked, looking first at his mom, then to Gavin, and then back to Michaela.

"I'm just on my way out the door, son. Hope you enjoyed lunch, you certainly can eat!" He turned and exited through the kitchen doorway through to the office.

Michaela didn't let out her breath until she heard the bell above the office door.

"Are you okay?" Chase asked.

"I'm fine now…what do you need, sweetie?"

CHAPTER 15

So do not fear for I am with you. Do not be dismayed for I am your God. I will strengthen you and help you. I will uphold you with my righteous right hand.

—Isiah 41:10

Usually, there were several guests booked over Labor Day weekend, and while Michaela appreciated the reprieve, it sure didn't pay the bills. Taking advantage of the interlude, she decided to relax and indulge herself. Maybe a manicure and pedicure or perhaps a leisurely soak in a bubble bath.

And after spending most of the day deep cleaning the common areas, Michaela was more than ready to relax for the evening. Picking up the romance novel she started awhile back, she decided a bubble bath was in order, and afterward, she felt like giving herself a facial. She couldn't even remember when she last had a facial!

Chase was spending the night with Marissa who had out-of-town family visiting. When he found out that Marissa's nephew, Colton, would be there, he resorted to begging. The boys had become fast friends a few summers back and now leapt at the chance to be together whenever Marissa's family was visiting.

Pouring a glass of red wine, Michaela headed upstairs and drew warm water into the porcelain tub. She set her glass and book on the small table near the restored claw foot tub and splashed in bubble bath, watching the water foam under the tap. Sighing in pleasure, she disrobed and stepped in.

Despite it being near the end of summer, the day had grown dark early when a wind from the west brought in storm clouds just as Heather predicted last weekend at Chase's party. And as the afternoon progressed, so did the wind. She could hear the limbs from one of the nearby trees hitting against the side of the house and hoped the electricity didn't go out on this dark and stormy night.

As she settled into the bath, her thoughts turned to Detective Ryan. At the party last weekend, she didn't know what to think, but her heart always raced a little faster when he was near. Aloud, she said his name, "Sean Ryan." She liked his name.

What a mess she found herself in though. This was a detective in the middle of a murder investigation and she the prime suspect. But still, it warmed her heart that he was nice to Chase and genuinely seemed interested in her son. Thinking back, James always tried to see her when Chase was either in school or after he'd gone to bed. Why didn't she recognize that at the time?

Her thoughts returned to Detective Ryan as she pictured his face; gray eyes fringed with dark lashes, a five-o'clock shadow that she liked, liked a lot. But it was the way he looked at her and interacted with Chase she held close to her heart. Thinking back to the day he helped her bring in the Hoosier cabinet, she recalled how when she turned to hand him the sack of muffins, his arm brushed her breasts. Though she was still embarrassed by the incident, she couldn't help but wonder if it had affected him.

The storm, brewing off to the west, worsened, and the branches from the tree continued to slap against the side of the house with a vengeance. At first, it was exciting after the warm summer and the fact it mirrored the storms brewing in her own life, but as the winds grew worse and the branches hit the side of the house viciously, what was thrilling at first was now turning ominous.

The longer she soaked in the tub, the feeling of trepidation grew. It had to be the lack of usual sounds around the B&B. She missed Chase, she missed the sounds of people mulling about in the common areas, the chatter of folks meeting for the first time, and car doors being slammed as guests returned from an evening out.

CHAPTER 15

Despite logical thinking and the reason for her uneasiness, it did little to dispel her feelings. And with the storm, it was almost pitch-black though it was only seven o'clock in the evening. She was in for a long night.

The phone in the office rang, startling her. She sat up straight and listened. It rang two more times, but when the answering machine picked up, no one left a message. Granted, she was far enough away and with the storm, she most likely wouldn't hear any messages. Her intuition told her it was another hang up. She sank back down in the tub, but now her desire for a leisurely soak dissipated.

She heard a thud that sounded different from the tree branches that slapped against the side of the house. She sat upright in the tub again with water trickling down her back as she listened. And then the hair on her nape rose. Getting out of the tub, she quickly toweled off and threw on her robe.

Stepping into the hallway, she tiptoed downstairs to the living area, holding tightly to the carved banister. Nothing seemed amiss or out of place, and in checking the windows and doors, all were still locked. She stepped into the kitchen and noticed a glass of wine had been poured and was sitting on the table.

She froze. Feeling her heartbeat in her throat, she scanned the room with wide eyes and then noticed the back door standing slightly ajar. It blew open further with a gust of wind, and Snickers ran through the doorway, stopping in front of Michaela. He looked up her and whined, sitting on his hind legs.

She felt her heart drop to her stomach, and holding her hand to her throat, she turned and ran for the front office door. She couldn't seem to run fast enough; her legs felt heavy and lethargic. She stopped short at the door, fumbling with the lock with shaky fingers and trembling arms. She wanted to weep in terror, and looking over her shoulder, only Snickers sat watching. Once she got the door opened, she threw it back and ran through only to run into a solid wall. A scream erupted from down in her throat, and then strong arms were wrapped around her to keep her from stumbling backward.

"Michaela...?"

The sound of Detective Ryan's voice broke through, and she looked up with tears in her eyes.

"What happened? Are you all right?" he asked with concern lacing his voice.

Still shaking, her teeth began to chatter. "Th-there's so-someone in t-t-the house!" She managed to get out.

Sean looked past her and then shoved her behind him, telling her to stay close. He entered the office with Michaela behind him, her hand grasping his shirt sleeve in a death grip.

Walking into the office, he noticed nothing unusual and continued through the gate and toward the kitchen doorway. With Michaela still close behind, they entered the kitchen, and Sean saw Snickers munching on dry dog food. The pup looked up from his bowl, licked his chops, and then went back to eating. *Some guard dog*, he thought.

Sean saw the glass of wine sitting on the table and the back door that led outside standing wide open.

Michaela tugged on his shirt sleeve. Turning his head, he peered down at her upturned face. "Someone was in here. They poured a glass of wine and left the back door ajar. When I stepped in, the door blew open with the wind. I didn't pour the wine, and I locked that door."

Sean stepped over to the back door and shut it firmly, turning the lock. "Stay here. I'll check the premises and all the rooms." He pulled a kitchen chair out and motioned for her to sit.

Moving through their private quarters first, Sean scanned the living and dining area before heading upstairs. On the left a doorway led to what was obviously Michaela's room. He entered, noting that it was tastefully decorated but not overly feminine. He looked under the bed and then opened the closet door, nothing. The soft fabric he held back garnered his attention, and he almost whistled. He'd really like to see her wearing this little number. Turning, he went through to the adjacent bathroom and saw the bathtub filled with water where she'd been bathing. A glass of wine sat on a nearby table that held other products. The tantalizing scent of the room had his imagination going places it shouldn't.

Crossing the hall to another opened door, he peered into Chase's room. It looked like a typical boy's room. He checked under that bed and the closet before checking out the other two rooms down the hall, another bathroom and what looked to be an office.

Returning downstairs, he went through to the common area for guests and then down the hallway toward the guest rooms. Having done research on the bed-and-breakfast earlier, he knew that the rooms had access from within the B&B but that also each room had outside access, at least the ones that faced the east. The west-side rooms had balconies since that side of the building overlooked a cliff to the ocean below. He didn't think there'd be anyone in any of these rooms, so he hurried back to the kitchen to find Michaela had made herself a cup of tea.

Looking up expectantly, she asked, "Did you find anything?"

"No. Are you positive you locked this door?" he asked, cocking his head toward the door in question. "And what about the guest rooms, are they all locked?"

"Yes and no…all the rooms that have outside access to the gardens are locked, but none are locked from within unless there are guests. Right now, there aren't any. And, yes, I'm positive I locked the kitchen door," she said, looking over at the door as she spoke.

"Where's Chase?"

"He's spending the night at Marissa's."

Sean's eyes lowered, taking in the thin robe that had fallen slightly open, revealing cleavage. Following his eyes, she looked down and quickly pulled the robe together tightly across her chest.

"I need to put something on," she said, rising. "If you'll excuse me…"

When she came back into the kitchen, Sean was seated, and he asked her to explain exactly what happened. She still had her hair piled up haphazardly on her head where a few damp tendrils had escaped, framing her face. Wearing an oversized sweatshirt and jeans, Sean thought she was attractive and watched her as she pulled out a kitchen chair to sit.

"I was in the bath when I heard a noise…" she began.

"The wind is blowing like crazy out there, are you sure it wasn't just the wind?"

"Yes, this noise was different. It came from inside the house." She looked around the kitchen until her eyes landed on the pantry door. "I keep the wine in the pantry that I serve guests for afternoon social hour…" She stopped talking and stepped toward the door and opened it. "Someone was in here."

Sean shot up from the chair he'd taken and joined her in front of the pantry, peering inside. It was more like a walk-in larder. The shelves were stocked with food items and in the back was a wine rack that held quite a few bottles. Some of the food items were strewn on the floor, and some of the bottles from the rack were lying on their sides on the floor. Nothing was broken. *This couldn't be the noise she heard coming from inside the house,* Sean thought.

She gaped at the mess with hands held at her throat. "Who would do this?" she gasped.

"These things could have fallen."

She looked up at Detective Ryan with disbelief in her eyes. She shook her head slowly. "You can't possibly think that. The wine bottles would have broken, and some items on these shelves that are on the edge certainly would have fallen!"

She turned abruptly, leaving Sean standing in the doorway. He picked up the food that had fallen over and stood them back upright and then replaced the wine bottles into empty slots in the rack.

"Why don't you have another glass of wine?" he said, emerging from the pantry to stand with an arm on his hip as he surveyed the room.

Michaela looked up at him with lips parted as if she were about to say something but hesitated.

"Look, I'm inclined to believe someone was here. But why would they push a few things over on the shelf and turn wine bottles on their side? It makes no sense."

"Does anything?" She stood up and walked over to the cupboard and pulled out two wine glasses. An opened bottle of wine sat on the counter she'd uncorked earlier, and she poured liberal amounts into both glasses. Turning, she handed one to Sean which he accepted.

He, too, sat again and found himself asking if he should spend the night.

Her eyes darted to his. "What?"

"I don't mean like that. I was thinking maybe you'd feel safer if I spent the night on the sofa in the living room."

"Oh…" She looked down at the floor, and then her eyes shot back up. "Why did you stop by?"

"I was in the area."

"That's not a reason. Were you here to ask me more questions?"

"Well, actually, just one."

Her brows furrowed. "Which is?"

"Is your brother-in-law still married to your sister-in-law? I mean, they seem to be living separated. Have they filed for divorce and she's still using the same last name?"

"They've been separated for a few years now. Brent is in Alaska and plans to stay there, but so far, neither have filed for divorce. I have no idea why they haven't, but I assume it's personal, and if Marissa wanted to tell me, she would."

Sean nodded. "Detective Hanson and I were wondering. We assumed they were either separated or divorced."

"And yet neither of you investigated…" She looked over at him with an arched brow. "I suspect that you probably have all the answers before you ask the questions. It's a means to see if I'm lying or if you can trip a suspect while interrogating them, right?"

"It's not like that. It can take hours to research some things. It's easier to just ask the question and, if need be, confirm." He reached up and ran his hands through his hair. Gray eyes met hers, and he studied her face.

Michaela blushed. He liked that she blushed easily. "Actually, I should step back from this case and hand it over to another detective. I'm too close…" His eyes moved down to her parted lips and then back up to her eyes. "I shouldn't be involved, and yet I can't help but want to protect you, get to know you better. Is that honest enough?"

"I'm uncomfortable with the way this conversation is going."

"Are you? And why is that?"

She stood up and walked over to the sink; with her back to him, she said, "Because I have feelings for you too, and I think it's a bad idea since you are involved with this case. And you look at me with interest and yet at the same time with suspicion."

Sean stood and walked up behind her. He brushed the hair from her neck, and she leaned back, barely brushing his chest. He put his arms around her waist, drawing her closer and laid his forehead atop the mass of curls.

She let out a shaky breath and relaxed into his hard frame, closing her eyes. He wasn't the only one conflicted. He slowly turned her around, and she peered up at him with large green eyes that slowly inched down to his lips and then rose back up to meet his eyes. He lowered his head and brushed his lips against hers. The kiss deepened, and she placed her arms around his shoulders and raised on tiptoes to better fit his frame. He could feel her softness molding him, and her scent wafted up, encasing him in her sweet fragrance. The kiss was slow and sensual, not demanding and yet promising so much more.

Michaela loved his five-o'clock shadow and how his whiskers felt against her soft cheeks. She wanted to run her hands through them. There was something rugged and handsome about a man who needed a shave, and his dark whiskers made her feel feminine. But it was more than that; his broad frame, muscled forearms that held her easily added to the attraction, and she found herself wanting more.

When he raised his head, she looked up at him. "Somehow, I trust you, Detective Ryan. I trust that you'll find me innocent and get to the bottom of what's happening."

He felt a jab to his heart. He didn't deserve her trust, and yet he could tell that she needed to trust him. He found himself saying he'd do all that he could to find who murdered James Collins.

*****

Sean woke to the smell of coffee brewing and bacon sizzling. He sat up abruptly, studying the room before he remembered where he was. Michaela told him he could use one of the rooms in the B&B,

but he declined, saying he'd feel better being closer just in case she needed him.

Together, they stretched a sheet down on the sofa after she returned with bedding and a pillow. Saying a halting good night, she practically fled the room, leaving him to get undressed. He smiled, recalling her big green eyes and the wariness behind them. She probably locked her bedroom door.

Only partially undressing before stretching out on the oversized sofa the evening before, he quickly donned his shirt and walked into the kitchen.

Michaela was at the stove, this time wearing jeans and a T-shirt that seemed to fit her too well. Once again, she was wearing an apron. He stepped into the room, and she turned. "Coffee…"

"Yes, please. How long have you been up?" he asked, pulling out a chair from the table.

"Since five. I'm used to getting up early. Most guests like to have coffee by seven at the latest."

She poured him a cup and sat it on the table in front of him. "Sugar or cream?"

"Neither, I like it black." He took a big slurp and appreciatively nodded his head in satisfaction. "I run on coffee!"

"Don't we all?" she added.

Bending over, she peered into the oven, and Sean admired the view. He found himself wanting to kiss her again. Last night, that kiss held promises, and he had a difficult time finding sleep just thinking about her. She always smelled good, a clean and yet sweet scent that tantalized his senses, and he liked that she didn't wear a heady cologne that was too strong.

"I hope you like biscuits, Detective Ryan…"

Catching himself daydreaming, his focus returned to her. "Sean," he corrected.

"Sean, I hope you like biscuits."

"Homemade?"

"Yes, it's a bed-and-breakfast. I don't think I'd get any five-star reviews if I served up the canned kind." She laughed, showcasing those stunning dimples.

"Anything you fix I'm sure will be delicious and a treat since I mostly grab something on the run."

He looked up at her to find her staring at him. "Last night," she began, "we should never have kissed." She licked her lips and nervously looked away.

"I disagree."

Shifting her gaze back to him, she didn't say anything. He could tell she was at war with her own feelings, and he wanted to reassure her. Reassure her about what though. That these feelings they have for each other would develop into a relationship? Did he even want one? What if she was looking for more? After all she had a son who needed a father. Did he want more? Did he even want a ready-made family? These thoughts sped through his mind, and when he peered up at her, it was as if she could read his thoughts.

She pulled out a chair and sank into it. "I like you and have feelings for you, Detective, but I'm not looking for a relationship just yet. It's only been over the course of the last couple of months I realized that I'm just now ready to start dating again. I'm still in love with my late husband, and it's going to take someone special to take his place in my life."

"Your husband was lucky to have you."

"No, Detective, I was lucky to have him." She smiled and rose from her chair to finish breakfast.

CHAPTER 16

But their evil intentions will be exposed when the light shines on them.

—Ephesians 5:13

"You what?" Tom sat up straighter in his chair. "Please, tell me no hanky-panky went on…" Though it was Sunday on Labor Day weekend, the squad room was full. Usually, crime picked up through the holidays, which meant almost everyone was working.

Sean almost laughed. "Hanky-panky, really? For your information, I only stayed the night because I was worried about her. Something odd happened there. The wine bottles didn't fall. They were carefully laid on their sides. And there was no obvious sign of a break-in, so it had to be someone who was already on the premises or has a key."

"When was the last time you stayed the night at a suspect's house much less a person of interest?" Tom arched his brows and pointedly looked at Sean. "Look, you're getting in too deep. You're no good to me if you get involved."

"She was scared out of her mind. I was about ready to knock on the door when it flew open and she ran out. She was understandably shaken."

Tom dropped his head and eyed the toes of his shoes before looking back up at Sean. "Are you falling for her?"

This time, Sean eyed the floor and was glad when a commotion on the other side of the room caught everyone's attention. A homeless guy had been brought in on charges of assault and was being uncooperative. As another officer walked by, the homeless man made a beeline for the officer's weapon. Thankfully, the scoff didn't result in the man arming himself, but the chair he was sitting in was knocked over and said officer had gone down hitting his head on the edge of a nearby desk.

Several officers had already gathered with a couple apprehending the homeless man and cuffing him while others attended the officer that went down. No blood, but there was sure to be a concussion.

Sean took the opportunity to start making calls without giving Tom an answer to his question. He honestly didn't know how he felt about Michaela.

*****

"Hey…" Michaela sat down heavily on the side of her bed. She needed to talk with someone about last night and the break-in. Next to Heather, Marissa was not only her sister-in-law but a good friend too.

"What's up, sweetie?"

Michaela sighed. "I thought you should know. Someone broke into the bed-and-breakfast last night."

"What? Are you okay? What happened?" Marissa fired off several questions in a row.

"I'm okay, no one was hurt, but it was very odd. I was soaking in the bathtub when I heard a noise from within the B&B. When I came downstairs, the back door was partially open. A glass of wine had been poured and sitting on the counter."

"That's more than weird, it's downright creepy. Was anything taken? I mean, what exactly happened? Please, tell me no one was inside…"

"No, nothing was taken, at least I haven't discovered anything missing and whoever was here had already left. But at the time, I didn't know that, so I ran. I was scared to death! But when I opened the front-office door, I ran straight into Detective Ryan. He was here to ask more questions. Honestly, I don't know what I would have done had he not shown up!"

"Maybe, I should come over and stay for a few days. Did you tell him about what happened?"

"I don't think there is a need for you to uproot yourself to stay here for a few days, but I appreciate the offer and love you for it! And, yes, I did tell him what happened, so he searched the place. In fact, he ended up spending the night for which I was grateful." Michaela was prepared for the outburst from the other end of the line.

"He what? Michaela, are you crazy!"

"Listen, he slept on the couch in the living room. He saw how upset I was and wanted to ensure my safety, that's all."

"I bet. What I mean is that I'm sure nothing happened between the two of you because I know you. But Detective Ryan is cunning, and I think he made opportunity of something terrible happening to further question you. By the way, why was he there again?"

"To ask a question about you..."

"Me?"

"Yes, both detectives wanted to know if you were still married to Brent or merely separated since you're still using the last name of McCrea. I told him about the situation with you and Brent. Look, I gotta run. I wanted to work in the vegetable garden before you bring Chase home, and then I need to make bread. The B&B is booked solid next week. After a dry spell, I welcome the onslaught."

"Well, at least with the place booked, you should be in good company, and I won't be worrying over you. But if you need me, don't hesitate to call. Promise?"

"I promise, love you."

"Love you too!"

Michaela jumped when her cell immediately rang. Looking at her device, she didn't recognize the number. After having a series of suspicious calls, she decided to ignore it. It rolled over to voice mail, and she listened to see if they left a message, but there was nothing but a click where they ended the call. She was starting to get spooked by these calls. When her cell rang again, she jumped before recognizing Heather's number. She smiled and answered.

"I just got off the phone with Marissa, what's up?" Snickers jumped up on the bed and curled up beside Michaela. She absently reached out to pet him as Heather launched into telling her about a brand-new restaurant.

"Let's meet up there tonight after I get off work to have dinner. If I recall correctly, you don't have anyone booked until tomorrow, right?"

"That sounds wonderful. I can probably ask Marissa if she'll just keep Chase over for another night instead of dropping him off a bit later today. What time do you want to meet? And why are you working on a Sunday?"

"That's easy, clients. They think you have no life and should be available 24-7, 365 days of the year. I know, belly aching won't help, and the income isn't shabby! How about seven thirtyish?"

Michaela laughed. "I wish I could feel sorry for you, but when you have overnight guests, you actually do have to be available 24-7! The time sounds great by the way, send directions to my cell, and I'll meet you there!"

After hanging up with Heather, Michaela made a beeline to the kitchen to start bread dough so she could get out to the vegetable garden while it was still cool. Thank heavens the storm from the day before headed out and left in its place a beautiful, sunny day.

Throughout the afternoon, Michaela took the time to clean their private quarters. After finishing her bedroom and bath, she grabbed her supplies to head downstairs. As she turned into the hallway, she stopped short and gasped. A man stood on the landing eclipsed by the light coming from downstairs. With heart pounding, she took a tentative step backward. Her hand flew over her heart, and she was ready to drop her tools when he stepped forward, no longer a silhouette; it was Gavin.

He was dressed in slacks and a shirt, buttoned clear to the top. He smiled upon seeing her, but the smile didn't quite reach his eyes, leaving Michaela shaken by the fact he invaded her private living quarters and was actually upstairs close to her bedroom. She took another step back, and he simultaneously took a step forward. Reaching up, he placed a hand on the doorjamb to support himself.

"Gavin!"

"I thought I'd drop by. I wanted to see you. You don't get to church often, and quite frankly, I want to see more of you." His eyes dipped down and lingered upon her breasts.

"We belong together, you and I." With his free hand, he reached up to rub an errant strand of her hair that escaped its confines between his index and thumb. Leaning in further, he sniffed her hair, causing Michaela to pull the offending curl from his grasp.

"Your hair is so soft. I'm sorry you didn't take my advice to wear it down." He quickly reached up and pulled out the clamp holding her hair, allowing the mass of curls to fall about her shoulders. "There now, that's much better."

"Gavin, I've been cleaning, and I'll wear my hair as I see fit. How'd you get into my private quarters?" Her fear was rapidly being replaced by anger. Placing a hand on her hip, she continued. "And taking the liberty of coming upstairs, how dare you?"

"I knocked, but you didn't answer. I saw your car in the lot, and I was worried. Otherwise, I wouldn't have been so bold. When I called your name from your living room, again, you didn't answer, so I came to see if you were okay."

His excuse could be accepted, but she didn't believe it for a minute, and by the gleam in his eye, she felt he was lying. Fear once again crept in, replacing her anger. She realized what a precarious situation she found herself. Being caught in her bedroom by a man with no one around didn't bode well. She was on her own.

"If you don't mind," she said, trying to brush by him.

"I do mind. I mind a lot," he said, blocking her.

Startled, she looked up at him. He grabbed her supplies and pushed her into the bedroom and set the supplies down on the nearby chair. Michaela was weighing her options. Should she try to make a run for it? Her bright eyes connected with his.

"There's no reason to be afraid, my dear. I just wanted to spend some time with you, alone. You always have guests or your kid's around. Sometimes, a person has to do what a person has to do for a little privacy and a one-on-one."

Grabbing her elbow, he forced her closer, and bending his head down, he kissed her. She tried to turn her head away, but he forced her chin back and continued to kiss her, plunging his tongue inside. Again, she felt sickened by his wet kiss and the plundering of his slimy tongue; it repulsed her, and she almost gagged.

She tried pulling back, but his other arm came around her waist, and he tightly held her there. He continued to ravish her mouth, holding her in a vice grip. As he ended the kiss, he dropped his hand from her chin, and Michaela instinctively turned her head, repulsed by his slimy tongue and wet kisses. She almost heaved.

"You're beautiful, and you waste that beauty sometimes by wearing the wrong clothes. You look much better in a dress. Let's pick one from the closet, shall we?" He grabbed her by the elbow, forcing her over to the closet. Opening the door, he pilfered through her clothes, stopping to look more closely at one of her negligees. Fingering it, his eyes gleamed, and Michaela started shaking.

Noticing her discomfort, he smiled. "When will you trust me? One day, you'll beg me to come to your bedroom to make love to you. In fact, you'll do everything in your power to make me happy." He once again pushed clothes aside until he came to a dark-blue dress. "Ah, this one, you look especially good in it." Pulling it from the closet, he held it up for her. "Change," he ordered.

"I can't put this on," she said adamantly.

"Michaela, you're being difficult. When we're married, you'll learn to abide by all my wishes. When I say come, you'll come. When I say do this, you'll do it. And you'll do everything you can to make me happy."

Flabbergasted over his audacity and ridiculous assumptions, she couldn't help but gasp. "Never! Not in a million years. Get out of my house!" she screamed.

His hand covered her mouth so fast it took her by surprise. "I dislike screaming." His voice was menacing, silencing her immediately. It was a veiled threat, and she fought back the bile that rose in her throat.

"Hellooooo," a voice from downstairs echoed. "Michaela, dear, it's your neighbor, Mrs. Hensley."

Gavin dropped his hand from Michaela's mouth and stepped away.

“I’m up here,” Michaela answered as soon as he removed his hand. “I’ll be right down.” Michaela stepped away and then turned to look at him. “It’s funny how we could hear her voice, isn’t it? Get out!” She ground out.

He blanched. “This isn’t over, Michaela. It’s not over until we’re together.” Turning, he left the room. Michaela took in a deep breath and then hurried down the stairs. She saw no sign of Gavin.

As she reached the first floor, Mrs. Hensley stepped forward and asked, “Are you all right, dear? I saw that man enter your private quarters and it just didn’t feel right.”

“I’m so glad you came over, Mrs. Hensley. He’s from our church, Gavin, the owner of the sporting goods store. Didn’t you recognize him?”

“I’m sorry, but, no, my eyes just aren’t what they used to be. Gavin? Why would he enter your private living quarters?” she asked.

“He’s been trying to date me, but honestly, I’m scared of the man. He’s just not right if you know what I mean. He cornered me in my bedroom, and if you hadn’t come over, I think he would have tried to rape me.” Michaela shivered, and Mrs. Hensley put an arm around her shoulders. “Did you see him come down?” she asked, looking back toward the hall.

“I did, but I really only saw his frame, nothing distinct. He didn’t come into the living area, he went toward the office or the kitchen. Shall we take a quick look to ensure he’s left?”

“Yes, please!”

*****

Once the squad room quieted down and the offender handcuffed to his chair, Tom glanced at Sean. “Mimi invited you over for a barbecue this afternoon. She said to bring a lady friend if you’ve one. I told her you weren’t seeing anyone.”

Sean replaced the phone back in its cradle. “Sounds good, what time?”

"Around five."

*****

Driving up in front of a ranch-style house, Sean cut the engine and grabbed flowers he had picked up from a guy selling them on a busy street corner. He knew Mimi would love them. Pulling the keys from the ignition, he got out and walked up to the door.

Mimi answered with a smile plastered to her face. "Ah, you shouldn't have, Sean!" She placed a kiss on his cheek and took the flowers from him. "Tom is in the back if you want to join him outside. I was so hoping you'd have some young thing on your arm when you came tonight."

In her late forties, Mimi was an attractive woman with shoulder-length brown hair that was always parted down the middle and flipped on the ends. Her laughter was infectious, and she always seemed genuinely happy.

"You look great, Mimi. Thank you for inviting me over."

"You don't have to flatter me… I'm just glad you could make it," she said over her shoulder, retreating to the kitchen to put the flowers in a vase. "So when are you going to start dating again?" She looked at him with a twinkle in her eye.

"I have no idea. I guess when the right girl comes along."

"Don't let Tom deter you. I heard that the young woman who owns the Bayside Bed-and-Breakfast is quite pretty and you have an eye for her. Of course, Tom isn't happy, but if she's the one, don't let this case stop you." She filled an empty vase with water and cut the stems on the flowers at an angle as she spoke.

"I'm afraid it's not that easy, and besides, we're not involved." Sean ran a hand through his dark hair and glanced toward the sliding glass doors.

"Go ahead, he's probably out there drinking a beer, letting the fire on the barbecue burn down a bit before he throws steaks on." She tilted her head toward the sliding doors and started arranging the flowers in the vase.

CHAPTER 16

Sean eased the slider back and sat down in one of the empty lawn chairs next to Tom. Tom reached into the ice chest and grabbed a beer and tossed it to Sean.

Popping the top, he took a pull and sighed contentedly as the ice-cold liquid slid down his parched throat. "Nothing like a cold beer on a warm day…"

"Noth'n like it!" Tom agreed.

Mimi joined them with a glass of white wine in her hands and sat opposite the men.

Tom spoke up, breaking the silence, "What a hell of a case we landed. Can you believe some of the people we interviewed at Collins's law firm?"

Sean shook his head. "The guy sure had a lot of enemies."

"And plenty of lovers too!" Tom laughed. "I still can't believe that Myerson came on to you when we interrogated her!"

"What's this?" Mimi asked sitting forward.

"Hon, you should have seen her. This woman doesn't have any morals whatsoever from what I can tell, and she even came onto Sean during the interview. I mean leaning forward to show cleavage, and she wasn't wearing a bra!"

"I have to wonder who ogled her more to notice such details." Mimi laughed.

"You don't have to worry about me, hon, I'm all yours!"

Mimi laughed and winked at Sean. "Oh, lucky me!" They all three laughed, and then she excused herself to season the steaks and get them ready for the grill.

"I interviewed a couple of McCrea's neighbors."

"When?"

"Almost two weeks ago now. You already left the squad room, and I wanted to take the opportunity to speak with a couple of people to find their take on her."

Looking over at Sean, he continued, "Don't look at me like that. You were busy, and I felt it was a good time to question a few neighbors. The woman next door adores her, and the old man across the street, while crotchety, liked her too."

Sean relaxed in his chair. "I wished you would have told me."

"I happen to see Mrs. McCrea in her vegetable garden while I was talking to her neighbor. It was quite…" Tom drained the last of the beer and crushed the can. "I can't explain, but I was looking out the window of the neighbor's house and noticed Mrs. McCrea leaving the garden. She turned to close the gate and happen to make eye contact with me. It was like, I don't know, being caught spying on her? I know you like her, and I admit she's quite pretty. But there's something about her I just don't trust. There are too many coincidences."

Sean shook his head. "You've a right to your opinion, but I feel she's innocent."

"Well, I guess we can agree to disagree, but don't let your heart or your dick do your thinking for you. Got it!"

Sean drained his beer and tossed it into the trash. "Don't tell me how to do my job!"

CHAPTER 17

God is our refuge and strength, a very present help in trouble.

—Psalm 46:1

Evidently, the new restaurant was the buzz about town because every parking space within a block was taken. Michaela ended up pulling onto a side street and found a space where she could park under a streetlight. Slipping into the restaurant and through the crowd, she noticed the bar area ahead and immediately saw Heather seated at the end of the bar itself. Turning, Heather waved and pointed to the stool beside her.

"Wow, this place is really hopping! I couldn't even find a place to park out front, so I parked on the side street." Michaela slipped onto the bar stool and dropped her purse on the counter in front of her.

"I took the liberty of ordering you a drink."

"I need it!"

"So I spoke with Marissa…" Heather leaned forward on the stool and eyed Michaela with concern. "She told me about the break-in. Why didn't you tell me this morning when I called or call me immediately last night?"

"I would have, but Detective Ryan stopped by, and he checked the place out. My mind was on other things, and I was upset, and this morning, I needed to get busy before it warmed up too much. Sorry!" Michaela raised her shoulders and angled her head toward

Heather in a sorry gesture. She thought about telling Heather of Gavin's visit but didn't want to worry her friend.

"She also mentioned that he spent the night and she was upset about it. Now, me, I'm kind of glad he stopped by and spent the night there. Did anything happen? I know you wouldn't have told Marissa, but come on, you can tell me."

Michaela whipped her head around. "Nothing happened!"

"Okay, if you say so." Heather rolled her eyes. "But seriously, Michaela, this could have been so much worse. What if they had still been in the house or tried to harm you? What I don't understand though is if nothing was taken and a glass of wine sitting out, were they simply sending you a message, and if so, what?" Her brows drew together above her eyes, and she pursed her lips before tapping an index finger to her lower lip.

Frowning, Michaela took a sip of the margarita set in front of her. "A message…come to think of it, why wasn't anything taken? It makes no sense but sending me a message does! But what?" She rotated her glass on the cocktail napkin, considering the possibilities. *Did this have something to do with James's murder?* She shook herself and felt a chill go down her spine.

"Do you think it has anything to do with James?" Heather asked, mirroring Michaela's thoughts.

"I was just wondering that myself."

"Do you think it could possibly be one of his other girlfriends?"

"I didn't even know about the others he was dating until after the fact, and I doubt they knew about me either." Michaela fingered the napkin her cocktail was sitting on.

"But what if one of them did know about you? He was rich, handsome, and rich. Did I mention rich? One of the other women he was seeing might have stepped up her game trying to get an engagement ring out of him. And you, my dear, would certainly have been a kink in her plans." Heather was talking faster as her idea formed and grew. "She might have gone ballistic and murdered him out of rage!"

Michaela looked at Heather with disbelieving eyes. "Are you hearing yourself? If that were the case, then why break into the bed-and-breakfast after murdering him just to harass me?"

"Well, put like that, it doesn't make sense. Party pooper! I was really onto something until logic came into play." Heather laughed and sipped her drink.

"Let's move on to another subject. This is really creeping me out. By the way, you look very nice tonight."

"Thanks, nice way to change the subject, and you look great yourself! When did you pick up that little black number and more specifically where?" Heather asked, looking Michaela up and down.

"Stop, people will think we're a couple!" Michaela blushed and quickly looked around.

"Back to Detective Ryan. Wouldn't it be something if he happened to be here tonight? I tell you, if he saw you in that dress, he'd be throwing you over his shoulder and carrying you home for a tumble under the sheets." Heather laughed when Michaela's face turned redder.

"Heather!"

"Oh, come on. Don't tell me that you haven't had thoughts along those lines!"

A hostess stepped into the bar and called out for Miles, party of two.

Heather stood up and pushed her purse strap over her shoulder. "That's our cue..."

The hostess led the women to a booth near the back of the restaurant. Passing tables draped in black tablecloths and pristine white napkins, they were seated in a booth with tall, dark cushioned sides. The opposite wall contained a large aquarium that gave the restaurant a serene feel to it. Heather carefully laid her cloth napkin in her lap and looked up at Michaela.

"Do you like Detective Ryan?" she asked.

Looking up from perusing the menu, Michaela laid it back down on the table before answering. "In an odd sense, I do. It's hard to put in words, but he, he makes me feel safe."

"It doesn't hurt that's he's good-looking either. I mean he has the look stories are made of. I can see him galloping away with the damsel in distress sitting securely in his lap." Heather laughed.

Michaela shook her head. "And I guess that makes me the damsel in distress since I am being investigated for murder? And besides, you have always been a romantic ever since high school when you had a crush over Jeff Dyson. Remember when you asked him to prom?"

"I do, I most certainly do!" Heather replied with a slight laugh. They continued the chatter after giving their orders, unaware of two men that watched them from a table close by.

When their food arrived, blackened salmon for Michaela and a filet mignon for Heather, they sighed in pleasure. The salmon was cooked perfectly, tender, moist, and seasoned just right. It was served with rice pilaf and steamed broccoli. Both women dug in, moaning between mouthfuls and enjoying their bantering over days gone by when they were in junior high and high school. The evening went by far too quickly.

As they made their way out of the restaurant, again, neither were aware of the two men following them at a distance. Standing on the sidewalk just outside the doors, the men hung back, one talking to the hostess and the other perusing photos on the wall in the waiting area.

"I'll be by tomorrow to help you set up for guests!" Heather reached out and pulled Michaela in for a hug as they exited the restaurant. "I worry about you, you know! Call me when you get home!"

"I will, and I'll be fine, really! Thanks for thinking of this. I had a great time, and heaven knows I needed an evening out."

"I think we both did, but you more specifically. We'll talk tomorrow, 'kay?" Heather turned and headed for her car as did Michaela.

It was close to nine in the evening, but Michaela didn't see anyone else on the streets. With it a legal holiday, most people weren't working or they had already left for home from their workplaces. And all the shops had long since closed for the day.

Turning the corner onto the side street, she noticed that the streetlight was out where she parked the car. And then she realized the light was broken with glass fragments littering the sidewalk. The light was working when she parked. The hair on her nape rose, and she scanned the street. It was eerily quiet, and she felt a need to get to the safety of her car.

She'd taken but only a couple of steps when she heard footfalls coming from the main street nearing the corner where she'd parked. Fear settled in, and she quickened her pace. The light from the main street lamppost cast her elongated shadow against the side of the building as she ran to the driver's side of her car. Fumbling to retrieve the keys from her purse, she dropped them on the asphalt and knelt down to find them. Peering over the hood of the car, she saw a shadow emerge of a man that was now cast onto the side of the building. The footfalls slowed and then stopped. Heart pounding and breathing heavily, she fumbled for the keys once again when he spoke.

"Mrs. McCrea, what you have done with it?"

Michaela held her breath. *What*? She panicked and swept the street again, searching with her hands trying to find the blasted keys. The roughness of the asphalt scratched her skin, and the darkness made it impossible to see anything.

"Mrs. McCrea, where is it? I want the package, and I want it now." He spoke again, his voice nearer than before.

With pulse pounding throughout her body, Michaela gave up her attempt at finding the keys and decided to make a run for it. Pulling her heels off, she shot up and darted for the opposite corner of the main street, running down the sidewalk.

Looking over her shoulder, she saw the man in pursuit. He wore an overcoat and baseball cap that kept his face hidden. She almost stumbled in fright and knew she couldn't outrun this man; she hadn't run in years though she was in shape. But she was quick and small, making it easy to out maneuver him if she darted around vehicles parked on the street, except there were few cars.

He was gaining on her. Her pulse was pounding and her fear palpable. She ran across the street to the opposite side, and seeing cars parked along the side street, she turned the corner, slipping in front of a van to hide. Breathing heavily, she tried to control her need for air, fearing he'd hear her. She could hear him running, and then a curse erupted from his mouth as he gasped for air.

She was afraid he'd hear her heart beating frantically against her rib cage. Leaning against the front of the van, her legs felt like Jell-O as fear settled deep into the pit of her stomach. Her heartbeat seemed to take control of every aspect of her body, hearing it in her ears, feeling it throughout her body.

Peering under the carriage of the van, she saw him creeping along the sidewalk in her direction, and she tiptoed to the street side of the van, hunkering down as she crept.

He was now on the opposite side of the van, and as he made progress toward the front of it, she continued to creep along until she was now at the rear of the van.

"Where are you hiding? It won't do you any good, you stupid bitch!" he lashed out angrily.

Peeking out from behind the rear bumper, she saw him proceed up the side street, looking between vehicles. Making another run for it, she dashed from behind the van and ran back toward the main street again, working her way back toward the restaurant. Seeing a door to one of the shops recessed, she dove into the alcove and struggled to find her cell within her purse.

The purse was slowing her down, and she couldn't continue holding onto it and run well. Ditching the purse, she started to dial 911, but the light from the cell lit up the space around her, giving her location away. She turned it off and hovered in the darkness the recessed doorway gave her. She desperately needed to call for help, but not this moment.

Gasping for air, she heard footsteps approaching, and there was no way she could outrun anyone this close. She pressed herself against the wall as close as she could, hoping to escape the notice of a passerby while holding her breath.

As the person came closer, she realized it wasn't the man who'd been chasing her. This was a kid wearing a hoodie, probably some punk or, worse, a gang member. How in the world had she gotten herself into this mess? Why didn't she have Heather drive her to her car or something, the buddy system! She was downtown for heaven's sake, and this was no place to be alone at night, especially for a woman.

CHAPTER 17

The kid pulled out a cell phone from his pants pocket as he passed her and hit a button. She could hear a voice on the other end, and the kid started mumbling something.

He didn't see her thank God!

She let out her breath but didn't know what to do. If she ran now, either man could grab her. She closed her eyes and rested her head against the wall, feeling utterly helpless. After about fifteen minutes, she decided to run for it, hoping the man chasing her wasn't waiting for her to reveal her whereabouts.

Pushing her cell phone down a pocket in the dress, she made a break for it and ran for all she was worth. Nearing the restaurant on the opposite side of the street, she looked back but didn't see anyone. Stepping off the curb, she ran toward the restaurant but stumbled, scraping her toe across the asphalt in the process.

"Damn!" she yelled out, hobbling the rest of the way across the street and onto the sidewalk ahead.

Limping to the entrance of the restaurant, she opened the door and stumbled in. The hostess looked up from her station, and her smile immediately vanished.

"I need help." Michaela gasped. "Someone is after me!"

The hostess was clearly flustered over the situation and peering at the few people waiting to be seated brought Michaela's attention to those around her. One woman sneered and stepped behind her husband while the man gave her a dirty look.

"I need help…" Michaela pled again.

"Wait one moment…" The hostess left her position, and in just a few moments, she came back with a rotund man at her side.

"I'm the manager of Cessi's. I need to ask you to leave at once. You're disturbing the other diners."

"I need help. A man tried to attack me outside your restaurant!"

"I must ask you to leave at once," he stated again, and grabbing her arm, he attempted to steer her toward the door.

"I was having dinner here with a friend earlier, and when I left, this man started chasing me. We need to call the police!"

"Go ahead and dial 911 if you want, but you'll do it outside this establishment," he said disgustedly.

"Please, I'm begging you…"

"Why don't you call 911?" an elderly lady piped up that was waiting to be seated. "It couldn't hurt, and she seems to genuinely need help."

The manager turned to look at the woman, and when he did, Michaela made a run for the restroom. She pushed open a stall door and locked it behind herself.

Placing the lid down on the toilet, she flopped down with her heart still violently thudding in her chest. She was shaking all over. Pulling her cell from her pocket she started to hit Marissa's name from her contact list but thought better of it. Chase was staying the night with her, and she didn't want to upset him. Heather was probably still on her way home.

Going through the numbers, she came upon Sean's. He had given her his number in case she needed him after the break-in last night. She hesitated and then punched his name. The line rang about five times, and she was about ready to end the call when it was picked up.

"This is Detective Ryan."

"Sean…" Michaela closed her eyes, and tears threatened. His voice sounded so good!

"Michaela, what's wrong?"

"I need help." She started crying.

"Where are you? Are you at the B&B? Has someone tried to break-in again? What?"

"No, I'm at a restaurant, and when I left, a man was chasing me. I managed to run back to the restaurant for help, but the manager is trying to push me out and refused to call 911."

"Are you hurt?" he rasped out, feeling his gut tighten.

"I'm not hurt. I was able to get away, but I lost my car keys among other things. Can you…"

"Which restaurant, I'll come get you," he interrupted.

She told him the name, and he instructed her to wait inside and to not go back out on the street.

She slid off the toilet seat and opened the stall door. A large mirror was opposite the stalls, and she peered at her reflection. No wonder they wanted to toss her out on her ear. Her hair was mussed, her face pale, and now streaks of mascara ran down her cheeks. She splashed cold water on her face and attempted to wash off the makeup from her cheeks. Finger combing her hair, she felt somewhat better, but she still was a mess. Without shoes and a toe that was banged up, she looked like an urchin. The blood was already starting to dry up on her toe and no longer bleeding. With her little black dress, which she almost talked herself out of wearing this evening, she didn't doubt the manager thinking she was a hooker.

She straightened her dress and stepped out of the restroom. The manager was waiting for her.

"Look, I'm sorry about disrupting your business, but I really need help. I called Detective Ryan from the police department, and he's on his way to pick me up. He instructed me to wait inside."

"You called a detective?" He looked around and then grabbed her upper arm and steered her toward his office. "You can stay in my office until he gets here. I can't have you disturbing diners and have them thinking the area is unsafe," he said harshly and practically pushed her into a chair. He firmly shut the door behind him, leaving her alone. She was surprised that he didn't try to lock her inside.

Looking around the office, she noted the place was a mess with paperwork strung out on the desk, books fallen over on a shelf, and file cabinet drawers standing ajar. Hunching over in the chair, she let the tears fall, hugging her waist. *Please, Sean, get here quick!*

Eventually, she heard voices outside the office door and was relieved to hear Sean's deep baritone. They spoke a little longer, and she knew they were discussing her and what happened. Finally, the door opened, and the manager was first to enter with Sean close on his heels. His eyes met hers in concern.

"Please, be seated." The manager pulled out a chair, and then he stepped around his desk to seat himself.

"I don't know what game this woman is playing," he began, "but she's disturbed other diners and is giving this new upend restaurant a bad name. I won't have it!" He shifted his gaze to Michaela. "This is a fine establishment, and I won't have hookers in here working the beat!"

Michaela gasped. Sean sat straighter in his chair and then leaned toward the manager. "Mr. Richmond, watch it...do I make myself clear? I won't have you malign this woman, and I think you owe her an apology..."

Michaela had never seen Sean more intimidating even when he and his partner were interrogating her for the first time. She shuddered and glanced over at the manager.

He held up his hands. "Look, I don't know this woman, and judging by her appearance, I took it that she was working the streets. Look at her..." He gestured for Sean to take a closer look, which he did.

His eyes took in her mussed curls, the hint of mascara that had ran on her cheeks, and his eyes slowly dropped to her neckline where they stopped for a brief moment before continuing their appraisal downward. His eyes stopped at her unclad feet and bungled toe. He inhaled deeply and then turned back to the manager.

"We'll be taking our leave now, but it might benefit you to have a paid security guard for guests leaving the restaurant alone at night, especially a single woman. And in case I didn't make myself clear, you still owe this lady an apology."

The manager glanced at Michaela and mumbled an insincere apology.

Sean stood and motioned for Michaela to stand too. Pushing his chair aside, he opened the door and laid a hand on Michaela's back to precede him out the door.

They made their way to the lobby and out the doors, all without Sean saying a word. He led her to his car parked just outside the establishment and opened the passenger side door for her. Once she was seated, he slammed the car door and went around the front of the car to slide in behind the wheel. He sat for a minute, and Michaela noticed the slight tick in his cheek. He was mad?

He finally turned to her. "What the hell were you thinking?" he ground out.

"What? What do you mean?" she asked with wide eyes.

"Look, wasn't it you who just had a break-in at the bed-and-breakfast? And now you're out and about, alone I might add, and wearing that…that dress!" His eyes once again focused on her neckline.

She wanted to cover herself up but didn't dare move a muscle.

"I'm fine now," she finally managed. "My car is parked on the side street, and I think I should be able to find my keys and drive myself home."

A cynical laughed erupted from deep in his throat. "You've got to be kidding. You're fine and can drive yourself home…" He shook his head from side to side.

"Look, I'm not at fault here!" Michaela lashed out, raising her voice.

Sean turned the key in the ignition and fired up the engine. "Where's your car?"

"It's parked on the side street behind us."

He punched the engine and made a U-turn and headed to the side street where he hooked another left. Seeing her car parked about five cars from the corner, he stopped in the middle of the street and put the engine in park. He got out and walked over to her car and bent over. When he returned, he threw her shoes into the floorboard at her feet and handed her the car keys.

Tears threatened, and she fumbled for the door handle to get out and drive home.

"What are you doing?"

"I'm getting out so I can drive myself home," she managed as tears brimmed.

"Michaela…" He opened the glove compartment and pulled out some napkins from a local fast-food restaurant and handed them to her. "You're not driving yourself home. Where's your purse?"

She hiccupped and looked over at him. "I think it's on the main street down a block on the opposite side."

He gave her a questionable look and once again pulled a U in the street and headed back to the main street, turning left.

"There," she pointed out. "That's where I ditched it, I think."

He pulled to the side of the road and told her to stay put. A few minutes later, he walked back with her purse in hand. When he got in the car, he handed it to her.

"Thank you," she said demurely and dropped her eyes to her lap. The tears were still coming, and Sean wanted to pull her into his embrace and comfort her. Where that feeling came from, he didn't know. So he put the car in gear and headed to the B&B without further words being exchanged.

CHAPTER 18

Let him kiss me with the kisses of his mouth for thy love is better than wine.

—Song of Solomon 1:2

Entering through Michaela's private entrance, Sean slammed the door behind him and locked it before following her into the kitchen.

Michaela tossed her purse and car keys down and leaned back against the counter, crossing her arms around her middle. "Would you like coffee or something stronger?" she asked.

"No," he snapped. "What I would like is a rundown of what happened tonight." He pulled out a kitchen chair and plopped down.

Snickers ran into the kitchen upon hearing their voices, and Michaela reached down and petted him. He had been fed before she left for the restaurant, but she checked his water dish to ensure it was full before pulling out a chair opposite Sean. "I guess I should start at the beginning…"

"You think?"

Her temper flared, and snapping back, she ground out, "Look, this wasn't my fault. I was merely out for an evening meal with Heather!"

Snickers whined at the raised voices and standing on his haunches placed his front paws on Michaela's lap. She ran her hand down his back to comfort him and then rubbed his head.

"You scared the hell out of me, Michaela! When I heard your voice on the other end of the line, I knew something was wrong for you to call *me*, and I knew it couldn't be good! But when you started to cry, I was beyond worried. I couldn't get to you fast enough. And then…exchanging words with that ridiculous manager of the restaurant didn't improve the situation, but the topping on the cake… seeing you in that dress like you're dressed for a night out hoping to pick up some guy." He waved his hand in front of her, and then his eyes came to rest on her chest again.

Michaela instinctively wrapped her arms about herself, hiding her cleavage.

His gaze found hers, and he said, "A bit late to cover up."

She blushed and looked away. "It's really not that revealing," she blurted.

He sighed and reached out, cupping her chin. "I'm sorry. It's just that I can't explain, but whatever this is between us…" He lifted his shoulders and dropped his hand from her chin.

Sighing heavily, Michaela launched into her story. "Heather and I agreed to meet for dinner at this new restaurant, but all the parking on the street was already taken by the time I got there, so I parked on the side street. When we left the restaurant, I noticed that the streetlight where I parked was broken." She lifted her eyes to his. "It wasn't broken when I parked there."

Pausing in her story, she looked around the kitchen without seeing it.

"And."

"That's when a man approached. I tried to hurry and get in the car but dropped my keys." She shifted in her chair. "I couldn't find them in the dark. I was scared. He asked me the oddest thing…he asked me what I had done with the package or something to that effect. I have no idea what he was talking about. Package…what package?" She lifted her shoulders and shook her head.

"He asked you what you did with a package…does this have something to do with Collins, you think?"

"I don't know. Now that I think about it, Heather and I were discussing the break-in. She thought maybe someone was sending me a message since nothing was taken, or for that matter broken!"

"Good point, so why did you take off your shoes and ditch your purse?"

CHAPTER 18

"I was scared to death and couldn't find my keys. I was afraid he'd walk around the car and grab me, so I decided to run for it and knew the heels had to go. So I pulled them off. I bolted across the road and up to the main street. When I looked around, he was giving chase…and gaining on me!" Her voice rose, reliving the nightmare. "I ran across the main street to the other side with an idea to run between vehicles and saw a few parked on that side street. I hid behind a van." She closed her eyes and tilted her head back.

Sean listened without saying anything, letting her spill out the events while fresh in her mind. His brows furrowed in concern, and he laid a hand over hers which were clasped in a tight grip on the table to where her knuckles had turned white.

She continued, "He was out of breath and cursing. As he walked by the van looking for me, I circled back around, and when he was past, I ran back toward the main street hiding in a recessed doorway of a store entrance. I must have stayed there for about fifteen minutes before I struck up the nerve to run again back to the restaurant."

"Your toe, do you have a first aid kit?" he asked.

"In the pantry…" As she pointed her finger toward the pantry, Sean noticed her scraped palm.

"What happened?" he asked, pulling her hand into his much larger palm.

"Trying to find my keys, I managed to scrape my hand on the asphalt."

Sean jumped up finding the kit on the top shelf. He returned and dropped down on his knees, and looking up into her large teary green eyes, he reached up, cupping his hand behind her neck; he gently pulled her forward. His lips found hers. They were soft and sensual, and his heartbeat kicked up a notch. The kiss deepened. He could feel her heartbeat with the pad of his thumb, but it was hard to discern if it was his pulse or hers. She moaned softly, and her lips parted, making way for his tongue to explore. She tasted so damn good.

Snickers whined, and their kiss ended. As Sean pulled away, her soft hair caught in his whiskers. He gently pushed her hair back behind her ear. She was flushed and her eyes half closed. He could see her pulse beating rapidly at the base of her throat and knew she was as affected by their kiss as he had been.

"You look so damn sexy tonight!"

Michaela's eyes popped open, and she laughed thinking about what Heather had said about Sean seeing her in this dress.

"What's funny?"

"I was just thinking about something Heather said at dinner tonight."

"Hmmm, she's something else, and if you ask me, I think she's rooting for us. Where's Chase tonight? It's obvious he isn't here."

"At Marissa's." Michaela laughed again, showing dimples, and Sean gently touched her cheek.

He loved those dimples. Feeling a need to touch him, she reached out and rubbed his shadowed chin with the back of her hand, enjoying their briskly texture. They both sobered as they looked into each other's eyes.

"Michaela…" His eyes dropped to her chest again, and his hand dropped from her cheek as his finger trailed the top of her collarbone, allowing his hand to graze the swell of her breasts above the neckline of her dress. She closed her eyes and leaned into his hand. This felt so good; it felt right.

"Michaela, we can't go on like this." He rested his forehead against hers. "Someone is after you, and I can't protect you or work this case if we're involved." He pulled away and locked gazes with her again.

"I'm afraid, Sean. Why is this happening?" She brushed her hair from her eyes. "I just don't understand. I don't have any package that James sent." She shook her head.

"We need to figure this out. Are you sure the break-in was the first time anything unsettling happened?" he asked as he rose from his knees and pulled a couple sheets off the paper towel dispenser near the kitchen sink. Turning the faucet on, he let the water warm before wetting the sheets to cleanse her stubbed toe and the palm of her hand.

Putting her elbows on the table, she dropped her chin into her upturned palms, flinching when her right hand hurt from the scrapes. Her head snapped back up instantly. "Do you think Chase is in any danger?"

"I doubt it. Someone is targeting you when Chase is not around unless something else has happened. Think, Michaela, any mysterious phone calls, a feeling that someone is watching you, anything that just struck you as odd?"

Sean held up her foot, laying it gently in his lap as he squatted in front of her. He gently washed the injured toe before spraying it with antiseptic. Michaela inhaled sharply with the sting from the spray, and then Sean bandaged the appendage with deft fingers. Then with the second paper towel, he gently wiped her palm, and with the gentle pressure, it was mesmerizing, his touch more of a caress than cleaning a wound.

"I've been receiving calls, mostly hang ups, but sometimes, there's someone on the other end breathing heavily," she finally answered.

"How long has this been going on?" Sean asked.

"For a couple of months or so. At first, I thought it might be kids with idle time on their hands, but not anymore."

Dropping her forearms to the table, she clasped her hands together. "Today, I was accosted by a man from my church. He's been interested in me for a couple of years now, but recently, he's grown more aggressive. He's off, if you know what I mean. He came to the B&B this afternoon, letting himself in through my private quarters. I had been upstairs cleaning, and when I turned into the hall from my bedroom, he was standing there. He's taking liberties and is demanding. He pushed me into the bedroom and forcefully kissed me. But then he forced me to the closet and wanted me to put on a dress that he picked out. He wants me to wear my hair down and cater to his needs. He actually thinks we'll get married. It's so hard to explain, but I think the guy is psycho! I'm not sure what he's capable of, but he scares me. If not for Mrs. Hensley coming over running interference, I don't know what would have happened. And then another day when I was working in the garden, I felt like someone was watching me. But when I looked around, no one was there..."

"Has he done anything like this before?" he asked, clearly angry. "The man from your church," he clarified. He decided not to tell her that it might have been Tom she felt watching her since he recently had spoken with some of her neighbors.

"Last Sunday, he practically forced the issue of us sitting together in church. Throughout the sermon, his hands were all over me. It was awful, and I didn't get anything out of the sermon I was so focused on keeping his hands off, uh, certain parts."

"What's this bastard's name?"

Michaela's eyes darted to his, and she could see the tick in his cheek return. "Gavin Brooks."

"If his advances toward you are escalating, it's possible he could have murdered Collins to get him out of the way. Remove the competition, but it doesn't explain about a package…"

As he reflected on that aspect, he said, "James could have easily hidden a package here that might contain evidence of some kind, something that a person would never want to see the light of day. Have you noticed anything at all, a package that you placed in a file to look at later?"

She shook her head. "I do all the paperwork and haven't seen anything like that. Heather and Marissa help a lot, but they check in guests and answer the phone, that sort of thing. I do all the cooking, cleaning, laundry, and paperwork myself."

"It wouldn't hurt to take a closer look around tomorrow. Something could have shown up, and you were extra busy with intentions of getting back to it later and then simply forgot about it. I can even help you look for that matter since I'm staying the night again."

Michaela's eyes darted to his, and she was about to protest.

"There's no room for argument," he said, holding up his hand. "And besides, you still need to change into something less revealing." His eyes dipped down and then back to hers. "I can even help with that if you like?" He glanced back up and smiled with a cocked eyebrow.

CHAPTER 18

Michaela shot up from her chair, hitting his chin with her shoulder in the process. It knocked him off balance, and he fell back on his butt.

"I'm so sorry!" Michaela leaned over him. "Are you all right? I didn't mean to knock you over," she asked, concern lacing her voice. She extended her hand to help him up.

Sean laughed and took her hand, but instead of letting her help him up, he gently pulled her down, and she found herself lying on top of him. He once again pulled her head down to meet his, and he gave her a warm, lingering kiss. Michaela at first resisted, but as the kiss deepened, she melted and relaxed into it. His tongue probed her lips, and she opened for him, moaning softly as his tongue pushed inside, tasting her. His arms wrapped around her, and he held her tightly, allowing his frame to cushion her from the hard floor beneath.

"Maybe, we should find a bed…" he murmured.

Michaela shot up like a bullet. "I'm sorry…" she whispered.

Sean sobered and sat up. "It's okay, we don't have to do anything you don't want, but I'm not going to deny that I want you."

Her eyes cast downward to his crotch, and she blushed seeing the bulge in his pants. She wanted to reach out and touch him, caress his hardened length, and she almost did but caught herself. Locking eyes with Sean, he smiled.

"There's no need to be ashamed, we both want the same thing. Why don't you change and get comfortable?" He cocked his head to better look at her from his angle since he was still sitting on the floor. "I think I'll make us something to drink, any preferences?"

"Uh, maybe a glass of wine… I'll be right back."

Once in her bedroom, Michaela tried to pull herself together. She closed her eyes in humiliation, and yet what she wanted more than anything was for Sean to wrap his arms around her and tell her that everything would be okay.

Her eyes flew open. "Like that's going to happen," she muttered.

Stepping into the bathroom, she washed her face and ran a brush through her hair. Gazing at her reflection in the mirror, she was torn. If she were honest with herself, she was attracted to Sean. No, more than that, she was starting to have deep feelings for him.

She stepped back into her bedroom and sat heavily on the recliner near the bed. If she were completely honest, she corrected herself, she wanted more than his arms, she wanted him, period. It'd been five long years of denial, celibacy.

Sean had poured two glasses of red wine from a bottle in the pantry. Michaela seemed to take much too long just to change, and he began to worry. His concern grew the longer she took. Finally, sitting his glass down heavily on the table, he rose from his chair.

Pushing open the door to her private living quarters, he stepped through and glanced about the space. Hearing a soft moan upstairs, he sprinted up the stairs and hesitated when he saw Michaela standing in her room in front of the window in a thin nightgown that reached to the floor. It wasn't one of the sexy numbers he saw in her closet earlier, but this one was sheer enough that he could easily see the outline of her back, buttocks, and slender legs. Her hair flowed freely about her shoulders, and the white gown she wore shimmered with her movement.

"Michaela?"

She spun around and blushed, lowering her eyes to the floor. He could easily see her body through the sheer fabric.

"Are you okay?"

She glanced back up and inhaled with a shaky breath. "No. I'm at war with myself, and I'm tired of the battle within…"

Sean stepped further into the room.

"I-I have feelings for you." She turned back toward the window as her blush deepened. "Strong feelings for you," she continued.

Sean approached quietly and wrapped his arms around her, and she jumped but didn't bolt. He kissed the top of her head. "I have strong feelings for you too." His voice was mere inches from her ear. She closed her eyes and leaned back into his frame.

She exhaled deeply, placing her hands upon his forearms which grazed the sides of her breasts. She loved the feeling and wanted more, and the battle within ensued. Peering into the window, she noticed their reflection. Sean's arms wrapped around her protectively with hands entwined above her abdomen. And while she watched their reflection, Sean untwined his hands and slowly moved them up toward her breasts. And she inhaled, her nipples turning into tight nubs. She watched fascinated as one of his hands explored the underside of her breast and inched upward to rub the hardened nipple. Her eyes closed, and she arched her back so that her breast pushed against his palm.

Sean lowered his head and kissed the top of her shoulder and then the side of her neck and finally her earlobe. She didn't know if she could take anymore. No, she wanted more, a lot more!

Sean captured her eyes in the reflection in the glass before turning her in his arms. Placing his hand under her chin, he tilted her mouth up to meet his in a slow, exotic kiss that left her breathless and her heart beating so fast she thought she'd die.

She brought her arms up and wrapped them around his neck as their kiss continued. Opening her mouth, his tongue explored and her limbs felt heavy, and heat flooded her lower parts as their tongues dueled, entwined, and explored.

As their kiss ended, she laid her head into the hollow of his shoulder and sighed heavily. He rubbed her back, letting his hands slide down further to the small of her back and then over her buttocks. She could feel his hardened length through their clothes, and she knew they had to complete what they started.

Reaching up, she rubbed the back of her hand through his whiskers. "I want to do this..."

Sean lifted his hands and plucked at the five tiny cloth-covered buttons on the front of her gown. Slowly, he unfastened the top one and rubbed his fingers across her exposed collarbone. He unfastened another, revealing cleavage and this time lifted her chin to kiss her lightly, nibbling at her lips. Another button slid from the hole, more cleavage, and then another and finally the last one, revealing more of her creamy breasts. He pushed the gown off her shoulders, letting it land in a pool around her feet. Before she could react or say anything, he lifted her and laid her gently on the nearby bed.

Sitting on the edge, he leaned over and kissed her thoroughly with his one forearm resting against her breast. She inhaled deeply, enjoying the sensation and wanted more as she entwined her hands around his neck. The kiss lingered, soft, smooth, slow, and sensual.

Finally, Sean pulled back and stood at the side of the bed to undress while admiring her nakedness. She instinctively crossed her arms to cover her breasts, and Sean said, "Please, don't…"

He unbuttoned his shirt and pulled it off, tossing it on the nearby recliner. Michaela watched him as he shed his clothes, tossing each article on the chair behind him. Strong muscular arms and shoulders framed his tapered torso, and a light sprinkling of dark hair feathered out across his pecks and then ran down the center of his body, dipping beneath his pants which was the next article of clothing to come off to be tossed on the chair. When he was completely nude, she focused on his erection and swallowed hard. He eased himself on the bed and lying beside her turned her face to kiss her. He trailed a finger along her collarbone and then over the swell of her breasts. She arched, wanting more, and he indulged her by cupping her breast and lowering his head down to suckle. She moaned softly, placing her hands on his shoulders.

Moving to the other breast, he gave it full attention. She moaned softly, closing her eyes and turning her head into the pillow. Her soft curls feathered the pillow, and with lips parted, Sean groaned, wanting more of her. He feathered kisses down her stomach to the top of her thigh, and her legs voluntarily parted. He slid his hand along her inner thigh to her apex. His slight touch nearly sent her over the edge. She bucked, needing more, and he gently pushed her legs further apart.

Moaning softly, she whispered, "Sean, please…"

He circled her center, teasing the sensitive area with his finger, and she raised her hips, wanting more. "More…" she murmured aloud.

Indulging her request, he slipped his fingers inside to find her damp and swollen. She raised her hips to meet the thrust of his fingers, and almost immediately, she convulsed against them, climaxing. Gasping, she opened her eyes and reached out for him.

Lying beside her, Sean pulled her into his embrace enjoying the feel of her soft skin, clean scent, and the fragrance of soft curls that tickled his chin. He was falling in love with this woman, and he was falling fast.

She laid her hand upon his chest and pulled her fingers through his chest hair and marveled that his heart was pounding against his ribs. Not only did she want more than just intimacy at the moment, she wanted him, and it was obvious he was affected by their lovemaking as she was.

As he rose above her, he stilled. "Are you sure, Michaela?"

Looking up at him adoringly, she nodded. His heart was melting; no one had ever looked at him with so much trust.

Supporting his weight on his elbows, he once again hesitated. "Are you sure, sweetheart?" he asked.

The endearment sent her over the edge, and feeling his hardness against the top of her thigh, she opened her legs, further inviting him. He settled in and was about to thrust inside when the landline shrilled beside the bed.

They both stilled. Sean almost cursed, feeling Michaela tense under him, and then placing her palms against his pecks, she pushed. He pulled up, supporting himself so that their bodies were no longer touching as they heard Heather's voice on the machine.

"Michaela, it's me, Heather. I was just checking in to see if you made it home safe and sound. I got waylaid as soon as I got home by Mom of all people. She just had to fix tea and find out all that's happening. She just left, so I thought I better call before it got too late. Give me a call so I know everything is okay. Love you! Bye."

The mood was shattered. The heavy breathing abated. Sean rolled onto his side beside Michaela before sitting up on the edge of the bed. Michaela's breathing was still shallow, and she felt bereft of Sean's body, more specifically his wonderful fingers. Shaking with need, she closed her eyes in frustration but also shame. This wasn't her. She believed with all her heart that sex outside of marriage was wrong. But, oh, how she wanted this! At war with herself, she finally rose to sit on the side of the bed with her back to Sean.

Frustration filled Sean. But more than that, he almost blew it. If he'd had sex with her, then he'd have to step down from the case; he would be too close and wouldn't be able to do his job well. Besides, he knew that given this liberty, Michaela had more at stake than he. She was giving him herself, including her heart. What was he bringing to the table? Granted, he wanted sex with her, but did he want more? His feelings were stronger than just a one-night stand or merely liking her. He cupped his head in his hands as he heard Michaela get up on the opposite side of the bed and then step into the adjacent bathroom.

Taking her absence as a means to get dressed, he donned his clothes and then sat down in the chair, waiting for Michaela to come out of the bathroom. Opening the door, she peered out and seemed a bit surprised to find Sean still in her room. She was now wearing a robe, and her eyes were red rimmed and teary.

"Michaela…"

She held up a hand. "Please, don't. I was completely at fault and shouldn't have pressured you into having sex."

"Pressured me?" He sat up straighter in the chair. "Just what the hell is that to mean? You think that you had to try and get me into your bed?"

She sat heavily on the edge of the bed facing Sean and wrapped her robe securely around her.

"I've been thinking about you from the first moment I laid eyes on you. I love everything about you, and I find myself lying awake at night, unable to sleep, because I'm thinking of you, your smile, those sweet dimples, the freckles across your nose, your hair, the color of your eyes, and fantasizing about what it would be like to have sex with you." He stood up. "And I won't apologize for that. What we did this evening was a gift, and I want more. Pressure me? Not for one damn minute. Where do you want me to sleep, on the sofa?" he asked, changing the subject abruptly.

Michaela winced. She was about ready to burst with need, and Sean had awoken desires that even James couldn't reignite. And she wanted Sean to stay the night in her bed, not the sofa! But she couldn't ask him to lay with her throughout the night and abstain from sex, especially when she wanted it as bad as he.

The sound of the doorbell brought them both up short in their thoughts. They looked at one another like a deer caught in the headlights.

CHAPTER 18

Michaela jumped up from the side of the bed, and Sean rose, placing his hand on her upper arm to stop her progress. "You don't know who's there. Let me check first."

He made his way downstairs to the front door with Michaela on his heels as the bell pealed out again at the private entrance. He flipped on the outdoor light and peered through the window to see Heather standing anxiously on the step.

Looking around at Michaela, he said, "It's Heather." Stepping to the side, he opened the door.

CHAPTER 19

Only by pride cometh contention, but with the well-advised is wisdom.

—Proverbs 13:10

"Why didn't you return my call or text me?"

"I'm sorry..." Michaela began, and then looking beyond Heather, she made eye contact with Sean.

Realizing Sean was still by the door, Heather turned sharply, giving him a once-over before turning back to Michaela. Taking in her appearance, she realized that she had interrupted them.

"I am so sorry, but I was worried half to death about you with the break-in last night and then when you didn't pick up or return my call... I just had to make sure you were okay! I see I'm interrupting, so I'll leave you two alone."

"It's okay, you didn't interrupt anything," Sean spoke up.

Heather looked perplexed as she swiveled her head back to Sean. "Am I missing something?"

"I was getting ready to leave. I'll let Michaela fill you in," Sean answered. He pulled out his car keys, and turning to Michaela, he said, "I'll be by in the morning to take you to pick up your car."

"Please wait..." Michaela rushed over to where he still stood by the door. "Thank you for helping me and being there when I needed someone," she said, tilting her head to peer up at him.

"There's no need to thank me. I would have come no matter what!"

Standing on her toes, she wrapped her arms around his shoulders and gave him a firm kiss right on the mouth, surprising Sean. He wrapped his arms around her, holding her close.

She felt good in his arms, and he prolonged the kiss even though he knew Heather was watching and would ask Michaela a thousand questions.

Before parting, she whispered in his ear, "I'm falling in love with you, Sean…" And then she was out of his arms and stepping back. "I'll see you tomorrow morning."

Sean felt his heart open to this woman, and he gently touched her cheek with the back of his knuckles. "See you tomorrow…"

When she closed the door and locked it behind him, Heather whistled. Michaela turned and laughed.

"So I really did interrupt things. Was it getting steamy? And what is it Sean wants you to fill me in on?" She arched her brows, but a broad smile was plastered on her face.

"While you may have had to deal with traffic and then your mom after leaving the restaurant, I had to deal with being chased by a man." Michaela turned toward the kitchen, and Heather followed.

"What? What do you mean you were chased by a man, and where is your car?" She watched as Michaela took an open bottle of wine and poured a glass for Heather.

Handing the glass to her, she filled her in on the evening up to the point that she and Sean almost made love. That she wanted to keep to herself and hopefully later reflect on the evening, holding it close to her heart.

"I'm sorry I wasn't available, but I am glad you called Sean. He sounds very protective of you. Again, this could have been so much worse. What do you think would have happened had he caught up with you, I mean the guy chasing you?"

Heather worried her bottom lip while Michaela didn't want to entertain the thought. Snickers snuggled down for a nap at her feet under the table, and Michaela patted the top of his head and muttered endearments.

Heather laughed. "Our pets will always be our babies no matter what. Clancy has been misbehaving, and I found where she started to claw the back corner of my sofa." Clancy was Heather's beloved fat tabby that definitely had an attitude.

"Changing back to this evening;" Heather went on, "that horrible manager at the restaurant. That's it, I'm boycotting the place. I don't care how good the food is! And package? What package? Do you have any idea what he may have been talking about?"

Michaela sighed heavily. "No. I don't have a clue and don't recall any package arriving. Sean suggested that we look around tomorrow morning to see if something came that got shuffled around and then forgotten."

"Why wait 'til morning? Let's start in the office. Maybe a package came while Marissa was manning the desk and she forgot to tell you about it."

Grabbing their glasses of wine, they headed into the office. Michaela took the desk while Heather looked around the counter space and cubbies. Finding nothing, they started in on the file cabinets and even looked behind larger pieces of furniture, thinking it could have fallen behind something. Exhausting their efforts, they went back to the kitchen, sitting down at the kitchen table.

"Well, that turned up zilch!" Michaela rasped. "And I'm tired to boot!" Following the women from the office, Snickers settled once again under the table at Michaela's feet.

"Okay, let's think about this for a minute. Do we even have a time frame for when said package could have arrived or been left and exactly by whom?" Heather refilled her glass and offered to refill Michaela's.

Michaela responded with a shake of her head and held her hand over the top of the glass. "I really don't know. But Sean seems to think that James might have hidden something here. And if that's the case, we're looking back to, well, over three months ago. And honestly, James was in almost every room in the B&B with exception of the upstairs."

"So let's take a look around the downstairs of your private quarters. When was the last time you pulled the couch out to look behind it or opened a hutch drawer, anything like that?"

Cocking her head, Michaela then jumped up with more excitement. "Not since James was here. I usually clean out drawers and behind furniture only twice a year or so, and that was before James stayed here, and I haven't deep cleaned since!"

Both women filed into Michaela's living room and started opening drawers, pulling open cabinets, and looking behind furniture. Still nothing turned up. They didn't find anything except for a loose dime under the couch and some dust bunnies.

Both women flopped down on the couch glassy-eyed and yawning. Michaela looked defeated while Heather put her feet up to rest on the coffee table. Snickers jumped up on the couch beside Michaela, and she absently petted him. "Okay, little guy, you need to go to bed. Upstairs you go, bed!"

Snickers jumped down and trotted over to the staircase. At least one of them had enough sense to get some sleep.

Suddenly Heather sat erect. "Didn't you say he was everywhere? What about the common rooms or for that matter even the kitchen?"

Michaela shook her head. "I'm in the kitchen every single day and in all the cupboards. Believe me, he didn't leave anything there. But the common rooms worth taking a look."

They jumped up and headed for those rooms. With few places to hide anything, they were able to cover both the dining and common room quickly.

Turning to Michaela from where she stood, Heather asked, "What about the room he stayed in?"

"I cleaned it. And I always check drawers and the closest for personal belongings so the room is ready for the next guest."

"What about under the bed?"

Michaela rolled her eyes. "Granted I don't always look under the beds, but I do vacuum periodically."

"Okay…appease me. I just have to see the room for myself."

"Be my guest, it's not locked from the inside. It's the last room on the right."

Heather disappeared down the hallway, and Michaela heard her open the door. Shaking her head, she returned to the kitchen and rinsed out her empty wine glass. She needed sleep.

Hearing a shout from the far end of the B&B where Heather was searching, Michaela's blood ran cold. Was someone else here? She ran toward the hallway when Heather ran out of the room.

"What about the air ducts?" she yelled.

Michaela stooped over, placing a hand to her stomach. "You gave me a scare. I thought someone was hiding in the room or something!"

"I'm sorry...but it just occurred to me, we haven't searched air ducts."

"The vents...of course. We see people hiding stuff in the air ducts in movies and TV shows all the time!"

"We need a cross-point screwdriver...two would be better so we can tackle them all in half the time."

"On it!"

With a step ladder and screwdriver each, they set to work removing plates and looking in the ducts which took up a good hour. Nothing!

"I've got to get some sleep. Do you want to sleep in Chase's room, the couch, or a guest room?" Michaela asked.

The next morning, Michaela called Marissa to tell her about the previous night and to see if it was okay if she picked up Chase later in the morning after retrieving her car.

But after punching in Marissa's number and asking her if she'd keep Chase for the morning, the landline rang, interrupting the conversation before she could tell her anything.

Ending her call with a promise to tell her everything when she picked up Chase, she answered the landline. It was someone making reservations for a couple of weeks later. By the time she ended the call, Heather was pulling food from the fridge for breakfast.

"I'm sorry, I should have answered the phone while you were talking with Marissa."

"No problem, in fact I'm sort of glad you didn't. Marissa would have asked a hundred questions about what happened last night and then get upset with me for calling Sean instead of her. I'd just as soon forego all that, I'm simply not in the mood, and I'm tired and sleep deprived."

"Me too, and now I'm starving. What sounds good? I'll cook!"

"Whatever sounds good to you sounds good to me."

"Okay, bacon and eggs it is. It was so disappointing not to find something last night after our extensive search. And actually, I think my muscles are feeling the exercise in climbing up and down the step ladder." Heather placed a few strips of bacon into a skillet she had set on the stove.

Michaela yawned and then asked, "Will you take me to pick up my car? I hate to bother Sean. And since you plan to help me this morning in prepping foods for the afternoon social hour, chores will be done in half the time."

"Sure, no problem." Grabbing a bowl from the cabinet, she proceeded to break eggs into it and whip them while the bacon started sizzling. Smelling bacon, Snickers ran into the kitchen and sat on his back haunches, begging for some.

Heather laughed. "Not on your life, big boy. I'm a bacon lover, so you're out of luck."

Michaela chuckled and filled his dog dish with food and refreshed his water. While Heather finished up breakfast, Michaela called Sean's number to tell him he didn't need to give her a lift to pick up her car. His cell went to voice mail, so she left a message.

It was a beautiful morning with the sun shining nice and bright. It perked up Michaela's spirits, and before opening Heather's car door, she took a deep breath, inhaling the perfume from the roses that lined the fence to the vegetable garden. Good weather always meant good business. Guests wanted to return in the future because they would remember the beautiful days they had during their visit. Whereas bad weather was what they remembered most often, even if the B&B exceeded their expectations.

"Come on," Heather barked. "We need to get your car and get back to start prepping for guests."

Michaela laughed and got in. As they left the parking area of the B&B, she noticed a car parked off to the side that wasn't familiar to her. And it appeared that someone was sitting in the car. Maybe, they were there to visit one of her neighbors. But as Heather negotiated the neighborhood streets to pick up the freeway, Michaela noticed the car was behind them and seemed to be turning on every street they turned on. Then again, if they were headed to the freeway, this would be the route to take.

She continued to watch her side-view mirror to see if the car stayed with them. And as Heather increased her speed and moved to the left in faster-flowing traffic, so did the car. And when she came upon a slower car on the freeway and ended up moving to the right to get around it, so did the car behind.

Finally, Michaela felt a need to speak up. "Heather, I think we're being followed."

"What?" Heather snapped her head around to stare at Michaela. Then looking into the rearview mirror, she asked, "Which car?"

"It's a couple of cars back, a dark sedan. It was parked across the street in front of my neighbor's when we left the B&B. They've been on our tail ever since, getting into the same lanes on the freeway you do."

"Well, crap! You ready to ditch them?" she asked, looking over at Michaela with an evil smile. "Tighten your seat belt, we're going for a wild ride."

She punched the accelerator and pulled the car into the far-left lane. Passing several cars in the lane next to her, she crossed several lanes back to the right and then exited the freeway. Turning left to go under the overpass, she headed west toward the downtown district.

Michaela continued to look over her shoulder, and she could see the sedan stuck at a red light after exiting the same off-ramp they had. "They got off this exit," she called out to Heather.

Turning left at the next stoplight and then turning right at the next side street, Heather was in and out of traffic, driving either like a pro or a madman. Michaela held on for life with white knuckles, but Heather seemed to be enjoying the chase.

Once they had turned right and were halfway down the block, the sedan also turned. "They're still on us…"

Heather turned another right and then a left, which Michaela could only assume was due to traffic; if heavy, turn right, if traffic was light with a green light, turn left. Heather knew these streets like the back of her hand. She'd been working at the home design center for several years with the head office located downtown.

"Who are these people…" Michaela muttered. "Even if we're out of their sight, when we make a turn, they still manage to find us!"

"Oh no…maybe they put a tracker on my car?" Heather exclaimed.

Michaela swiveled her head to look at Heather. "Tracker? What do you know about trackers? I hate to even ask…" She waved her hand and turned around in her seat.

Heather laughed. "You know how I love spy movies. See it does pay to watch them after all, doesn't it?"

Michaela only shook her head.

Pulling a left and entering a ramp into a parking garage, Heather drove through the narrow, cemented drive, circling the square cement block of the building until they were a few stories up.

"Get ready to jump out and look under the carriage of the car on your side, and I'll check mine for one."

"But what are we looking for?"

"You'll know when you see it…believe me."

She turned into a parking space, and as soon as she put the car in park, they both jumped out and peered under the carriage.

"Found it!" Heather shouted. She pulled it from the undercarriage. "Here, hold this and strap in!"

She backed the car out, screeching tires, and then punched it. A car pulled out of a spot ahead of them, and Heather stomped on the brakes, throwing them both forward in their seats.

Michaela turned to look behind them as Heather accelerated again, but moving at a snail's pace behind the car that pulled out in front of them had them both feeling anxious. Looking down at the tracker in her hands, Michaela found herself being thrown against the car door as Heather pulled into a space between an SUV and a van.

"Toss it over the side," she directed to Michaela once they were stopped.

Michaela jumped out and tossed the tracker, watching it hurl to the bottom and splinter into pieces. Running back to the car, she threw the car door open, and Heather told her to get down.

They both hunkered down inside the car, hoping the bigger cars on either side would conceal their whereabouts. It wasn't long before they heard a car's engine get louder as it neared. It passed picking up speed, and Heather dared to look up over the back of her seat.

"It's a dark sedan, the same one that was following us. I think finding this little space near the end helped. Hopefully, they won't backtrack."

Michaela let out her breath. "We can't just sit here. If they see the tracker below, they'll know our location if we don't move."

"You're right, but let's give it a minute or two before we leave."

After about five minutes, Heather turned the key, and the car fired to life. She backed up slowly and then headed to the exit. "Be sure to watch for that sedan, they could be waiting for us."

But as they exited the building neither saw the car, and Heather proceeded to the restaurant where Michaela's car was parked.

"You need to call Sean and tell him we were tailed," Heather announced, parking behind Michaela's car.

"You're right." Michaela pulled out her cell and punched Sean's name from her contact list. Again, the line rang several times and was picked up by voice mail. Looking at the time, she noted it was now close to ten thirty. Her brows drew together in frustration. Was he avoiding her after telling him that she was in love with him?

After the beep, she left her message. "Sean, Heather and I were followed on our way to pick up my car. Heather managed to lose them…" Noticing Heather mimicking with her hands, she turned to her.

"Tell him about the tracker…"

"Oh, they put a tracker on Heather's car which we found and ditched. I just thought you should know." Michaela ended the call and placed the cell in her purse.

"Okay, I'll pick up Chase for you so you won't be confronted by Marissa, and I'll just give her a quick rundown by telling her that I spent the night. I'll leave the details and what you want to fill her in on up to you. But I'm worried. What if the car that was tailing us is back at the B&B? If you're by yourself, they might be bold enough to just walk in on you or, worse, break in!"

Before Michaela could reply, her cell rang. Pulling it out of her purse, she looked at the screen, and her heart skipped a beat; it was Sean.

"Hi," she answered.

"What's this about being tailed and finding a tracker?" he broke in without preamble.

Heather pulled the cell from Michaela's hands. "Sean, it's me, Heather. I was taking Michaela to pick up her car when she noticed that we were being followed. But in trying to lose them, they managed to keep up with our location, and that's when I realized they must have put a tracker on my car. We found it and got rid of it and managed to lose them. Right now, I'm parked behind Michaela's car at the restaurant, but we're worried about the people chasing us watching the B&B again. If Michaela is alone…"

"Okay, right now, I can't break away. I'm buried in work. Put Michaela back on." Heather handed the cell back to her.

"Michaela, be sure to lock up tight when you get home. If you're not expecting any guests until this afternoon, don't worry about answering the door. I'll try to get a police car to drive by periodically during the interim. Got it?"

"Yes, thank you."

He hung up without saying anything more. She was disappointed but realized he was busy and this wasn't the time for endearments.

CHAPTER 20

The thief comes only to steal and kill and destroy. I came that they may have life and have it abundantly.

—John 10:10

"We have a new lead on the case," Sean said, entering the squad room and pulling off his jacket before taking a seat at his desk.

Tom set down his stained coffee mug and looked across at Sean. "A new lead?"

"Yeah, it turns out there's a guy attending the same church as Mic-McCrea. He assaulted her yesterday afternoon…"

"And we know this how?"

"She told me." Sean looked across the desk at Tom's skeptic face. "Hear me out. Apparently, he went over to the B&B yesterday afternoon and took the liberty of letting himself in through her private entrance and then proceeded upstairs where Mrs. McCrea was cleaning. He pinned her inside her bedroom. She thought he was going to rape her, but her neighbor stopped by."

"Okay, so how do we know Mrs. McCrea didn't arrange a rendezvous and then tell the nosy neighbor this story to hide the fact they're having an affair."

Sean sighed clearly exasperated. "Like all persons involved in this case, we need to talk with him. If this guy is enamored with Mrs. McCrea, it also means he could be capable of murder if he felt that Collins was homing in on his territory."

"Granted, it's worth a visit. So who is he?"

"His name is Gavin Brooks. I did some research, and the guy owns a sporting goods store over on Main. He's forty-two years old, has never married, and up until a few years back, he lived with his mother. Her death certificate indicates she died of natural causes, but when I talked to the coroner, he had private notes on the case indicating that he couldn't find a definitive reason for her death without further tests. Her body was cremated."

Sean felt he should wait to fill Tom in about the man who chased Michaela the previous evening. Tom would be just as skeptical, and for now, it was on a need-to-know basis.

*****

After entering the sporting goods store owned by Mr. Brooks, the detectives were stopped by a salesman asking if he could help them.

Tom produced his badge and said they needed to speak with the owner, Gavin Brooks. The salesman's face paled, but he nodded and led them to the front counter. "I'll get Mr. Brooks for you. Please, wait here."

When Gavin walked out from his office, both detectives eyed him closely. He was tall and muscular, and Sean could see how he could easily manhandle Michaela.

"Gentlemen, to what do I owe the pleasure?" he asked smoothly.

Both Tom and Sean showed their badges, and Sean spoke up, "We need to ask you a few questions. Perhaps we could use your office for privacy..."

He inclined his head and extended his hand to indicate the door he'd just come from. After sitting, he looked across at the detectives. "What's this about?"

Again, Sean took the lead. "We understand that you've taken an interest in Mrs. McCrea, the owner of the Bayside Bed-and-Breakfast..." Sean began.

"Whatever she told you, it's not true! I didn't do anything when I was there, and I told her that I called out, but she never answered, so I investigated to ensure she was okay. I mean, after all, she's being investigated for James Collins's murder, and for all I know, someone could be after her too!"

Tom and Sean exchanged glances. "What did happen?" Tom asked.

"Nothing, I stole a kiss, and as far as I know, you can't be arrested for stealing that!" He leaned back in his chair, crossing his arms with a smug look on his face.

"What else did you do while there?" Sean asked.

"Nothing."

"Did you try to get her to change into a dress you picked out for her to wear?"

Tom's head snapped around to look at Sean.

"I just want her to look nice. She's a beautiful woman and a Christian. She should look like one and dress appropriately. It's something I hope to instill in her once we're married. She needs someone to teach and show her what's right, to advise her."

Tom sat up straighter in his chair. "And what makes you an expert?" he asked.

"By all means, I'm no expert, but I can help Michaela to make better decisions. She's as much told me that she loves me, and she looks forward to being with me. Just last Sunday, she sat with me in church."

"From my understanding, she didn't get much out of the sermon because your hands were all over her," Sean ground out.

"That's not true. At one point, she even held my hand!" Gavin said, leaning forward looking indignant.

"What were your plans after you discovered Mrs. McCrea was fine?" Tom asked.

"I had no plans really. I just wanted to be with her, and I know she'll come to worship me once I show her the error of her ways, and we can correct them together."

"Where were you the night of August 5?" Tom asked.

"August 5, let's see, I believe that was the three-day convention I attended in Atlanta. What happened August 5?"

"That was the night James Collins was murdered. Do you have proof you were out of town?"

"I do. I have my airline ticket stub and credit card statement not to mention the room I booked is also on the credit card. But why are you asking me about this? I thought you were here about Mrs. McCrea. If she's saying that I hurt her, I assure you, gentlemen, that she was wanting my advances!"

"Maybe, you didn't want the competition and decided to remove Collins from the picture. We'll need to see those statements."

"That's absurd! I'll get the statements for you, gentlemen."

"Detectives," Tom corrected.

*****

"You're not going to believe this!" Tom sat across from Sean in the squad room. He replaced the phone in its cradle. "Collins's place was broken into last night, and it appears someone was looking for something in particular. The place was ransacked. Let's get over there!"

Pulling up in front of Collins's home, one of the officers on duty approached the car. "Detectives, this way…" As they all approached the entry, they donned shoe covers to keep from contaminating the crime scene.

"By the way, I'm Officer Coleman. We got a call early this morning from a neighbor who said they saw lights on in the house and knew it was supposed to be empty. They didn't see anyone arrive or leave. From what we can garner, there was nothing taken, so we're assuming they were looking for something specific."

"They?" Tom arched a brow.

"Figure of speech, we have no idea if there was just one perpetrator or more, or for that matter, gender."

They made their way through the house. Cabinet doors stood open, the recliner and sofa in the living room had been slashed and most of the stuffing removed that lay in heaps upon the floor. Even the mattress in the bedroom had been slashed. Again, drawers stood open and clothing littered the floor.

"Whoever it was, they were definitely looking for something, and it must have been small enough to hide in a drawer. We need to get a team in here to dust for prints though I doubt we'll find any," Sean said with hands resting on his hips as he looked around at the mess.

Tom looked over at Officer Coleman. "Any chance we know how they got in?"

"Yes, it appears they jimmied the lock on the back door to gain access."

"The security system was turned off?"

"It was turned off when we arrived on the premises."

"How in the hell can it be turned off without first breaking in?"

Sean glanced over at Tom who was a bit computer challenged. "Someone could have turned it off remotely."

"Any idea what they may have been looking for?" Tom questioned as they made their way back to Sean's car.

Reflecting on the evening before and the man who chased Michaela asking about a package, Sean thought he might know. "Actually, I think they were looking for a package," Sean answered as they climbed in the car.

"A package, what makes you think that?" Tom turned sharply to look at Sean.

Sean hesitated in inserting the key into the ignition and replied, "After I was at your place for a barbecue yesterday, I got a call from Micha… Mrs. McCrea. She was having dinner downtown with a friend. After she left the restaurant, she was approached by a man demanding she turn over a package." Seeing Tom's reaction, Sean held up his hand. "Wait, there's more to the story than that. Let me fill you in."

"I don't like it. I don't like this at all. She's playing you!" Tom said, shaking his head.

Sean started up the car, and they headed to the nearest fast-food place to grab a quick bite to eat and, more importantly, coffee. They both needed caffeine. After getting their order, Sean parked the car while Tom pulled their food from the bag.

Sean sighed and tapped his fingers on the steering wheel, and Tom laid the wrapped burgers on the console between them. Taking a slurp of coffee, he waited for Sean to fill in him. Sean wasn't about to tell Tom how close he'd been to making love to Michaela; he'd keep that to himself. With the thought still lingering in his mind, he remembered her last words to him. Was this a case in which the circumstances were so dire that a person thought they were falling in love with their protector? He had no idea, but he never felt this way before on any other case, even if it entailed a pretty woman needing help. And this was a woman he was investigating, not protecting.

After taking a huge bite from his burger, Tom piped up, "I know what you're thinking. You think she's innocent, but when you add everything up, it shouts guilty as hell to me. Think about it. First, she loses her husband to homicide, then her aunt up and dies, leaving her that bed-and-breakfast. And let's not forget about the insurance money either. Then she claims someone broke into the place, and yet nothing was stolen or broken. And now we have a man who supposedly chased her wanting a package. I bet she has a package. She's guilty, and I think she murdered Collins."

Sean shook his head. "We're both entitled to our opinions, but for now, it's purely speculative until we have proof. Proof I don't think you're going to get because I don't think she's guilty."

Tom harrumphed and ditched the last of his coffee out the side window. "Let's go. I need my car since I have errands to run."

Sean took a huge bite out of his tasteless burger and threw the rest back in the bag before starting the engine.

Both men were silent on the way back to the station. As Tom exited the car, Sean spoke up, "I plan on interviewing a couple of the people who lost their cases against Collins's clients."

Tom nodded looking back over his shoulder. "Good luck!"

*****

Tom had his own ideas. He didn't have errands to run, but he planned on stopping by the church Michaela attended to talk with her pastor. After getting in his own vehicle, he put in a call to the church office and found the pastor wasn't in but at a member's home having lunch. It sounded odd to Tom that a pastor would be having lunch alone at a church member's house when he knew from research the guy was married. Maybe, there was more to this church than he first thought. After getting the address, he was going to stop by regardless.

The Victorian house was set back on the property, and Tom could see two cars parked in the long driveway; one he recognized. Offhand he couldn't place where he'd seen it. The other was just an old Buick; it was probably the pastor's car.

Ringing the doorbell, he could hear shuffling on the other side of the door before it was finally pulled open by a petite elderly woman with graying hair. So much for the idea that something untoward was going on…

"Mrs. Adams?"

"Yes!"

"I'm Detective Hanson, and I was wondering if Pastor Hodges is here. I'd like to ask him a few questions." Tom held up his badge, but the woman didn't even bother to look at it.

"Oh yes, Pastor Hodges is having lunch with me today. Please, do come in." She shuffled back and turned, expecting Tom to follow her inside.

Following Mrs. Adams into the dining room, he recalled where he saw the other car, at the bed-and-breakfast. And confirming that thought sat Marissa McCrea at the dining table looking tall, sleek, and exotic, just as he recalled when he and Sean stopped by the B&B. Today, she was wearing tight leather pants and a blouse where one spaghetti strap had slipped off, baring a shoulder.

"Pastor, this gentleman says he needs to ask you some questions."

Pastor Hodges placed his cloth napkin on the table and stood holding out his hand. Tom leaned in to shake hands, and both men warily eyed the other. Pastor Hodges was younger than Tom imagined and of medium height with light-brown hair that was cropped short.

"Oh, please be seated," Mrs. Adams said, indicating a chair. "Sierra dear, would you please bring another place setting for this nice young gentleman?"

Tom spoke up, "That won't be necessary. I'm here to ask Pastor Hodges a few questions. I didn't realize I'd be interrupting your luncheon."

"You're not!" Marissa spoke up. "Pastor Hodges, this is Detective Hanson. He's investigating the James Collins's murder, and he thinks our Michaela is the one who did him in!" She arched a brow and then turned to the pastor.

Pastor Hodges turned a sharp eye on Marissa, and Tom could see that he was a bit irritated with her outburst.

"Detective." Pastor Hodges inclined his head. "Please, be seated, Sierra already has a place setting, and we have plenty to eat." He indicated the young girl who had a plate and silverware in hand. Placing everything on the table, she stepped back.

"Thank you dear!" Mrs. Adams smiled, and the young girl retreated to another room.

"Oh, please do sit!" Mrs. Adams insisted.

Tom sat, and once seated, the pastor sat too.

"So what's this about Michaela?" Pastor Hodges asked, briefly glancing at Marissa.

Tom cleared his throat. "What can you tell me about her?"

Pastor Hodges passed the sandwich plate down to Tom. "Please, take one, we've plenty."

Before he knew it, his plate was laden down with food that did look and smell good. Pastor Hodges began. "We are aware that you want to know more about Mrs. McCrea because she dated that young man who was murdered. I don't know anything about the late Mr. Collins, but I can tell you that Mrs. McCrea is a young widowed mother who loved her late husband dearly. What you probably don't know about her though is that she was born to young parents who had a difficult time. Her mother found herself pregnant out of wedlock, with Michaela. The couple married, but they fought constantly. If not for Michaela's late grandmother and aunt, the poor girl would never have known love and peace. In fact, her parents neglected her when she was a child though they never abused her. They just weren't ready to be parents. Michaela found solace and love with her grandmother who ended up raising her, and during the summer months, she spent much of her time with her aunt. She was shy but thrived under the care and love of her grandmother and aunt."

"How do you know so much about her youth?" Tom asked, clearly puzzled.

"Both her grandmother and aunt were members of the church."

"How long have you been a pastor there?"

Paster Hodges chuckled. "Clearly, I'm not old enough to have been pastoring the church that long, but I have been there for the past six years."

"And what happened to her parents?" Tom asked, looking up from his plate.

"Her mother remarried and moved to Europe. France, I believe. None of us know what happened to her father."

"Is she well-liked by members of the church?"

"Yes, she is. She doesn't attend often because she runs the bed-and-breakfast, full-time work and then some. But her son usually attends church with either Heather or Marissa here, and sometimes, other church members are happy to pick him up."

"It almost sounds like she's raising her son much the same way she was raised, neglecting him out of duty to make a living," Tom reflected.

"No, that's not the case. She's very attentive to her son, and though she's extra busy, she makes time for him," the pastor assured Tom.

"How can you know for certain, are you there to witness that?"

Marissa piped up. "I'm there quite often, and I can assure you that Michaela is a very loving mother."

"Michaela is generous and kind, and Chase is a wonderful boy," Mrs. Adams added, handing the sandwich tray to Tom. "Here, sample the cucumber sandwich though typical to be served at a May Tea, it's simply divine!"

Inwardly, Tom winced, cucumber sandwiches? Sounded awful to him! Putting manners forth though, he took a wedge and dropped it on his plate.

CHAPTER 20

"I'm assuming then that you knew about Mrs. McCrea's late husband and that he died under mysterious circumstances?" Tom turned to Pastor Hodges.

"Yes, and as a church family, we were all in mourning with her. It was an awful time, and she had a terrible time coming to grips with his passing and never knowing what actually happened."

"Did you ever think for a minute that maybe Mrs. McCrea was partly responsible for his death?"

Marissa gasped. "I told you what happened when you came to the bed-and-breakfast that night. She had nothing to do with those brake lines, and that was proven already! She loved Brad and was a devoted wife. In fact, she still has all his trophies from football in the upstairs office like it was a shrine! Those things are cumbersome and heavy. We had to reinforce the shelves when she put them up!"

Tom turned his attention to Marissa, and those intense blue eyes of hers were shooting enough venom to kill, and they were directed solely at him.

"I think it might be wise if everyone took a nice, deep breath. We have lemon pie for dessert after all!" Mrs. Adams chirped, looking at each person in turn. "Sierra, I think we're all ready for dessert. But don't take this young man's plate just yet, he's not finished with his cucumber sandwich."

Dishes were removed and pie placed in the center of the table by the young girl, and much to his chagrin, she left his plate in front of him so he could choke down the blasted sandwich. He shoved the rest in and gulped iced tea to get it down. It was all he could do to keep from grimacing.

As talk turned to small chitchat around the table, Tom's thoughts turned to the trophies Marissa mentioned. Usually, when a spouse passed, or in this case, murdered, all their personal effects were removed save for a few mementos, items that had meaning to both parties. Why would she keep trophies?

"Did Mrs. McCrea know her late husband long before they married?" Tom queried.

Marissa turned to him. "They didn't meet until a few months before they married. They met at a bar." Looking over at Pastor

Hodges, she apologized. "Sorry, while Michaela wasn't wild, she did go to bars occasionally. And that's where she met Brad. It was like love at first sight." She forked some lemon pie into her mouth and peered over at Tom. "Why ask?"

"I was just curious. Usually, trophies are only keepsakes if their memory is shared by both parties. I was just wondering if Michaela knew Brad when he was awarded those trophies."

"Brad was in high school when he received most, but not all. The rest was while he was at college. They didn't meet until later." Marissa dropped her eyes to her plate and took another bite of pie, forking it in, and then dabbed her mouth with a cloth napkin.

Tom looked over at Pastor Hodges who was openly watching Marissa. She turned her gaze to the pastor, and there was meaning behind their locked gazes. Marissa smiled and then forked another piece of pie.

CHAPTER 21

The Lord is close to the brokenhearted and saves those who are crushed in spirit.

—Psalm 34:18

Before pulling into the parking lot of the B&B, Michaela checked the street but didn't see any unfamiliar cars. After cutting the engine, she grabbed her purse and headed straight to the office door with keys in hand and locked the door behind her after entering.

She was glad for the interlude waiting for Heather and Chase. She needed to think. And she wasn't happy with where her thoughts were going. Was Sean playing her? Was this a ploy to fish out information? Closing her eyes, she tried to withhold the tears that threatened. This was the first time she let down her guard since Brad, and she felt vulnerable.

With Chase home soon, she didn't want to worry him or, for that matter, Heather. She needed her game face on so she could welcome guests when they arrived later in the day. Snickers ran to greet her, and she squatted down to embrace him as she finally gave in and let the tears flow. Snickers covered her in kisses, and she couldn't help but smile.

She eventually stood and headed to the kitchen where she pulled ingredients to start appetizers for the afternoon social hour. As she worked, her thoughts turned to Sean again. Closing her eyes, she wished she could undo last night. And yet she wished they had been able to make love. She enjoyed being in his strong arms. It was killing her not knowing if he was actually using her to work the case or if he had genuine feelings. Her knife slipped, and she cut her finger.

"Ouch!" At the sink, she let cool water run over the cut and then washed it thoroughly. But the darn thing just kept bleeding. Holding the paper towel to the wound to staunch the bleeding, a knock sounded at the private entrance.

Slipping into the living room, she peered through the peephole and saw Sean standing on the stoop. She let her breath out and unlocked the door for him.

"I came by to see if you were okay. I have an officer that will be driving by every half hour or so..." Looking down, he saw the paper towel clutched over her finger, and it was blotted with blood. "What happened?"

"I cut myself, it's nothing."

"Let me see." Sean pulled the paper towel away, and the cut immediately started bleeding again. "That's a bit deep to be nothing. Let's get some bandages on it."

Walking past her, he entered the kitchen and stepped into the pantry to get the first aid kit. She stood by the kitchen sink, experiencing déjà vu, only this time it was her finger and not her toe. When Sean stepped from the pantry with the kit in hand, he made eye contact with her.

"We need to set things straight," she said.

"Straight?"

"Yes, we should never have let things get as far as they did last night. I don't even know what I said to you before you left. I was just feeling so, so strange. It's hard to put into words." She lifted her chin, knowing she lied about not remembering what she'd said.

He put the first aid kit on the table and popped the lid open. Pilfering through the contents, he pulled out a bandage and antiseptic spray. He pulled out a kitchen chair and motioned for her to be seated. Walking across the kitchen, she complied and put her arm on the table so he could better tend her finger.

Her heart was beating so rapidly she didn't know if he could hear it. He sprayed her finger and then started applying the bandage.

When he made eye contact again, she blushed. He didn't smile or say anything.

As he returned the kit to the pantry, she felt the need to say something, anything. Instead, she closed her eyes, and tears made their way to the surface. Before she knew it, Sean knelt down in front of her and took her into his arms. She sobbed into his shoulder, and he held her until her tears were spent.

"I'm sorry. I don't know what's wrong with me…" Wiping her nose with the back of her hand, she grimaced. "I need a tissue!"

Sean stood and grabbed a tissue that was on the counter. "You've been under a lot of duress lately. You're under an investigation for murder, you've had break-ins, someone chasing you at night, and now someone following you by car." Handing her the tissue, he lifted his shoulders. "Don't be hard on yourself."

"I'm sorry I can't stay," he apologized, changing the subject. "I arranged for a police car to drive by every half hour."

With an ache in her heart, she stood. "I'm sorry I've put you through extra work."

"Michaela, look at me." He slipped his finger under her chin and lifted her head slightly. "You're not putting me through extra work. I want to keep you safe."

He hesitated and then dropped his hand. "I need to go." At the door, he turned. "Collins's place was broken into last night and ransacked. I'm assuming they were looking for a package." He watched her closely for any signs that she may have already known. But her reaction was void of any prior knowledge.

"What!" She sat heavily on the edge of the recliner. "Heather and I searched the place here last night for a package. We didn't find anything, and we even checked the air ducts."

"Air ducts." He smiled and could tell they thought they were clever to think of it.

She nodded. "Heather's idea, not mine." She raised her shoulders.

"Well, it's good to know…"

CHAPTER 22

Let him kiss me with the kisses of his mouth for thy love is better than wine.

—Song of Solomon 1:2

After Detective Hanson left and lunch dishes cleared from the table, Pastor Hodges spoke up, "I think it's time for Marissa and I to conduct church business in the study. Are you ready?" he asked, turning to Marissa.

"Of course!"

"I'm so delighted that I can provide a space for your work, Pastor Hodges!" Mrs. Adams gleamed with a proud smile on her face. "Now you two get busy doing the Lord's work!"

Closing the study doors behind them, Marc turned to Marissa and fingered the spaghetti strap that had fallen from her shoulder. "I love this time we've together, my love. But it's not right, it's not the Lord's way."

Placing a hand over his fingers to still them, she looked into his eyes. "You're wrong my love, Clara can't bare you children and does not love you anymore, so the Lord has given you me to carry on in her place. To bring you pleasure and hopefully children. You're too great a man to be stifled by a frigid wife who abhors the sight of you."

Marc turned away to stand before the window with his back to her, clearly troubled by their affair. Marissa came to stand behind him and wrapped her arms around his waist. He could feel the softness of her breasts pressed against his back, and he reveled in the feel of them.

CHAPTER 22

"I love you, Marc. I need you..."

He turned around and traced his finger across the swell of her breasts. She peered up at him through her long, dark lashes. "My love, the Lord says in his word to not hold back thy breasts."

With the verbal encouragement, Marc pulled her blouse down to expose a bare breast. He toyed with her nipple until it hardened beneath his touch. He groaned. Marissa reached down and grabbed the hem of her blouse and pulled it off over her head. Marc brought both hands up to cup her tender flesh and rolled her nipples between his index and thumb. Marissa reached for him and could feel his hardened length beneath his slacks.

"I shall not withhold my love from thee." She breathed. Letting her head fall back, she enjoyed his attention, and his lips found a budded nipple which he sucked into his mouth.

He pulled away swiftly. "No, this is wrong, Marissa..."

She wrapped her arms around his neck, and they kissed passionately. When the kiss ended, Marissa stepped back. "Please, don't say that, Marc. In my heart, I believe the Lord has sanctioned our union. In Solomon, it says, 'The king hath brought me into his chambers. We will be glad and rejoice in thee. We will remember thy love more than wine, the upright love thee.'"

Placing her hands on his cheeks, she pulled his head down and slowly kissed him. It was a slow, exotic kiss, and she drew her tongue across his lips, and they parted. He acquiesced and opened his mouth, allowing her tongue access. He moaned as she let her tongue duel with his.

Stepping away, she pushed the fabric of her tight pants down slowly over her hips and down over her thighs, continuing the slow hypnotic disrobing. She pushed them off and kicked the pants away. She wore no panties. "I could hardly eat lunch today I was so aroused..." she whispered. "I yearn for you, my love..."

Marc stepped forward and pulled her into his embrace and slowly backed her up to the edge of the desk, where they often made love each week. She pushed herself up on the edge. Marc was weak; he could not withstand such temptation, and as Marissa told him many times, the Lord had sanctioned their love in the spirit, if not in matrimony. Standing between her thighs, he traced a finger around her core, and Marissa cried out.

"Shhhh," he whispered.

Stepping back, Marc unzipped his khakis and pulled out his hardened shaft. Marc had been blessed with a large penis that in his youth, had his parents' young neighbor teaching him everything about sex. She marveled at how big he was and often had him over for "cookies" after he mowed their lawn. And then he met Clara, who introduced him to God, and he left the wild life behind. But due to his size, Clara found their lovemaking uncomfortable. In part, he knew it was because she was tiny, that and the fact she just didn't enjoy sex, which left him in need. But when Marissa joined the congregation there was an immediate attraction that slowly led to love, which first started with quiet candlelit dinners together at nearby towns. At first, the stolen kisses were enough until they weren't. Their infatuation turned into a full-blown love affair, and if not for the congregation, Marc would have divorced Clara long ago so he and Marissa could be together forever. With that thought, he let his head fall back, imagining the intimacy they could enjoy.

He pushed his hardened shaft to her apex and asked, "Do you love me, Marissa?"

"I do, my love. Let's pray that your seed will bring life within mine." Marissa breathed heavily, and then Marc thrust inside until his shaft was completely buried, and then he slowly withdrew before pushing himself in deeply again, enjoying the rhythmic play of lovemaking. With each thrust, he buried himself deep within her core, and Marissa whispered his name over and over until she convulsed with an orgasm, and soon after, Marc, too, shuddered with his release.

Marissa reached for his hips to keep him from withdrawing. "That was beautiful," she whispered.

Marc leaned to kiss her softly. "It was beautiful. You're beautiful! But I still feel this is wrong. It's a betrayal to Clara, to God."

Marissa placed her hands to each side of his face. "No, my love, don't shame me or what we've done. I'm bringing you pleasure, and hopefully, a child will come from our union. You deserve offspring to carry on your name and your work. Our union is blessed by the Lord."

Marc withdrew and grabbed a tissue from the box on the desk to wipe himself before pulling up his khakis. Marissa sat up on the desk and pushed her heavy dark tresses behind her shoulder. "Please, don't grow cold toward me, my love. I already feel bereft of your body and now your presence. I can't bear it!"

Stepping closer, he tipped her chin and kissed her. "I love you and love our weekly luncheons and meetings here. I just want so much more. Meeting here and there outside of town at a hotel… I want more, I want you by my side, always."

"It will happen. We have to trust the Lord." Marissa lowered her head to his shoulder, and Marc wrapped his arms around her body.

She felt so good and sitting on the edge of the desk, he couldn't help but reach out and run his index finger around her areola. She softly sighed and pulled back, offering her breasts.

Marc groaned. "I want to make love to you again and again and again." He laughed softly.

"I'm here…" They heard a noise outside the study door. Marc stepped back and helped Marissa down. She grabbed her clothes and ran to the adjacent bathroom, closing the door just as the study doors opened.

"I didn't want to interrupt, Pastor Hodges," Mrs. Adams said, "but Clara just called and asked for you." She held up the phone and looked around the room for Marissa. "Where's Marissa? I thought she was in here with you?"

"She had to use the bathroom, but we were wrapping up business for this week," he said, taking the proffered phone from Mrs. Adams.

"Hi, sweetheart…"

"Are you still there with Marissa?" she asked in a clipped tone.

Marc squeezed his eyes shut. "We were just finishing up…" Mrs. Adams left, closing the study doors behind her.

"I bet!" Clara interrupted. "I'm tired of this shenanigan. You aren't fooling me like you are poor Mrs. Adams. What if I told the congregation that you and Marissa are having an affair? I bet you wouldn't like that!"

"Clara, I've told you before, we're not having an affair. Please, be reasonable, sweetheart."

"Don't call me sweetheart!" she yelled.

Marissa opened the door, now fully dressed and walked up behind Marc, wrapping her arms around his waist. She lightly kissed his back.

"Please, Clara, let's not fight."

Marissa's hands slowly made their way down the front of his pants, and she fumbled, trying to unbuckle his belt, distracting him.

"Put her on!"

"What? You want to talk with Marissa?"

Marissa took the phone from Marc. "Mrs. Hodges, this is Marissa..."

"Leave my husband alone, do you hear me!" Clara yelled.

"Mrs. Hodges, we were meeting on church business and nothing more. I have a boyfriend."

This time, Marc took advantage of Marissa while she was on the phone. Reaching down, he pulled her nipple into his mouth and sucked. She moaned.

"What was that?" Clara asked indignantly.

"No-nothing," Marissa breathlessly replied.

Marc lifted his head, leaving a large wet spot on her blouse over her nipple. He gently took the phone from her hands and disconnected the call.

CHAPTER 23

Flee from sexual immorality. Every other sin a person commits is outside the body, but the sexually immoral person sins against his own body.

—1 Corinthians 6:18

Sean's cell indicated a call from a number he didn't recognize. "Hello…"

"Hi, Sean, this is Trina. You remember me, don't you? Trina Myerson?"

Sean pulled his cell away from his ear, looking at it as if he'd never seen the contraption before. Putting it back to his ear, he replied, "Of course."

Trina giggled on the other end. "I haven't seen you since the other night at the bar, and I have some information I wanted to share with you, but I can't tell you over the phone. Can you come by this evening?"

Sean hesitated. What if she did have information? "What time?"

"Around seven thirty…will that work for you?"

"Sure." He hung up without saying goodbye.

At seven thirty, he pulled up in front of her house. He rang the doorbell, and he heard Trina inside calling out for him to enter. He pushed the door inward and then walked through the threshold.

"I'm in here…" she called out.

Shutting the door behind him, he followed the sound of her voice to find her in the kitchen cooking. That surprised him. He didn't think a woman like Trina would even know how to toast bread.

She had her back to him, and whatever she was cooking smelled delicious, another surprise. When she turned, as he suspected, this was simply a ploy to get him over here. She was wearing a dress that put the one she wore to the bar to shame. The bodice was cut even lower. When she stretched to grab a couple of wine glasses from the overhead rack, he thought for sure her breasts would pop out of their limited confines. In fact, he stood almost mesmerized to see if they actually would before he realized he was staring.

He shifted his gaze to the table that was set for two with candles and a bottle of wine that was uncorked. A small bouquet of flowers was included in the intimate setting.

"Hungry?" she asked, drawing his attention back to her. "I was just fixing some dinner, and knowing you'd be coming by, I fixed extra."

Stepping to the table, she placed the wine glasses by each plate and then turned toward him. "We didn't get to have fun the other evening, so I thought I'd make it up to you."

"I thought you had some information for me," Sean stated, placing his hands on his hips.

"I do! But first, let's eat. There's wine on the table, why don't you pour us each a glass." She moved away and proceeded to pull a casserole from the oven. She placed it in the center of the table on a hot pad before grabbing garlic toast.

"Shall we sit?" she asked. She stood in front of her chair, fully expecting Sean to seat her. Instead, he pulled out a chair across from her and sat down.

She exhaled loudly and took a seat, pulling herself up to the table. The casserole was lasagna, Sean's favorite, but he refrained from trying it though he was tempted. Trina took care of that by plating some for him.

"This lasagna is heavenly. It came from Martin's deli down the street."

He should have known. "What information do you have? I can't stay, I can't eat, and I'm not going to fuck you." He was done and wanted the insult to hit home.

Bright eyes settled on his, and if he didn't know better, she seemed offended and a little hurt, making him feel like an ass. But Trina's kind simply didn't get innuendos. You had to be right up-front and honest, no matter how brutal.

"I do have information," she faltered. "I overheard some other secretaries at work who dated James talking about how that owner of the bed-and-breakfast I told you about had also threatened them! One of them, Lillian, happened to drop by when James was staying there for a little rendezvous. She said the owner confronted and threatened her right there on the premises. That woman can't be trusted!"

Sean shook his head. He pushed his chair back from the table and stood. "Don't bother me again, Trina. This was just a farce to get me over here hoping we'd screw."

She jumped up and placed a hand on Sean's arm, stopping him. "Don't leave. I really like you, and, yes, I do want to make love, but I won't beg. What's wrong with having sex with me anyway? Don't you like what you see?" Placing her hands under her breasts, she lifted them, and Sean thought once again they'd be popping out to greet him. When they stayed within the confines of the dress, Trina deliberately pulled down the fabric enough to uncover one breast.

Sean sucked in his breath. She grabbed his hand and placed it over her breast, and Sean kneaded the flesh, stroking her nipple with his thumb. He sighed and found himself responding. Dropping his hand, he shifted. And Trina reached out to trace his erection through his pants.

"Oh my, what have we here..." She smiled seductively and peered up at Sean through long lashes. "I think it wants to come out to play."

He slapped her hand away. "Look, I'm not interested."

"Tell that to your penis." She laughed.

Sean shook his head and turned to leave. When she put out her hand to stop him a second time, he brushed it off, giving her a disgusted look. At the door, he turned giving her one last glimpse before he left.

*****

The next morning, Sean replayed the scene from the night before. What was it that bothered Trina so much that she kept referring to Michaela? As far as he knew, she didn't know Michaela, and with Collins gone, why would she keep bringing her up?

When Tom came in, he told Tom about the visit, hoping to get his take on it.

"Collins did date a lot of women working at the law firm, and it's quite possible one did meet with him while staying at the B&B. We should check it out."

Once again, the detectives were back at Henderson, Rose, and Collins Law Offices. By now, everyone knew who they were, and as soon as the receptionist seated at the entrance saw them, she inclined her head, waiting for them to stop at her desk. The silent acknowledgment did not include a friendly smile but more of a scowl.

Tom pulled out his badge, but she didn't bother to look at it. "We're here to see one of the secretaries, her name is Lillian. It's all we have to go on. Is she in today?"

Her scowl deepened, but she turned to her computer and with a few key strokes brought up a screen. Studying it, she said, "You must be referring to Lillian Callahan. She's not in today."

"Her address?"

She glanced up at Tom, her eyes narrowing. "I'm sorry, but that's private information." Her lips thinned before looking away and back at the computer. She closed the program but not before Sean managed to snag a look. He recognized the photo of the woman from seeing her here at the firm, but he had no idea what floor she worked on. But they wouldn't need that information because he was able to get her home address.

Tom cleared his throat and was about to launch into a verbal sparring with the receptionist when Sean spoke up, "Please inform

Miss Callahan that we need to speak with her right away, it's very important."

Tom's gaze shifted to his partner, realizing Sean had information, and once they left, Sean clued him in. With just her full name, they could have looked up the address back at the precinct, but having it up-front saved time. Sean punched the address into his cell and did a reverse address look up to get her phone number. He punched the number in, and the line rang several times before going to voice mail. Sean left a message as both men headed back to the office to see what they could dig up on Lillian Callahan.

CHAPTER 24

A false witness will not go unpunished, and he who breathes out lies will not escape.

—Proverbs 19:5

Sean expected to find zip on Callahan. So he was surprised to find she had a few minor infractions on her record. But it all added up to nil—charges when she was a teenager fined with possession of an illegal drug, another for having stolen earrings from a department store, and so the record went. Nothing big, but still a record that was troubling.

His cell rang and he picked it up. "Detective Ryan."

"Detective Ryan, I'm returning your call. This is Lillian Callahan." Her voice was light, and she spoke without any hint of an accent despite that her record indicated she was born in Ireland.

"Yes, we need to ask you some questions. We can either come to you, or you can come to the precinct." He sat back in his chair, and Tom stopped typing to listen to Sean's end of the conversation.

"I'm on my way out again, so I'll come to you, but I need an address."

Within the hour, Ms. Callahan was directed to the squad room. Sean rose and extended his hand. "Ms. Callahan, thank you for coming in. We have only a few questions, and then you should be on your way."

He pulled out a chair for her, angled to his desk. She wore a navy-blue skirt and white blouse, and her light-brown hair was pulled up with a clip, keeping her hair off her nape. With black framed glasses, she was a plain-looking woman with what seemed a no-nonsense attitude.

"We need to ask if you ever visited the Bayside Bed-and-Breakfast to meet with James Collins?"

She penned her gaze on Sean and frowned. "I've heard that name before, but I was never there. Maybe, it was Mr. Collins who mentioned it in passing…"

"We were informed that you not only met Mr. Collins there but it was an arranged rendezvous point which erupted into a verbal spat with the owner of the B&B. Can you tell us more about that?"

She sat forward. "What? I was never at the bed-and-breakfast, but what's more, I never had an affair with Mr. Collins. I'm probably one of the very few women working at the firm who didn't! Who told you that?"

"It doesn't matter. Has the owner of the bed-and-breakfast ever called and fought with any of the women at your firm in regard to Mr. Collins, possibly threatening them or you?"

"I don't know who owns the bed-and-breakfast that you're referring to. And I can't say if I know anything about the owner calling and threatening other women at the firm either. There is always talk among the secretaries and paralegals, but I never get involved with any of that. I do my job and I go home."

"It wasn't always that way though, was it?"

"What do you mean?" She frowned.

"It appears you were arrested a few times in your past." Sean pushed the paperwork around on his desk, and her eyes shifted to the papers and then back up at him.

"I was a teenager when that happened. I learned my lesson, and I've been clean ever since."

Sean stood. "I think you've helped all you can. Thank you for coming in."

"I don't quite understand. I haven't helped in any way that I can see."

"You have. I believe the person who gave us information was probably trying to steer the investigation away from herself."

After Ms. Callahan left, Sean asked Tom if they should take a closer look at Myerson. They both agreed she was hiding something.

As they pulled up to the curb outside Trina's home, she was leaving the house. "Hey," she called out upon seeing them. "I was just on my way to the firm."

She walked over to the car and leaned down to peer in. Glancing at Tom, she turned her attention to Sean. "You're back!"

"We need to ask you more questions. It'd probably be best if we went inside."

"I'm on my way to work. If we go in, I'll be late."

Tom looked at his watch; it read two forty-five. "Late for what? It seems that if you're just now going in, you're already late."

Trina turned to Tom. "I was called in." His eyes fell to her cleavage and then rotated back up to her face.

Leaning forward to peer past Tom, Sean said, "What exactly do you have against the owner of the bed-and-breakfast? We questioned Lillian Callahan, and she said she never visited the B&B to meet with Collins. And she doesn't know anything about anyone being threatened by Mrs. McCrea. Would you like to elaborate on why you lied, or do we need to take you in to the station?"

"I didn't lie. She probably forgot. I can give you names of other secretaries who will tell you themselves!"

"Okay, shoot!" Tom got out his notepad and was ready to start writing.

"Why are you so focused on this woman when Collins is dead?" Sean spoke up.

Her eyes riveted to his in anger. "James was about ready to propose, and she ruined everything!"

Tom opened the door and got out with Trina backing out of his way. He quoted the Miranda Rights to her before opening the back door. "You can get in now, or I can handcuff you."

She obliged and got in the back seat but not before she gave them both a piece of her mind. "And to think I was ready to have sex with you!" she yelled.

Tom turned around to look at her. "Not you, him..." She pointed toward Ryan.

CHAPTER 24

Back at the precinct, they put Trina in an interview room to stew for a while as they gathered more information. When Tom researched Myerson before, he didn't find anything that was criminal, and having spoken with others at the firm, along with what Collin's secretary told them, the most they could find on her was she led a promiscuous lifestyle.

When Sean walked into the room, Trina sneered at him. "Why am I here?" she demanded.

Sean took a seat and laid a folder on the table in front of him. Trina glanced at it and then back up at him. "Where were you the night of August 5?"

"Why?" she snapped.

"Where were you between the hours of 2:00 a.m. and 4:00 a.m.?"

"I'd have to look at my calendar."

Sean opened the folder and pulled out a picture of Collins. "What'd you use to bash his head in?"

Trina looked down at the photo and paled. But she didn't look away.

"Where's the weapon you used to murder James Collins?"

"I didn't murder him. I was hoping for a proposal. So why would I want to murder him. You're the detective…" She sat back in the chair and crossed her arms over her midriff.

"Did Collins find out you were sleeping with other lawyers at the firm and get pissed off? Did he end your relationship?"

Trina laughed. "You really don't get it, do you? James enjoyed sex and sleeping around. He also enjoyed threesomes."

"That bother you?"

"I was in on many of those threesomes if you must know."

"And yet you expected a proposal for what…certainly not marriage." Sean scoffed.

"None of that bothered me because I'm always up for some fun in the bedroom. But since James met that owner of the bed-and-breakfast, things changed, and I could tell he was no longer as interested in me. It's all her fault!" Trina's voice rose an octave with each word.

"I bet that pissed you off and you decided to kill James before letting that other woman have him..."

"Sure, it pissed me off. It pissed me off plenty, but if I were to murder anyone, it would have been her! Besides, she has a kid, and James hates kids."

"How'd you know she has a kid?"

Looking around the room, her head swiveled back to stare at Sean, and after a moment's pause, she said, "James told me."

"What else did Collins tell you?"

"He often confided to me on many things. He basically wanted to sleep with her, and he seemed adamant on doing just that. I told him I could arrange a threesome, but he squelched the idea, saying she would never consider it like she was so noble..."

Sean replaced the photo of Collins back in the folder and closed it with a slap. Drumming his fingers on the desk top, he stopped talking, hoping that Trina would say more. Five minutes passed with the only sound, the ticking of the second hand on the clock above the door.

Finally, she spoke up, "I drove by there once. I just wanted to see what the place looked like. But I didn't see her though I thought about stopping." She looked off toward the corner of the room.

"Did you murder James Collins?"

She jerked her head back to face Sean. "No, I never murdered him," she ground out.

Sean stood. "You're free to go."

She jumped up and flew across the room to the door before he could open it. She was out and down the hallway as he exited. The door adjacent opened, and Tom walked out, shaking his head. "She didn't do it."

CHAPTER 25

But let justice roll on like a river, righteousness like a never-failing stream!

—Amos 5:24

Tom sat in silence, beating the pencil between his fingers against the desk top.

Tap. Tap. Tap.

Finally, Sean couldn't stand it any longer. "What's got you all wound up?"

Tom stopped tapping the pencil. "I think the murder weapon was a trophy."

"What makes you think that?"

"Something Mrs. McCrea said when I ran into her. She was talking about Brad McCrea's love of football and how Michaela stored all the trophies in the upstairs office. They're like mementos she can't part with, a shrine if you will."

"So you were talking to Marissa McCrea, but when and where did you run into her?" Sean asked, clearly puzzled.

"I wanted to get a feel of how others regard Michaela. I decided to chat with a few members of the church she attends. It just so happened that Marissa McCrea was at the church member's house I stopped by."

"Why are you so fixated on Michaela?"

"I told you, you're too close to her and developing feelings. If you weren't such a fine detective and good friend, I'd be asking you step down from this assignment. You're not clearheaded."

"You can't believe for a minute she murdered Collins, seriously?" Sean stood up and scowled at his partner. "What else have you been up to, clearly leaving me in the dark?"

"I've only been asking questions about her from neighbors, church members, even other relatives, although they are far and few between. Those who should be closest to her don't know her at all while neighbors and church members seem to think she's great. There has to be a dark side to this woman, especially when you look at the damaging evidence."

"A dark side? Good God, listen to yourself! You've become a cynic in your old age!"

"Maybe, but I talked to the ME and asked him if the impression in Collins's head could have been made by a trophy of some kind. He spun the idea around and thinks it's definitely plausible. I think we should get a search warrant."

"No, damn it, no! If you think it's possible, then let me ask her to see the trophies."

"Are you out of your mind? If you gave her a heads-up, she'd dispose of them immediately. It's better if we just show up with a warrant."

"I don't want anything to do with this, not one thing!"

"I don't think you get to choose in this case. Just because you don't want it to be her doesn't mean you can step down when the job gets tough. Either you step away from this case entirely or you step up to the plate and do your damn job!"

Within the hour, the judge signed off on a search warrant, and both detectives were on their way. Tom seemed to relish the idea that it was Michaela while Sean sat rigid, hating the idea of confronting her as a prime suspect.

The crunch of gravel seemed loud to Sean's ears as they pulled into the parking lot and cut the engine. He had come to care for Michaela and Chase and hated to think what this would do to them or how she might come to think of him as the enemy.

Stepping inside the office, they saw Michaela setting up a cart in the common room with utensils, napkins, and tableware. She was preparing for the social hour. She looked up when she heard the door chime and smiled when she saw Sean. Her smile waned upon seeing Detective Hanson.

Walking into the common area, Hanson pulled the warrant from his side jacket pocket. "We have a search warrant to go through the premises to your private living quarters."

She frowned. "Why? What do you hope to find?" she asked.

Tom refolded the paper and placed it back in his pocket. Sean wouldn't make eye contact. Both avoided her question.

"Please stay here and don't leave the premises," Hanson added.

An officer who had followed them to her residence stood to the side after they left. She sank down into one of the chairs by the fireplace with her heart racing. This was absurd!

Ten minutes later, they were back downstairs with some of Brad's trophies in marked clear plastic bags.

Michaela's eyes widened. "Why do you need Brad's trophies?" She looked up at Detective Hanson, and seeing his eyes harden, she looked over at Sean, but he still avoided her gaze. None of this boded well, and she had a sinking feeling deep in her gut.

*****

Over the next couple of days, Sean refrained from calling Michaela. As this case seemed to be wrapping up, it was more imperative than ever to stop all contact with her. It didn't stop his heart from aching, and he hoped to hell this all worked out. He'd fallen head over heels for her.

Tom slapped a report on Sean's desk and then walked around to his own.

"What's this?" Sean asked.

Tom sighed. "It's a report you're not going to like, and this is where I should say 'I told you so.'"

Frowning, Sean opened the report. "This indicates there was blood found on one of the trophies we took from the B&B," Sean said, looking up at Tom.

"And that isn't the all of it. It's a match for Collins's blood. That trophy also matches the impression on Collins's head wound. It's the murder weapon," Tom added.

Sean paled at the implication. This couldn't be right. He knew Michaela well enough to know she wasn't capable of murder. But how can you explain away facts? They don't lie.

"Look, I know this is hard for you. I have to arrest her, and though I don't like it one bit, this is one time I think you should stay out of it. I'll be the one to arrest her, alone."

Sean looked up. "I can't let you do this."

"Like hell…"

"What I mean is I can't let you arrest her by yourself. I should come, we are partners."

"Yes, but one of us has dick for brains. Why don't you investigate further, see if in some way, on God's green earth, that this trophy was planted to make her look guilty. I don't think so, but it'll give you something to do."

*****

Detective Hanson opened the door to the B&B and seeing no one behind the counter rang the bell several times in succession.

Marissa walked into the office. "Now what?" she asked abruptly, all pretext to civility gone.

"Where's Michaela McCrea?" he asked.

"She's cleaning the guest rooms."

Tom walked through to the hallway leading to the guest rooms and seeing one open door peered inside to see Michaela finishing up making a bed.

He cleared his throat to get her attention. As soon as she turned, he pulled out the handcuffs. "Michaela McCrea, you are under arrest. You have the right to remain silent. Anything you say can and will be used against you in a court of law. You have the right to an attorney. If you cannot afford an attorney, one will be appointed for you."

As he cited the Miranda Rights, he turned her around and placed her arms behind her deftly, slipping the handcuffs into place.

Grabbing her upper arm, he steered out of the building to the waiting patrol car. Opening the back door, he helped her in while placing his hand on the top of her head and slammed the car door once she was inside. The sound was deafening. This couldn't be happening. The waiting officer had the motor running, and Tom slapped the driver's side door before turning away to get in his own vehicle.

Michaela barely noticed Marissa. When she peered out the side rear window of the car, Marissa was screaming and walking toward Detective Hanson with arms held high and fingers pointing.

The ride to the police station seemed surreal, and yet Michaela wondered where Sean was; why hadn't he been with Detective Hanson? Tears blurred her vision, and without the means to wipe her eyes, they started falling relentlessly. And what about Chase? What would he think? She let her head fall back against the backrest, feeling totally helpless.

At the police station, she was guided to a small interview room and left alone for what seemed like an eternity. The room was hot and small, void of windows, save the huge mirror that hung on the wall, which she now faced. She couldn't help but think of the movies and dramas she watched that set up an interrogation room in such manner. She was probably being watched on the other side, but by whom? Detective Hanson for sure, but was Sean also watching her?

Sean drew in a sharp breath. Michaela sat rigid with red-rimmed eyes and sniffling from time to time. Her handcuffs at least had been removed. For that he was grateful because Tom could have cuffed her to the table as well. He hated seeing her like this, and his gut told him she couldn't have done it, and that meant only one thing: she was set up, but by whom? As far as he could tell, she was well-liked, ran a clean establishment, and even attended church as often as possible given she was the sole caregiver. Granted she had help from Marissa and sometimes even Heather. But that only afforded her at best a couple of Sundays a month to attend church with Chase. Chase? Oh god, he must be upset, and that was putting it mildly. Should he attempt to talk with him? Probably not; as one of the lead detectives in this case, he knew it wouldn't be well looked upon. He could count himself lucky that his relationship with Michaela, up to this point, was under the radar.

Tom entered the room, and Michaela looked up at him. He set a tissue box down in front of her, and she immediately reached for it.

"Thank you," she murmured.

Tom sat without speaking while he opened a folder and shuffled papers inside. A tactic meant to make the perpetrator nervous and more willing to talk. In Michaela's case, she only seemed to appreciate the solitude before questions started pouring out.

"When was the last time you saw Mr. Collins?" Tom asked.

Michaela jumped when he finally spoke. "Uh, I believe it was around the first couple of weeks in June."

"An exact date…"

"I don't recall."

"What happened?"

"He came to the bed-and-breakfast late in the evening after Chase had gone to bed. I was surprised by his visit since I wasn't expecting him."

"Were you dating him?"

"Yes."

"Isn't it true you were about to end the relationship because he was seeing other women?"

"Yes…no…"

"Which is it?"

"I was thinking of ending the relationship, but I didn't know he was seeing anyone else at the time."

"What happened? Did you end the relationship that night?"

"We were in the kitchen, and he took the liberty to grab a bottle of wine from the pantry. He then pulled a corkscrew from the drawer and opened it. He filled a glass up to the brim and handed it to me. I told him I didn't want any wine, but he put the glass up to my lips, insisting I drink. So I took a sip."

"You remember a lot of details, but you don't recall the date."

She warily eyed Tom and sighed. "I don't recall the date other than it was a weeknight."

"Then what happened?"

"He set my glass down on the counter and pulled me into his arms and kissed me."

"That must have hurt."

Ignoring the sparring, she continued, "He then grabbed my hand pulling me toward the stairs, saying he wanted to take me up to my bedroom so we could make love. I told him no and shoved him away. He'd been drinking before he arrived at the bed-and-breakfast. I could smell hard liquor on his breath. I told him no, and it angered him."

"And then what, you threatened to kill him?"

"No! I didn't have time to think about anything else other than getting him to leave."

"What happened? Did he fondle you, try to get you excited?"

"He grabbed at my breasts, and when I pushed his hands away, he got even angrier and pushed me against the wall, holding my arms behind me."

"And then?"

Michaela shot Tom a nasty glare.

"Did he rape you?"

"No!"

"Are you positive?"

"I think I'd know if I was raped or not," she ground out.

"Did you murder him out of revenge?"

Michaela rasped out. "I didn't murder him."

Tom opened the folder and pulled out a picture of the trophy that had been used to murder Collins. "Do you recognize this?"

Michaela leaned forward and peered at the photo. "It's one of Brad's trophies."

"It's the murder weapon that you used to kill him."

She paled and looked again at the photo. "This was used to murder James?"

"You tell me."

"How do you know it's the murder weapon?" she asked.

"We found blood on it that matches Collins's blood type, but more than that, it matches the impression left on the side of his skull. That pretty much leads us to believe that since this trophy is owned by you with traces of James's blood found on it, it's likely you're the murderer. Let's not forget you had motive, his assault. Either that or you were jealous of the women he was seeing."

"I didn't kill him!" Michaela raised her voice.

"What happened next?"

Pushing her curls behind an ear, it appeared she was trying to recall the question. "He pushed his free hand up my gown and… and roughly pushed his fingers…inside. I tried pulling away, but he shoved me back against the wall, pinning my arms. He continued to…you know, and his kisses grew slobbery while he was continuing his assault." Michaela took a long, shaky breath and then continued, "And-and then he started kissing my breasts through the fabric of my gown. I yelled for him to stop, and he got even angrier. He finally removed his hand and pulled my nightgown down, exposing my breasts… I continued to struggle, which angered him further. He finally pulled back, and raising his hand, he slapped me."

"Go on."

"I was stunned, and then someone rang the bell on the office counter. He stepped back, freeing me as if realizing he was taking things too far. Then he apologized and left."

"And that was the last time you saw him?"

"Yes."

"Where were you the night of August 5?"

"August 5? I was at the B&B. I had guests booked."

"You were there all night?"

"Yes!"

"Do you have an alibi?"

"My son was there…"

"Does your son sleep in your bedroom, Mrs. McCrea?"

"Of course not, he has his own bedroom."

"He can't really alibi for you then, can he?

"How does your involvement with Detective Ryan play into all this?"

Michaela frowned. "What?" His change of questioning grew confusing.

"I think you're trying to play him like a fiddle."

Sean stiffened and almost left the room to interfere, but his sergeant stood beside him, having entered the room just a few moments earlier. When Sean moved, he laid a hand on his arm, stopping him. He gave a warning look and then resumed watching the interrogation.

So much for keeping this quiet; he'd be lucky now if he wasn't removed from the case and reprimanded.

"I don't know what you mean…"

"It seems to me that you've taken a liking to Detective Ryan and are playing up the damsel in distress. But did you know that he was married?"

Michaela stopped breathing. Sean closed his eyes. He never intended for her to find out about his personal life until after the case was solved, but worse, Tom made it sound like he was still married to his ex.

"Did you threaten Mr. Collins because he was seeing other women while dating you?"

"No. I didn't know he was seeing anyone else."

Tom pulled another photo from the file folder. He placed it so it was right side up facing Michaela. She looked down and paled seeing James with his head bashed in. His eyes were open and void of life. Her hand flew to her mouth, and she squeezed her eyes shut. The room was starting to spin out of control. Taking deep breaths, she tried to recover, and finally she opened her eyes and looked straight at Tom.

"I didn't kill him." Tears threatened from shimmering eyes.

"How did James's blood end up on your trophy, Mrs. McCrea?"

She shook her head. "I don't know…"

"Did you plot his murder?"

"No!"

"While you've been detained, we took the opportunity to further search your private quarters. Guess what was found?"

Michaela shook her head. Sean, still watching the interrogation, wondered what the hell was going on.

"We found hair. Mr. Collins's hair to be exact, and we found it in your bedroom."

Sean stiffened. For the first time, doubts started to flood his mind.

"No, he was never in my bedroom ever!"

"The way I see it, you had sex with him, and when he continued to have affairs with other women, you got mad and plotted his murder."

"No, no, no!" Michaela's tears started falling.

"Why not just confess and get this over with?" Standing up, Tom replaced the photos in the folder on the table. "I'll leave you to think about this, and when I come back, maybe you'll fess up to Collins's murder."

Sean turned and walked out the door, meeting Tom in the hall. "What the hell is this about? When did you get hair that matches Collins from her bedroom?"

Tom held up a hand. "She's guilty. You're not thinking straight." He looked past Sean to their sergeant. "You already suspected the truth, after all, you gave me the idea to search her private quarters, right?"

Sean knew their sergeant was standing behind him and that Tom was giving him an out. He nodded. Tom swept passed him and headed for the squad room. Their sergeant left, heading for his office, leaving Sean standing alone in the hallway.

*****

Two hours later, Michaela was released on bail. With a young son at home, they felt she wasn't a flight risk, and thankfully, the judge impinged a light bail that she could afford.

In leaving the building, she saw Sean. He turned and made eye contact with her. Dropping her gaze, she opened the door and walked out into the sunlight.

Sean wanted to speak with her, but this wasn't the time or place to be seen together. He wanted answers.

A squad car was waiting to return her to the bed-and-breakfast. The officer got out upon seeing her and opened the back door. She slid in without saying anything. He closed the door and promptly got back into the driver's side. The ride home was quiet with neither speaking. After pulling into the parking lot, the officer got out, but she opened the back door without waiting. She nodded at him and walked toward the private entrance.

After turning the corner, she stopped and waited for the police car to leave. She couldn't go in yet. She needed time to think, so she walked to the back gardens and sat on a bench.

How did James's hair get in her bedroom? Maybe, his hair got caught on something she wore. Her thoughts jumped to Sean. He was married? Oh god, she almost made love to him and told him she loved him. Folding, she hugged her waist. She was so stupid! He must be making fun of her at this very minute. The trophy, it was used as the murder weapon? How? When? She had so many questions, and with each, she felt like she was dying inside.

CHAPTER 26

Whoever conceals hatred with lying lips and spreads slander is a fool.

—Proverbs 10:18

It was getting late when Michaela finally rose from the bench and entered through her main living quarters, avoiding other people and, more specifically, Marissa who would fire questions at her. With her head pounding and a sick feeling deep in her gut, she just wanted to rest.

Still, curiosity piqued; she opened the office door to peer in. Marissa wasn't manning the desk. She must be somewhere else in the bed-and-breakfast, and as Michaela started to turn away, she noticed the sign on the front door of the office was turned to closed. That didn't make sense; Marissa's car was still in the parking lot.

Furrowing her brows, she wondered what happened that Marissa would close shop. While the police were looking at Michaela as the primary suspect in James's murder, the real killer was still at large. If something was wrong, Marissa would have left a note on the desk and the answering machine turned on.

Michaela entered the office and checked the desk. No note was left and the answering machine was on. Scared for Marissa's safety, she wasn't sure what to do. Who could she possibly call?

With heart pounding, she tried to calm herself. She was jumping to conclusions, and Marissa was no doubt okay. She'd text her. Reentering the living area, she pulled out her cell.

CHAPTER 26

A thud from upstairs gave her pause. And then she heard another thud. Truly terrified now, she didn't know if she should investigate. But what if Marissa was being held captive upstairs, someone possibly hurting her, or worse? Thank goodness Chase was at soccer practice.

She quietly made her way up the stairs, halting every so often. With her heart in her throat, she crept along the hallway when she heard another sound from the upstairs office. She stopped and took a deep breath. The office door was open, and she crept to the door. If someone had Marissa, then she'd duck into Chase's room and call the police.

Peering through the crack of the opened door, Marissa was the only one in the room. And she was going through file cabinets.

"Marissa, what are you looking for?" she asked perplexed, stepping into the doorway.

Marissa turned abruptly. "What are you doing here?" she asked.

"I was released…what are you looking for?"

Marissa threw her long dark hair over her shoulder. Leaning against the desk, she crossed her arms in front of her. "You need to sit…"

Michaela's stomach hit bottom. *Please, no more bad news!*

"I'm looking for a package…" she began as Michaela warily sat down.

"A package?"

Marissa cut in, "Yes! Where is it?" She pushed away from the desk and crossed over to Michaela.

With her face mere inches away from Michaela's, she spoke through clenched teeth. "I need it before anyone else gets hurt. Do you understand?"

"What are you talking about?"

"The papers, Michaela! The files that will expose everything, the packet Brad sent you just before he was murdered!"

Michaela paled and shook her head. "Marissa, I don't have a clue as to what you're talking about. But, please, please, tell me you are not behind the man who's been chasing me!"

Marissa smirked. "You have no idea, do you? I mean you are so damned stupid!"

Crossing the room, Marissa slammed the door shut before turning back to Michaela who sat dumbfounded by this turn of events. It was the proverbial jaw-dropping moment when she realized the emphasis behind this.

"Brad wasn't the person you thought. You just loved the new house and all the things he bought. Did you really think his business was taking off because he was so good at what he did?" She shook her head and rolled her eyes, turning away from Michaela.

"I've heard enough! Don't you dare malign Brad. He was a good man, a good father, and a great husband!" Michaela shouted, jumping up from her chair.

Marissa spun around and shoved Michaela with such force that she fell back in the desk chair, landing hard on the seat. Her head hit the wall behind her with a thud. She sat momentarily stunned. Marissa took the opportunity to grab the duct tape sitting on the desk and tore off a strip from the roll and set about wrapping the length around both Michaela's arm and the arm of the chair. Sitting upright, Michaela tried to pull the tape off with her free hand. When Marissa tore a second strip off, Michaela pushed her away with as much force as she could muster with one free arm.

Stumbling backward, Marissa found her footing and grabbed Michaela's hand again and pushed her full weight against Michaela's body, deftly wrapping the tape in place. Michaela strained against the trappings. Stepping back, Marissa surveyed her work and then reached for more tape.

"What the hell are you doing? Stop, just stop!" Michaela screamed. Marissa ignored her and started to tape her legs to the pedestal of the desk chair. Michaela kicked out, catching Marissa's shin with the toe of her shoe.

Cursing, Marissa stepped back. "Damn you!" Grabbing the phone from the desk, she hit Michaela on the side of the head, and she slumped in the chair, head hanging. Marissa took advantage of her dazed state and taped her legs to the desk chair, wrapping the tape around both legs and the pedestal.

CHAPTER 26

Michaela's vision blurred with pain, and she once again strained against the trappings to no avail. Duct tape would be impossible to break the bonds that held her.

"I'm through with trying to find the package on my own. And several times over the years, I have tried to find it. But there was always something to stop me. But time is running out. Let me tell you a story. Brad was into selling and buying black-market goods. I know because I'm the one who set him up though he didn't know it was me. He got in too deep and wanted to come clean. But he couldn't just walk away without consequences. He feared for his life, and yours, and Chase's. He knew that to come clean, he'd need evidence, but I was always one step ahead of him. When you told me that he'd been acting strange, I figured out what was going on. But it wasn't until you told me he was leaving for a meeting down south that I knew for sure." She pushed herself up onto the edge of the desk and crossed her legs.

Michaela had gone quiet, listening closely with hands furled into tight fists.

"I set it up for my boyfriend to follow Brad that day. When Brad stopped for a break, his brake lines were partially cut. And driving along the scenic route, it was a given he'd go over the cliff. It was done swiftly, and no one was the wiser, certainly not Brad, the fool!"

"You murdered Brad!" Michaela hissed, trying to wrestle free of her confines with renewed strength.

"Calm down! You can't get free. But, yes, he left me no choice, and though I didn't actually murder him per se, it was at my command that he was set up. We found out a couple of weeks earlier that he stole files that would incriminate not only me but my boyfriend and a few other key players. We started planning how to handle the situation, following him, trying to figure out where he hid the evidence. But when you told me that Brad had been acting funny and later that he planned a business trip down south, we put two and two together. He had the evidence on him to turn state evidence. But then after the 'accident,'" she air-quoted, "we found only copies in the wreck, which we quickly destroyed. It was a no brainer, he planned to mail the originals to you. The thing is, I really liked Brad."

Marissa once again threw her long hair over a shoulder. She raised one shoulder and smiled. "He was good in bed…"

Michaela's gasp had Marissa laughing. "Oh, don't worry. We only did it once. In fact, it was an evening when you were helping your aunt here at the B&B. I stopped by your place, and Brad had been drinking. I tried to comfort him, of course, and before you know it, one thing led to another. To be honest, he felt awful about it afterward. I told him it was our secret and I would never tell."

Marissa chuckled. "Oops, I guess I just let the cat out of the bag!" She mockingly held a hand over her mouth and then continued, "After his funeral services, I decided it would be best to find the package without alerting you. You were in a state of depression, and it was truly hard watching you try to recover and move on with your life. Then the move from your house to here. I helped because I was trying to find the package he sent. What better way than helping you move. But then you started renovations of this place, and there were workers here. And if workers weren't around, it was guests. It became increasingly more difficult for me to look! It got to the point I was being reckless as time moved on. In fact, I was caught just a month ago." Marissa shoved off the desk and walked to the shelf that was now void of Brad's trophies.

Turning sharply, she said, "I was caught by none other than James!"

"James…"

"You had gone out that morning, and Chase was at a friend's house. I was here all alone and took my time looking through your drawers and closet. I heard a noise and turned around to find James standing in the doorway. He asked me what I was doing. I tried lying to him, but he could see right through it. He threatened to tell you that I was going through your stuff. I couldn't have that!

"So I told him that if he helped me look, he could get in on the deal. It was after all lucrative! He bought it. But, well, you know how James liked his women. There we were in your bedroom with your bed right there. The bed he'd been trying to get you into for a few weeks I might add." Marissa smiled, staring at the floor.

Angling her head toward Michaela, she proceeded, "He stepped up behind me as I was searching in the closet and kissed my neck. I leaned against him, and he placed his arms around me and turned me to face him. We kissed. Then he reached for my breasts, and I let him cup them with his strong hands."

Marissa brought her hands up and cupped her breasts, rolling her head back with eyes half closed. Michaela was sickened by the display and turned her head away. But when Marissa resumed her story, Michaela's eyes shot back to the woman she thought she knew.

"And then he asked me if I'd like to use the bed. What more can I say? We had sex. He was good!" Marissa's eyes sparkled. "Of course, I had to tell my boyfriend about it. Unfortunately, Collins did the stupidest thing ever!"

Michaela now understood how James's hair came to be found in her bedroom. Everyone was going mad around her, and she was taking the fall.

Marissa reclined against the desk again. "He tried to blackmail me. He wanted money in exchange for his silence, and he wanted 50 percent of the profit from the black-market goods. The man was greedy beyond belief, but because of his name and what he did for a living, he said he was taking the bigger risk and he needed compensation for that. Of course, we had to do something." Marissa sat back on the desk and crossed her legs.

"I borrowed one of Brad's trophies which I knew you wouldn't miss since you rarely come into this room. That night, we made plans to meet at his home. I wore a very revealing dress, and we had sex, which was quite good by the way. I swear, Michaela, you really didn't know what you were missing out on." Marissa laid her head back and sighed before continuing, "And, well, you can guess the rest. He was after all found dead in his home, blunt force trauma to the head as they call it. The best part was setting you up to take the fall."

Michaela shook her head. "I can't believe you murdered James too!"

"I didn't want to. The man knew how to treat a woman even if it wasn't sincere." She raised her shoulders. "He left me with no choice though. And as for you, I hope you're learning that if you don't tell me where the package is, there could be severe repercussions."

"If this package is so important, then why didn't you act sooner? Five years, Marissa. What am I not getting?"

"Simply put, we didn't tell top players the real files were missing, damning evidence that could put us all behind bars. We thought we could handle it on our own and created false documents, but then a month ago, that all changed. It's come to light the files we duplicated are not authentic, so now we have to pay the piper!"

"And what do you plan to do with me?"

"That definitely poses a problem, but for now, I think with evidence stacked against you, you'll be sentenced for James's murder. What happens before or after is out of my hands. That's why you need to tell me where it's at."

"I don't know! I never received a package from Brad!" Michaela shouted.

"You still don't understand..." Marissa looked at her watch. "You could be putting Chase into danger. His ride should be arriving soon since soccer practice has been over for the past ten minutes."

"You harm one hair on his head and I'll kill you!" Michaela threatened through clenched teeth.

"It's not me, dear, you have to worry about. I love the kid as if he were my own. I kept him, watched him, burped him, I even changed his diapers when he was a babe."

"He's nothing like you!"

"Yeah, I know. I've always been bad which is why Brent and I split. I was unfaithful to him before we got married and after. He caught me a few times and each time forgave me, thinking I'd change if he just loved me enough. In the end, he couldn't take my indiscretions and moved to Alaska."

Michaela shook her head. "I almost feel sorry for you."

"Well, don't. But for now, I need to put tape over your mouth so you won't alert Chase when he gets here. Don't worry, I won't harm him. Like I say, I love the kid!"

She stretched out another length of tape from the roll. Michaela twisted her head from side to side to avoid being gagged, but Marissa picked up the phone again with intentions of using it. Upon seeing the veiled threat, Michaela complied.

"This goes away if you only tell me where the package is..."

Michaela shook her head.

"Fine..."

Once Marissa left, Michaela tried pulling the tape in earnest to release her arms from the confines, but it was strong, and she only succeeded in irritating her skin.

It wasn't but a few moments later she heard voices down the hall as Marissa met Chase.

"Chase sweetie! Your mama had business today, and she just texted saying she won't be back until late. She asked if you'd like to go to the pizza place tonight as a treat!"

"Sure! When do you think she'll be back?" he asked.

"Not until probably seven or eight tonight, maybe not until after you've gone to bed. Let's go have some fun!"

Michaela fought back the rising hysteria bubbling up from within. She heard their footsteps retreat as they descended the stairs, and she wondered how long they might be gone. Did Marissa hope to hold her hostage for long and then what?

When she could no longer hear their voices, she prayed that Marissa wouldn't harm Chase. Looking about for something she could use to help her break loose from her restraints, but it was futile, the desk had been swept clean with exceptions of the phone and roll of duct tape that remained. And nothing else was within reach. The more she moved, the more the tape pulled her tender skin.

As the light in the office faded, she dozed off and on, only to awaken stiff and out of sorts before the events of the last few hours bombarded her thoughts and fueled her fear. It seemed hours had passed when she was awakened by voices. It was Chase and Marissa.

"I had lots of fun, Aunt Marissa. I wished Mom was home so I could tell her about the good time we had!"

"I'm sure she'll be home soon enough. Time for bed for you though. I'll be in shortly to tuck you in, sweetie!"

She heard Chase's door open and close and then footsteps retreating again back down the staircase.

She waited.

She dozed.

She woke.

Feeling a bit fuzzy-headed, she felt the presence of someone else in the room with her. Raising her head slightly, she whispered as best she could through the gag, "Marissa?"

"Yes… I was hoping that you'd come to your senses and tell me where the package is…" She yanked the tape from Michaela's mouth, causing her to yelp.

"I don't know! Let me go!"

"Were you aware that I was the one who gave Detective Hanson the idea about the trophies? You see, I ran into him at Mrs. Adam's house. He stopped by to question Pastor Hodges about you, and I started talking about how you adored Brad and still had his trophies upstairs in the office. I could see the wheels churning in his balding head. It was kind of fun to watch really. About the envelope, you are running out of time. Tomorrow morning after Chase is in school, maybe you'll be more willing to talk."

Replacing the tape over Michaela's mouth, she left the room, locking the door behind her.

Bound to the chair watching the night sky through the office window, Michaela fought the urge to vomit. Her head ached from where Marissa hit her with the phone, and she hadn't eaten a meal since midmorning when she was arrested. Nausea churned in her gut, and it was all she could do to focus on other things. As time passed, moonlight made its way to the small window where it cast light into the small space.

At first, she thought she was seeing things, but down on the floor, something was reflecting the moonlight. Squinting to see, she finally realized it was the knife she used to open envelopes. She'd lost the letter opener and had gotten a knife from the kitchen that she now kept on the desk. With a desk calendar still lying in the middle of the floor along with other items that had been on the desktop, it was clear Marissa must have been frustrated in trying to find the package and simply took an arm and swept everything off onto the floor in anger.

CHAPTER 26

Dragging the chair forward, inch by inch, she finally managed to get close enough she could pick up the knife with her feet. Thankfully, she'd worn slip-on shoes, and she was able to use her toes to remove the heel of her shoes and then slip her feet out. With feet free, she tried gripping the knife by the handle using her toes but kept losing it as it slipped from her grasp. This was harder than she realized.

She wanted to scream in frustration. Each time she dropped the knife, it scooted further under the desk. If this kept up, she wouldn't be able to get it at all.

Exerting more effort, she was finally able to grasp it, but now what? Her legs were still bound to the chair. Attempting to turn the knife over so the sharp edge was pointing toward her, she might be able to saw through the tape. But turning the knife using just her toes and feet so the blade could cut through the tape was difficult at best, and through the process, she managed to nick herself a few times. But she eventually turned the knife to the right position. And she started sawing. The procedure was slow and agonizing. At this rate, Marissa would find her in the morning still sawing away. Her feet were starting to cramp with the effort she exerted. Focusing solely on the sawing motion and nothing else, she kept the pace and ignored the pain; she had to do this.

She stopped to rest for a short bit and realized the tape seemed loose. Maybe, she was making progress. Spurred on by the thought of cutting through to release her legs, she sawed in earnest. The tape was getting looser, and finally, she found her legs freed. Pulling her legs from the tape, she could feel the fabric of her pants adhering to the sticky tape before they gave way. Her legs were freed!

With her legs now free, she attempted to bring the knife up to where she could grasp it with her hand. Success! She was breathing hard from the exertion of all the sawing and trying to grasp the knife, but she couldn't stop. Turning the blade without dropping it was chore enough, and with it in position, she started sawing the tape that held her wrist bound to the arm of the chair, nicking herself good at one point. She could feel the warmth of her blood oozing down over her hand and hoped the cut wasn't too deep.

Again, it took time, but she could do this. The moonlight faded as the moon continued its orbit across the night sky. And still she sawed. Then all at once, she was free. She felt the hair on her arm being pulled out by the stickiness of the tape as she released her arm from its confines. Now that she had a free hand, she removed the tape from her mouth and then freed her other arm.

She sat for a moment, marveling that she was able to free herself. But then spurred by fear, she pushed out of the chair and almost cried out when her legs started to give way under her. She lost circulation from being bound for so many hours. She circled the room a few times, holding onto furniture around the room for support. The tingling pain that ran down her legs as circulation finally made its way through capillaries eased, and she felt she was strong enough to leave.

She started to open the door and came up short, remembering that Marissa had locked it. If she recalled, there was a spare key hanging on the side of the file cabinet. Making her way into the back of the room, she placed her hand between the wall and the side of the cabinet and slowly moved her hand down the side, feeling for the key. Without light, she'd have to be careful not to dislodge it.

She felt the top of the magnet as her hand slid down slowly. Holding her breath, she was able to grasp the key without knocking it off. She unlocked the office door and cracked it open to peer down the hall. All was dark and quiet. She had no idea if Marissa was asleep in her room or downstairs. She tiptoed down the hall to Chase's room and slowly opened the door. His night-light was on, and he was alone. She could see the rise and fall of his chest as he slumbered. Snickers lay at the foot of his bed and immediately raised his head and thumped his tail.

Stepping across the room to his bed, she leaned over and placed her hand over Chase's mouth. His eyes flew opened, and he started to yell.

"Chase it's mom. Shhhhh!"

He was startled.

"We need to get out of the house, but we can't make a sound. Do you understand? Nod your head if you do."

He nodded. She removed her hand from his mouth, and he sat up in bed.

"Mom, what's going on?" he whispered.

"I can't tell you now. Do you know where Marissa is sleeping?"

He shook his head and frowned. "Did Marissa do something wrong?"

"I'll tell you later. Get your shoes on. Don't worry about dressing."

She helped him out of bed, and while he put his shoes on, she took the extra pillows and placed in his bed, pulling the covers up over them. Turning, she grabbed a few articles of clothing from Chase's drawer and stuffed into his backpack. She held it up, indicating for Chase to put it on.

"Mom, your wrist, it's bleeding," he whispered.

Looking down, she saw it was still oozing blood and took one of Chase's socks to wrap around her wrist for the time being. She grabbed Snickers and crept to the door. Peering out, Michaela didn't see any signs of movement, and the lights were still off.

They tiptoed to the stairs and started down. Knowing where every footboard creaked, Michaela held Chase back and whispered, "The next step has a creak. Don't step in the center but to the right on that step." Chase had run up and down these stairs for years but seemed oblivious to the creaks and noises it made.

Each time they came to a place on the stairs that had loose boards, Michaela would stop Chase and instruct him where to step. This took longer than she liked, and it was difficult holding Snickers as they made their way down the stairs in the dark.

At last, they made their way to the first floor. She still didn't know if Marissa was sleeping in a guest room or on the sofa. If she was on the sofa, they'd need to leave through the kitchen and then out the back door.

Thank goodness Chase followed her without asking more questions. The kitchen was cast in darkness as they made their way to the door. Michaela unlocked it and slowly opened it. Thankfully, she had oiled the hinges just a few days prior. The good Lord was definitely watching over her. She grabbed her car keys hanging by the door, and they stepped out on the landing, drawing the door shut behind them.

She gave Snickers to Chase and told him to stay close. She relocked the door from the outside and then huddled under the outdoor lights. Michaela motioned for Chase to follow, and they ran for the car. Michaela unlocked the doors manually rather than using the key fob that would sound the alarm. Helping Chase into the car, she took his backpack and grabbed Snickers again. She didn't close the door firmly and told Chase to leave it ajar. Walking around the front of the car, she dropped the backpack into her seat and asked Chase to set it in back on the floorboard behind her. She slid in behind the wheel and dropped Snickers into the back seat where he instantly cuddled into a ball and closed his eyes. She left her car door ajar too and inserted the keys into the ignition and turned the key over.

The car came to life, and she thought the motor deafening. She held her breath, glancing toward the bed-and-breakfast but didn't see any lights flicker on. She shoved the gear into reverse and backed out of the lot. Once they made the turn onto the road, she turned on the car lights and stepped on the accelerator. Turning onto a side street, she pulled over so they could close their doors.

"Mom, what's going on?"

"Oh, Chase!" She shook her head.

"Where are we going?"

"I don't know…but away from here for now."

CHAPTER 27

Assuredly, the evil man will not go unpunished, but the descendants of the righteous will be delivered.

—Proverbs 11:21

Looking at the clock on the dash, it was now 3:45 a.m. as she parked the car in one of the guest's parking spaces at Heather's condo complex. After cutting the engine, Michaela sat in the dark totally exhausted and hungry. She hated waking Chase again, but she didn't know how much time she had before Marissa discovered them missing. And the boyfriend; well, it was obvious that Clara, the pastor's wife, was correct. How did she know about a boyfriend when Michaela knew nothing of the sort? Shaking her head, she still couldn't believe all that happened. Tears threatened when she thought of Brad. Was it true that he was into selling black-market goods? Why? She felt inadequate and had let Brad down as a loving wife. Was she so focused on herself that she failed to see the warning signs or, worse, that she really enjoyed the luxuries Brad was able to supply that she never questioned them?

Chase had fallen asleep almost as soon as they hit the road, but now it was time to wake him. Michaela told him briefly that Marissa was not to be trusted and that at a later time she would tell him everything. She neglected to tell him that might not be until he turned twenty-one. He would have plenty of questions, and she didn't know how much she should tell him.

Opening the car door, the interior lights flickered on and woke her son. "We're there?" he asked, sitting straighter in his seat and rubbing his eyes with the back of his hands.

"Yes, grab Snickers please."

Ringing the doorbell, Michaela heard shuffling from inside before lights came on and eventually the exterior light on the front stoop. A curtain brushed back from the plate glass window of her living room, and Michaela saw her friend's face.

After unlocking the door, Heather opened the door wide and asked, "What's wrong!" Her eyes were big as saucers, and when she saw Chase with Snickers in hand, she stepped back so they could all enter.

"What's wrong?" she repeated.

Stepping inside the decorated interior, a sofa chaise was on the right with plenty of pillows and a throw displayed on the end. An overstuffed chair was angled to the sofa and beyond a dining area with a large mirror on the adjacent wall, making the space appear larger than it was. To the left was a breakfast nook with a large bay window looking out to her front garden area. The kitchen, beyond, opened to the breakfast area with stainless steel appliances, quartz countertops, and white cabinetry.

Michaela told Chase to lie down on the couch, and she grabbed the throw that was artfully displayed across the arm and placed over him. Heather seemed to understand they couldn't talk in front of Chase and quietly watched as Michaela tucked Chase in and kissed him on the forehead. Snickers jumped up on the end of the couch and settled in close to Chase.

In the kitchen, Heather turned on the coffee pot before turning to Michaela, and seeing the dried blood on her head and that her wrist was wrapped in a sock, she whispered, "Oh my god, what happened?"

Michaela blurted, "Marissa murdered James."

"What!" She placed her hand to her lips, eyes even wider now.

"She confessed after tying me to a chair in the upstairs office. It took me most of the night to break free." She looked at her arms which still hurt and could easily see the burn marks from ripping the tape off her arms. Heather's eyes followed, and she gasped.

"You're not kidding! Did she do this too?" Heather reached for Michaela's arms and inspected them closely before lightly touching the area on the side of Michaela's head.

"Yes, she hit me with the phone on the desk trying to subdue me long enough to tie me to up. It worked." She shrugged in despair, and she felt like she might shatter into pieces any moment.

"I can't believe this! And your wrist..."

"I did that. I nicked myself with a knife trying to saw my way out of the bindings."

"But why...why would Marissa tie you up and hurt you like this?" Heather asked.

"Because she's looking for a package she thinks I have, but I don't know anything about a package. Sound familiar?"

"Oh my god. I can't believe this!"

"Do you have something to eat? I haven't eaten since yesterday midmorning;" Michaela asked, changing the subject.

"Of course, you want eggs or something like that?"

"No...fruit or anything. I've put you in danger by coming here. I need to leave soon before we're discovered missing."

Heather pulled her lunch from the refrigerator she made before going to bed. "Here, it's a tuna sandwich and an apple I prepared for today's lunch."

Michaela reached for the sack and dug out the sandwich.

"I don't understand. Why did she murder James?" Heather asked as Michaela pulled back the plastic wrap from the sandwich.

Taking a bite, she spoke with her mouth full, "She not only murdered James but she also had a hand in murdering Brad." With the last statement, tears flooded her eyes, and she swallowed hard. "I can't turn to anyone but you, and I'm putting you in danger."

"Brad? This is crazy! We've got to call Sean at once!"

"No. We can't call him. I was arrested yesterday for James's murder..."

"What the hell, Michaela! Why am I just now finding all this out?" Heather asked with arms akimbo.

"I simply didn't have time. Detective Hanson put handcuffs on me after reciting my Miranda Rights, and then I was interrogated in a small windowless room for a long time before finally being released on bail. After that is when I found Marissa going through the files in the upstairs office. And then this," she added, looking down, flinging an arm wide.

Slumping into a nearby kitchen chair, Michaela continued, "I think maybe we should leave. I'm not kidding when I said I may be putting you in danger. Marissa was working with a boyfriend, and he's the one who cut Brad's brake lines. Once she realizes I'm gone and have taken Chase, she may call her boyfriend. And with few places I could go, yours would be the first place she'd check."

"Okay, slow down. Do you think she knows you're gone, and by the way, what boyfriend?"

"I don't know. We sneaked out, and I don't know who the boyfriend is. Clara was the first to mention anything about a boyfriend."

"If it makes you feel better, we can always go to my mom's. She has a big basement, and we can settle in there while you tell me everything that's going on, and we'll figure out our next course of action."

The next hour was a blur as they loaded up the car and headed to Heather's mom's place. Chase grumbled over being awakened again but fell promptly back to sleep once they were underway. Heather insisted they not wake her mom since she had a spare key to her place. That way they could avoid questions, and it was probably best that her mom didn't know they were there right away.

Parking a block away, they walked the distance to the house, letting themselves in through the back door. The house was cast in darkness with only the light from the refrigerator helping them find their way. The door to the basement was off the kitchen, and they filed down with Heather turning on lights as they made their ascent.

The basement was quite spacious with a bedroom and bath at the back accessed through a short hallway. A large living area was located in front with sofas and a bar area. Heather's dad had renovated the space years earlier for a place to convene with his cronies to play poker once a week. But now, it was rarely used.

CHAPTER 27

After getting Chase and Snickers settled in once again, Michaela poured out her story.

As the two women settled on the couch with a cup of steaming coffee, Michaela retold the story from the beginning. "Yesterday, Detective Hanson came to the B&B and put me under arrest. At the police station, I found out that one of Brad's trophies was used to kill James. It has his blood on it, and, of course, it will have my prints, but it matches the impression made on James's head. They also found his hair in my bedroom."

"Wait, Brad's trophy was used to murder James, and how in the hell did James's hair end up in your bedroom?"

"Marissa took the trophy and planned it all so I would take the fall…"

"But how did James's hair end up in your bedroom? You never had sex with him, did you?"

"No!"

"Thank God!"

"Once I was released and back home, I found Marissa upstairs in the office looking for something. We struggled, and she managed to tie me up by duct-taping me to the desk chair. She confessed she had Brad murdered because he was dealing in black-market goods and was getting ready to turn state evidence. Then she said that James caught her looking through my stuff, and she was forced to tell him what was going on. They ended up screwing in my bed, hence how his hair came to be found in my bedroom. She left me tied up, demanding to know where the package was…"

"The man that chased you, he was looking for a package. Any ideas at all?"

"None! I told Marissa that, but she refused to believe me."

"Okay, so why did she murder James?" Heather asked, taking another sip of coffee that had now grown lukewarm.

"According to Marissa, he got greedy. He not only wanted in on the black-market goods but thought he should get 50 percent of the profits to keep his mouth shut because he was taking the greater risk."

"Wow." Heather shook her head from side to side.

"By the way, I also found out Sean's married."

"What! You mean to tell me he's been playing you all along? I can't believe it! Wait, you said that Brad was dealing in black-market goods?"

"That's what Marissa said. She added that I just loved the fancy house and cars etc. but not once did I question where it all came from. She's right. I never questioned Brad about the money he made from his business. Oh, Heather, how could I do this to him? But that's not all, Marissa claims to have slept with Brad too!"

"Oh, hon, no. I can't believe that about Brad. He adored you, and you didn't do this to Brad. If he got into the black market, it was a decision he made alone and not because of you but probably in some odd way for you."

"If that's the truth, then in essence, I'm the one who might as well have cut his brake lines!"

"That's nonsense and you know it. How did Marissa know he was dealing in black-market goods?"

"She said she was the one who set him up, but he didn't know it was her. I can't believe all this about Marissa. She's been a supporter and friend all this time. Or so I thought." Michaela hung her head, shaking it from side to side in defeat.

"That's hard for me to wrap my head around." Heather's eyes lit up. "Wait just one damn minute!"

Michaela looked up when Heather jumped from her seat.

"About five months ago, I received a package mailed to the B&B. I was watching the place for you, but I ended up with an emergency call from clients and had to leave right away. On the way out, I was stopped by a postman with a package, but because I had already locked up, I just took it with me. Once at the office, I placed it in the back of the desk drawer with intentions of giving it to you as soon as possible. I can't believe I totally forgot! I bet it's the package everyone is after."

"Is it still in your desk?" Michaela asked.

"Yes!"

"We have to get it!"

"No, I need to get it. You and Chase need to stay here. He'll be waking any minute, and you need to talk with him. It won't be easy."

Michaela sighed heavily. "I'm so confused on what to do. And I now feel like I can't trust Sean. I've fallen in love with him and told him as much. We almost made love!"

"I knew I walked in on something big…" Heather sat back down and placed a hand on Michaela's arm. "I'm truly sorry."

CHAPTER 28

Fools give full vent to their rage, but the wise bring calm in the end.

—Proverbs 29:11

Marissa slept in the next morning only to be awakened by the doorbell. She turned over, and her eyes fluttered open. It wasn't the sound of her doorbell, and as her eyes adjusted, she realized she was still at Michaela's, downstairs on the couch.

Sitting upright, the events of the day before flooded her mind, remembering Michaela was tied up and locked in the upstairs office. The doorbell sounded again and then repeated as someone kept pushing the button, which angered her. Looking at the time, she gasped. It was already eight in the morning. Where was everyone? Where was Chase? What about the two guests staying here? Shit!

Wrapping a robe around herself, she went to the door and peered out through the peephole. It was Detective Ryan. She threw open the door as he was ringing the bell again. "What do you want at this ungodly hour?" she hissed.

Taken aback on seeing her, he hesitated. "I'm trying to find Michaela. She's not answering her cell. Is she okay?"

"She's fixing breakfast and can't be disturbed. I was supposed to help her, but she let me sleep in. I have to go." She started to close the door in his face, but he put his foot over the threshold and placed his hand on the door.

"I need to speak with her, it's important."

"Look, she doesn't want to see you, not after being arrested. Give her some time." This time, she managed to close the door in his face.

Running up the stairs, she opened Chase's door and saw he was still in bed. He should be up and getting ready for school, but she needed to check on Michaela first. She threw open the office door and gasped. Michaela wasn't there. She managed to break free from the tape. She saw the knife lying on the floor and cursed herself for not seeing it yesterday. She spotted some blood, which gave her a bit of satisfaction that at least Michaela didn't escape unscathed.

Turning, she fled back to Chase's room and leaning over the bed saw that pillows had been stuffed under the covers to fool her. "That bitch!" she yelled.

Entering the office, a man was standing at the counter. "Miss, when will we have breakfast?" he asked.

Turning on him, she yelled, "I'm not the owner!"

Taking a step back, he asked, "Where is the owner?"

"Well, how should I know?" Marissa fired back.

The man turned and rushed back toward his room. She didn't have time for guests, and she needed to find Michaela! She sat down heavily in the desk chair, exasperated. Michaela must have worked through the night to cut the tape with that knife, but how the hell could she do it bound as she was? Where was she and how did she manage to sneak out with Chase in hand without making a sound?

Fuming, she found her cell on the end table in the living area and hit Damon's name in her contact list.

As soon as he answered, she started talking. "We've got a problem. Michaela escaped sometime last night and took Chase with her."

"How in the hell did she escape? You said you bound her tight with duct tape!"

"Evidently, there was a knife on the floor she managed to use."

"A knife…if her legs were bound to the chair, how did she manage to pick it up? You couldn't have had her taped up well."

"I did! You weren't here, so don't tell me what I did or didn't do!"

"Calm down." She could hear Damon breathing on the other end of the line. "How'd she get away? Her car, walk, run? And where would she go?"

"I don't know. Wait a sec and let me look outside to see if her car's still in the parking lot." She pulled back the drape; Michaela's car was gone. "Shit, she took her car. The only place I can think of off the top of my head is Heather's."

"Give me the address."

*****

Sean turned from the door after Marissa slammed it in his face. Something was off. Turning toward the front entrance to the business, he saw the blinds still drawn. Michaela would have opened them earlier. He tried the door, but it was locked.

As he headed back to his own vehicle, he noticed Michaela's car was gone. Why hadn't Marissa just told him she wasn't there? The thought hit him square between the eyes; she was on the run. That brought him up short, and he felt his heart drop to his stomach. Michaela wouldn't run; she wasn't the type of person to run from the law even if she was guilty, he reasoned.

He felt awful knowing she was hurting, and indirectly, he was responsible. Being arrested, held for hours through an interrogation, and then thinking he used her. He had to talk with her. Once he was back in his own vehicle, he tried calling Heather's cell. If anyone would know, it would be Heather.

*****

Waiting for Damon, Marissa mulled over the possibilities of what this setback could potentially mean. If they couldn't find Michaela soon, chances are the police would be called in. Marissa sighed heavily. The last thing she wanted was to flee, if it came to that, and thinking along those vague terms, she needed to call Marc. He deserved more from her than simply disappearing, but hopefully, it wouldn't come to that. For now, she needed to break off her relationship with Marc. Leaning over, she gasped at the idea of losing her love forever. She loved him deeply, quite possibly the only man she ever truly loved.

"Marissa, sweetheart," Marc said, answering his cell when it rang. Seeing her picture come up on the screen, his heart notched up a beat. He stepped over to his office door and closed it. He didn't want the church secretary overhearing their conversation. "I can't wait until Thursday to have you all to myself."

"Marc, I've been thinking."

"Thinking?"

After a pause, Marissa continued, "We need to stop seeing one another, I've given this a great deal of thought, but I may be leaving the area…"

"What? What do you mean you're leaving the area? As in moving away?" His voice had risen.

"Please, Marc, don't make this hard on either of us. I love you so much…but I may have to leave, and right now, I'm not sure where I'll be going. It's hard to explain, and I can't give you details, but know I love you very much no matter what happens."

"If you leave, I'll come with you, wherever you're going, I'll come. Whatever the reason, I'll understand, but please don't leave me, sweetheart."

There was a pause on the other end of the line, and Marc was about ready to ask if she was okay.

"And what of Clara?"

"I don't love Clara. I love you, and I couldn't bear to live life without you. I simply couldn't go on like I did before-before *us*."

"You can and you will! You're a strong and wonderful man. Please, know I never intended to hurt you, but something's come up, and I may have to leave…forgive me?"

"I can't, I can't forgive you if you leave me. Please, don't forsake me, my love!"

"Bye, Marc…" Marissa hung up and felt as if she closed the door firmly to any happiness she might ever have.

Clara stopped by the church to get Marc's credit card to do some shopping since she misplaced her own card. Entering the office, no one was manning the desk, so she cracked the door open to Marc's office to see if he was counseling anyone or on the phone. She could hear his voice, and what he said gave her pause.

"I don't love Clara. I love you, and I couldn't bear to live life without you. I simply couldn't go on like I did before-before us."

Clara froze. She felt her cheeks flush, and while she no longer loved Marc, she just couldn't abide that he was in love with someone else, and she knew who was on the other end of the line. She softly closed the door and left quickly before Mrs. Walker, the church secretary, returned.

Getting in her car, she felt ill. She no longer loved Marc, but she'd be damned before letting another woman have him, especially the likes of Marissa. Shaking, she put her keys into the ignition. Knowing for some time they were having an affair and meeting once a week at Mrs. Adam's house on the pretext of doing church business, galled her.

Turning the key over, she knew what she had to do…

*****

When Heather's office opened at eight in the morning, she left to fetch the package using her mom's car since hers was still at the condo.

On the way there, her cell pinged indicating, an incoming call from Michaela. Michaela didn't have her cell on her, and, therefore, it couldn't be her. It had to be Marissa. Trying to sound calm and natural as possible, she answered.

"Hey." The line clicked off. She grimaced and threw the cell into the holder. It rang again. This time, she didn't recognize the number.

"Hello…"

"Heather, this is Sean. Do you know where Michaela is?" he rasped out.

"Probably at the B&B. I mean, she does have guests if I recall correctly. She'd either be serving breakfast or starting to clean rooms I imagine. Why?"

"Damn! I went by there this morning and tried to see her. Marissa answered the door. She's acting funny, and I think she knows where Michaela is, but she's not telling me."

"Why would she do that?" Heather hedged.

"Because Michaela was arrested yesterday by my partner and she's now out on bail. I really need to talk with her. I have to know, was she intimate with Collins?"

"What! Why would that be any of your business…" she snapped.

"I'm in love with her, and I think she may be playing me."

"And here she thinks you've been playing her…"

"You know where she's at." A statement.

Shit. Her big mouth!

"Did she tell you that I was married?" he asked.

"You're married!"

"Heather, you're too nice to play these games. I know that you know a lot more than you're saying. I'm divorced. My partner made it sound like I'm still married. I need to see her."

"Why don't you just call her?"

"I tried, but her cell goes right to voice mail."

"Look, she doesn't trust you and neither do I. She's safe for the time being. Maybe, you should do more checking on Marissa McCrea."

Silence…

Finally, his voice came over the line. "What's going on?"

"Look, I shouldn't be talking to you, but Marissa is the one who murdered James and not only James but Brad too. She confessed everything to Michaela after she tied her to a desk chair in the upstairs office."

"Fuck! I'm sorry…"

Heather went on, "Michaela was finally able to escape, arriving at my condo just after three o'clock this morning with Chase. Right now, they're both safe, but they won't be if Marissa finds out where she's staying."

"If she's at your place, she's not safe!"

"She's not there."

"We need to talk. Meet me somewhere."

"I can't."

"Are you sure she's safe? If anything happened to her…"

"She's safe."

*****

Pulling into the condo complex where Heather lived, Damon noticed that her car was still parked in front. According to what Marissa told him, Heather's car wouldn't be here if she was working. Either she took a personal day off or Michaela was here.

He decided he'd try the door. He rang the bell and knocked a couple of times, but no one answered. The drapes were still drawn.

Walking around to the back of the place, he easily jumped the fence into her courtyard and tried the slider. It was locked, but it would be easy to break into. It didn't take him long before he was inside and closing the slider behind him.

Walking through the place, he noticed that Heather's bed was unmade but what was particularly interesting was the fact that the couch had been used as a bed. One of the throw pillows was angled down, and a throw was rumpled like someone had been using it as a blanket.

The coffee pot in the kitchen still had a full pot that had grown cold. He was as certain as anything that Michaela and the kid came here before everyone left, taking Michaela's car.

He pulled out his cell. "Where would Heather and Michaela go if they left?" he asked without preamble as soon as Marissa answered.

"They were there?"

"It looks like it to me. And they must have all left together in Michaela's car."

"I've been friends with Heather for a while, but we weren't close. Let me see what I can dig up. I'm going to call her work." They both clicked off.

Marissa dialed Heather's office and spoke with the receptionist. "Yes, I'm looking for Heather Miles. I'm a friend of hers, and I need to speak with her about an important matter. Can you put me through?"

"I'm sorry, Heather isn't in the office today. She's out on a personal matter. She usually has her cell with her though."

"I'm actually planning a surprise party for her and was going to weasel some information about her friends, family, etc. so I could contact them. Do you by chance have any other contacts for Heather listed? That would save me of ton of work!"

"Well, just a moment." The receptionist put her on hold for a short while and then came back on the line. "I have a couple of contacts. Sorry there's no more than that. She listed her mother and also a friend of hers."

"Can you provide their addresses by chance?"

"Sure, the first is Heather's mother, Lana Miles, and her address is 2929 East Cottonwood Lane, and the other is Michaela McCrea over on..."

Marissa cut her off. "Oh, I have Michaela's information already. Thanks so much!"

Calling Damon, she gave him the address for Heather's mom. "I'm sure they're there!"

*****

After Glenda hung up, she thought about the conversation. Maybe, she shouldn't have given out a personal address. She knew better than to give out private information to just anyone. The conversation bothered her. Why would she want to throw a surprise party for Heather? It wasn't her birthday; she was sure of it. Getting up, she returned to the supply room to get Heather's file.

Sitting at her desk, she perused the papers. Heather's birthday was in April. Perplexed, she decided she would notify Heather right away.

CHAPTER 29

Though a righteous man falls seven times, he will get up, but the wicked will stumble into ruin.

—Proverbs 24:16

Heather rushed into the office just as Glenda was picking up the phone to call her. Returning the phone to its cradle, she started to rise, but Heather swept by her desk in a rush, nodding in her direction.

Once in her office, Heather closed the door firmly behind her and pulled open the top drawer on her massive mahogany desk that housed a computer, photos, and books. The area around her desk was littered with paint and fabric samples, and several volumes of thick books on design leaned not only against her desk but the surrounding walls. The file cabinet in the corner was filled to the brim, and papers were sticking out. She'd been so busy with recent renovations and decorating assignments she simply hadn't the time to organize.

Reaching into the back of the drawer, she pulled out the package. Turning it over, she noticed the return address and frowned. She dropped the package into her oversized purse. She felt vulnerable not knowing if the building was being canvassed. Marissa knew where she worked, and if she thought for a moment that Heather had any idea where Michaela was, she'd put a tail on her in no time. But she had one advantage; in having driven her mom's car they'd be looking for a Toyota Prius and not a Lincoln Continental. Still, she would feel better if she knew what Marissa's boyfriend looked like.

Opening her office door, she walked out and thanked Glenda for cancelling her appointments for the day having left a voice mail earlier instructing her to do so. Glenda, once again, started to say something, but Heather continued on her way out the door.

Surveying the parking lot, she didn't notice anyone sitting in a car watching. Maybe, it was safe. With keys in hand, she headed straight for her car and once inside, she locked the doors immediately.

"I've got it!" she called, heading down the stairs to the basement.

Sitting on the sofa was her mom. "You didn't tell me that Michaela and Chase were visiting! And you certainly didn't tell me that you borrowed my car."

"Uh, sorry!" she offered with raised brows with a slight grimace.

Michaela piped up, "I was telling your mom how I needed a sabbatical and that you offered me use of her basement for a few days."

"Right, I didn't think you'd mind, Mom!" Heather said, turning to her mom.

"Not at all. I always considered Michaela the other daughter I didn't have! I'm so happy you're all here even Snickers!" Mentioning the dog, Snickers ears perked up. Everyone laughed, and for the first time, in several hours, everything felt normal.

"Mom, why don't you fix your famous pineapple upside-down cake? Michaela's still itching for the recipe to make for her guests."

"Oh, what a wonderful idea...but I do need to go to the store first. I need a can of pineapple rings. Chase, would you like to go with me and pick out a treat if it's okay with your mom?"

"Sure, can I, Mom?" Chase asked, turning from the TV.

"That's sweet of you, Lana, and, yes, you can go," she said, looking over at her son.

"Here are the keys." Heather held out her hand and dropped them into her mom's open palm.

"We'll be back soon, girls!"

"Thanks, Mom!" Heather yelled as her mom and Chase ascended the basement steps.

"'Girls.' I think Mom still lives in the nineties!"

Michaela laughed. "Oh, this feels wonderful. It feels almost normal!"

Heather sat down in the space on the sofa her mother just vacated. Opening her purse, she pulled out the envelope.

"I'm a little confused why this was mailed to the B&B so many years after Brad was murdered. It should have arrived shortly after Brad was killed to our old address," Michaela said, taking the envelope.

"I have no idea why either. Look at the return address."

Michaela peered closer at the return and raised her brows. "It's from Brad's business address, McCrea Arts & Antiquities, 1300 Main. But how can that be? The business was sold." She looked over at Heather with brows furrowed. "If it was mailed five months ago, where has it been all this time?"

Heather wanted to soothe her friend, but what could she offer in the way of explanations?

Michaela took a deep breath and then tore open the envelope. A letter was folded inside, and as she removed it, a key fell out.

"That's a key to a safe deposit box," Heather said, picking it up from Michaela's lap to inspect it.

Michaela unfolded the letter and read aloud,

> My dearest Michaela, if you're reading this letter, it means I'm no longer with you. I regret that I've done some despicable things. Things I'm not proud of. I've gotten in too deep, and trying to find a way to come clean has not been easy. I've stolen documents that contain evidence. The key is to a safe deposit box where this evidence has been put in safekeeping. I caution you, love, be extremely careful. These documents contain evidence that will take down some very wealthy and influential people who will try anything to keep this information from leaking out. I've placed this burden and task on your shoulders, and for that, I'm deeply sorry. My intentions were never to put you at risk. Take this to the police. Be careful, my love! Love you always, Brad.

She refolded the letter and placed it back in the envelope. Tears fell, and Heather reached over and put her arm around Michaela's shoulder.

"Sean called me."

Michaela stiffened. "You didn't tell him where I'm at, did you?"

"Of course not!" Heather opened her mouth to say more than thought better of it. Now wasn't the time.

"He doesn't say which bank."

"No. Maybe, he wasn't thinking clearly when he wrote this letter or maybe assumed you'd know."

"We banked at Midtown Bank because it was close to his office downtown. I wonder if that's where he opened a safe deposit box." Michaela wondered aloud.

"It wouldn't hurt to find out. Do you want to drive over there now?"

Michaela shook her head. "We need to wait for Chase. I don't want him thinking I abandoned him here. He needs stability, and he's confused. I'm not sure what I should tell him. I can't fathom why this package showed up five months ago when Brad has been gone for over five years. It doesn't make sense." Michaela absently caressed the package with troubled brows.

"Let's call and find out!" Heather said. She googled Brad's old address and found the business was still used as a fine arts and antiquities store by another name. She called the number and put it on speaker before handing her cell to Michaela.

"Le Mann's Fine Arts & Antiquities, how may I help you?"

"Yes, my name is Michaela McCrea. My husband used to lease the building you're in now, and about five months ago, I received a package from my late husband with your return address. Do you know anything about that?" Michaela peered over at Heather.

"Did you say Michaela McCrea?"

"Yes, I did."

"I'm so sorry about the package. We actually found it behind a file cabinet. It'd been there for some time, collecting dust, and recalling that your husband was deceased, we didn't know if we should mail it or not. We figure the cleaning crew must have accidentally knocked it behind the cabinet where it remained until we found it. I'm deeply embarrassed for not having found it sooner."

"I was curious and wondering why it was mailed when it was. Thank you, I appreciate your help very much."

After hanging up, Michaela handed the cell back to Heather. "Well, I guess this means Brad planned to mail it to me right away. Can you imagine it being lost and then found just five months ago?"

"It doesn't say much for the cleaning crew, does it? I wonder who was supposed to mail the package though. From the letter, Brad indicates you should only receive this package if something happened to him…" Heather mused. "So who was supposed to mail it?"

Michaela sat up straighter. "You're right, if Brad wanted this sent to me, he must have planned for another person to mail it. And come to think of it, I'm curious why he would have it mailed to the bed-and-breakfast."

Turning to Heather, Michaela added, "I think I might still have Brad's secretary's home number in my contact list, if only I had my cell."

"What's her name?" Heather asked.

"Marian Walker."

"Let's see if we can find her on Google."

After finding the number, Michaela called using Heather's cell and put it on speaker so they both could hear. The line rang several times before being picked up. "Hello…"

"Mrs. Walker, this is Michaela McCrea. I'm sorry I haven't tried to stay in contact with you over the past few years, and I hope my call finds you doing well."

"Michaela, it's so nice to hear from you, dear. Like you, I apologize I haven't tried to stay connected either. I actually moved into the granny flat behind my home, and my daughter and her husband moved into the main house. I've since retired, and the grandchildren keep me busy."

"That's good to hear. The reason I'm calling is that I'm looking for answers. Brad had a package that was to be mailed to me, but—"

"Oh, dear!" Mrs. Walker interrupted. "Did you get it then?"

Michaela frowned. "The package?"

"Yes, Mr. McCrea asked me to mail a package to you. It was the day before he was killed, and he asked me to ensure I mailed it if he was late getting into the office the following morning. But the next morning, the package was gone, so I assumed that it had already been mailed. And then, of course, I found out later in the day that Mr. McCrea was killed in that accident. I didn't want to bother you about it at the funeral. You had enough on your plate, and I figured it was business related and didn't want to cause you further pain."

"Actually, the package was lost behind a file cabinet presumably by the cleaning crew. The new owners at the same address found it a few months ago and sent it on. I was trying to figure out who originally was supposed to mail it."

"I'm so sorry you never received it until fairly recently. I never thought about the package falling behind a file cabinet though. And one would think the cleaning crew would have noticed something falling, but then the poor man who usually came in to clean Mr. McCrea's office was hard of hearing."

"Thank you again, Mrs. Walker. Do you have any idea why Brad addressed the package to be sent to the bed-and-breakfast instead of our home address?"

"He set the package on my desk as he was leaving the office. I never bothered to look at the address. I'm sorry. But I do recall Brad mentioning you were spending a great deal of time at the B&B, and with your aunt's recent passing, you were tending to paperwork in getting the title transferred to your name."

"That makes sense. Thank you for your help in clarifying some of my questions."

"You're more than welcome, and again, I'm so sorry you never received the package until recently. I hope it hasn't caused you any problems."

"It hasn't and not to worry," Michaela assured her before glancing over at Heather and rolling her eyes. "You should come by for coffee or lunch someday soon. I'd love to see you."

"That sounds like fun. But I know you're busy, so only when it's convenient for you, dear."

"Wow…" Heather murmured after Michaela disconnected the call.

The door to the basement opened, and Lana yelled down that they were home and getting ready to put groceries away before starting the cake. That was their cue to leave for the bank in hopes of retrieving the documents Brad had put in safekeeping.

*****

Damon pulled across the street and stopped. The American craftsman-styled house sat on an elevated lot, and though the yard was plain, it was well-manicured. He didn't see Michaela's car parked in front or in the driveway and checked the address again to make sure he was at the right place. He pulled the keys from the ignition and climbed out, slamming the door behind him.

Ringing the doorbell, it took only a few moments before it was opened. "Yes, can I help you?"

The elderly woman on the other side furrowed her brows. The man had black eyes and brown hair that needed trimmed and a beard that gave him a rakish appearance, like a pirate. Being tall and trim with wide shoulders, one could say he was handsome except for the fact his eyes held malice, and the way he looked at her sent chills down her spine.

"I'm looking for a friend of mine I thought lived on this block. I was hoping you could help."

Chase entered the room licking a big spoon and stopped short staring at this stranger. He paled instantly.

"Your friend's name?" Lana asked uncertainly.

"Uh, yes, it's Bryan Allen…"

She shook her head. "I'm sorry, I don't know anyone near here by that name." She started to close the door, but he spoke up.

"That's a shame." He pushed the door back with such force that it caught Lana by the shoulder, knocking her against the wall. After crossing the threshold, he kicked the door shut behind him…

CHAPTER 30

Jesus said, "Let the little children come to me and do not hinder them…"

—Matthew 19:14a

Recovering, Lana screamed, "What do you want!"

Chase stood frozen in the kitchen doorway with big, round eyes. Damon turned toward him, and Chase knew he was in trouble. Turning, he ran back into the kitchen and straight for the back door with Damon close on his heel.

Lana screamed for him to stop, but Damon ignored her. Chase tried unlocking the door but fumbled with the latch and then the knob wouldn't turn. Looking over his shoulder in fear, Damon was almost on him. Turning back, he managed to get the knob unlocked when he was grabbed by the back of his shirt and hauled backward.

"Not on your life, kid. You're our insurance policy!"

He pushed Chase in front of him and walked him toward the front door. Lana tried to grab his arm. "Let go of him now!" she yelled. Damon turned and slapped her hard enough she hit the living room wall and almost collapsed.

He bent over and whispered in Chase's ear, "You scream or draw attention to us once we're out this door, your mom's dead."

Chase stilled at the threat with large eyes and nodded his head. Once they were out the door and headed across the street to the car, he didn't look to either side.

*****

Clara headed home after leaving the church with her mind reeling from the betrayal. She knew Marc and Marissa were having an affair, but what bothered her most was finding out that Marc was actually in love with the woman. That galled her. She overheard gossip about Marissa's past and how she used men. And before she'd let Marc leave her high and dry, she'd kill 'em both.

Driving home like a crazy woman, she pulled into their narrow driveway and hit the garage door opener. It slowly eased up, and Clara pulled inside.

As she was unlocking the kitchen door, her cell rang. It was Marc. Scrunching her thin lips together, she debated if she should accept the call or not. She ignored it and went straight through to Marc's study. Opening the double doors to a dark wood-paneled room with built-in bookshelves lined with books, objets d'art, and faux plants, she stepped inside closing the doors behind her. A large fireplace dominated one wall where a couple of leather recliners were angled with a small table between the chairs. The study was masculinely decorated by none other than Heather Miles, a member of their church.

They had been so thrilled over the look of the room they hired Heather to decorate the rest of the house. And while Clara didn't much care about cooking, she did love the kitchen with its modern, dark, sleek cabinets and stainless-steel appliances.

Clara brought her hand up to her throat when she recalled how Marc criticized her for not fully using the kitchen after the remodel. But truth be told, she not only hated cooking, but she disliked most foods and always felt awful after eating a full meal. For her, the kitchen was simply another room to be tastefully decorated but not used.

A grouping of photos sat on the corner of Marc's massive desk in the study, and Clara glanced at them with a sneer. Most were photos of Marc while on a missionary pilgrimage several years back. The larger photo was of her and Marc standing together with his arm around her shoulders. She shoved it face down on the desk. Opening the center drawer, she pulled out keys to unlock the gun safe which held not only the handguns but ammunition for them both.

CHAPTER 30

Most church members would abhor the idea of owning weapons, but over the last few years, there was an influx of home invasions in their area. Fearing for their home and personal safety, Marc purchased two handguns and insisted they learn to fire them properly. She smiled to herself, with practice, the instructor told her she had a good eye and a great aim. Little did she think it would be so useful in what she had to do. She loaded one of the weapons and placed the firearm in her purse. There would only be one or two places that Marissa was likely to be, her home or at Michaela's.

*****

"Sean..."

"Yes." He looked across his desk at Tom typing a report and tried to keep his tone neutral. It was better that Tom didn't know he was talking to Michaela just yet. It wouldn't bode well and possibly get him thrown off the case.

"Chase was taken."

"What...how, when?" Tom looked up, and Sean held up his hand.

"I'm at Heather's mom's place, but Marissa and her boyfriend must have found out where we were. Heather and I left to go to the bank, and when we got back, we found Heather's mom, Lana, in tears and half frightened to death. A man barged into her home and upon seeing Chase grabbed him and left. We don't know where they've gone. I need your help?"

"I'm on my way. Just give me the address."

Sean shoved his service weapon in its holster and grabbed his keys. Tom frowned.

"A personal matter I need to tend to," Sean offered.

Tom's frowned deepened. "I hope it doesn't involve Michaela."

"Not to worry then. I'll be back before you know it."

Tom nodded but watched him as he left the room. Sean cringed, knowing Tom didn't buy it for one minute.

When he pulled up to the address Michaela gave him, she was out on the stoop and came running when he quit the engine. Before he could open the door, she was there with tears running down her face.

"You've got to find him. You've just got to!" she said almost in hysterics.

Softly touching the wound on the side of her head, he frowned. "You're hurt. Did Marissa do this?"

Michaela shrugged off his hand. "Chase has been kidnapped. You've got to find him!"

"First tell me what happened…"

"We don't have time for that now. He's been taken…don't you understand!" she cried.

He put his arms around her shoulders. "I understand, but I can't find him without more information because I won't have anything to go on." He rubbed his chin against the top of her head, enjoying the softness of her curls. When he pulled back, his shirt was wet from her tears.

Heather had come out on the stoop and ran a shaky hand through her hair.

He gently nudged Michaela toward the front door, and as they neared, he could see that Heather, too, was upset with red-rimmed eyes.

Upon entering the house, he saw Lana sitting on the recliner, leaning forward with her arms wrapped around her middle. Looking up at them, Sean saw a bruise on the side of her face.

"What exactly happened?"

Lana spoke up, "Chase and I were in the kitchen. We just finished putting cake into the oven when the doorbell rang. I opened it, and a man told me he was looking for someone in the neighborhood and thought I could help. It was a lie though. As soon as he saw Chase come out of the kitchen, he barged in. Chase ran into the kitchen, and the man went after him. He took him, and when I tried to intervene, he hit me."

"Can you describe the man?"

"I think so…"

"You can probably follow Marissa to where he's got Chase stashed," Heather spoke up.

CHAPTER 30

Sean, who had sat down on the sofa near Lana, peered up at Heather and then turned his attention to Michaela. "How did you get this?" he asked Michaela, pointing to the wound on the side of her head.

"Marissa hit me with a phone."

Sean winced and tenderly touched the wound with a caress.

"And tied her up for several hours…" Heather broke in.

"Why would she tie you up and hit you with a phone?"

"She was trying to find the package everyone seems to be looking for," Heather spoke up once again.

"She was at the bed-and-breakfast when I stopped by there at eight this morning. She said that you were fixing breakfast for the guests, and when I told her I needed to speak with you, she said that you wouldn't see me because you'd been arrested. And then I saw that your car was gone."

"She probably thought I was still tied to the desk chair in the upstairs office. She confessed to having murdered James and Brad. But what she was after is a package." Holding up a package, Michaela continued, "This one to be precise."

"What's so important about this package that everyone is trying to find it? And what has this got to do with a man breaking in and abducting Chase?"

"I think she plans on using Chase to force me into giving her this package. But what she doesn't know is that I didn't know of its existence until early this morning." She looked over at Heather.

Heather took over. "Brad planned to mail the package to Michaela in case he was murdered. Only the package was lost behind a file cabinet and wasn't discovered until a few months ago. It was shipped to the B&B on a day I was watching the place but was called into work. On my way out the door, the postman asked if I would sign for it just after I locked up. Being rushed back to work, I just took it with me. Unfortunately, the couple I was working with were upset when I arrived at the office, and I slid the package into the back of the top desk drawer. Over the course of the day, it completely escaped my mind, and I neglected to give it to Michaela. While we were talking in the wee hours of the morning, it hit me just as plain as day. The package everyone is looking for is the one I accepted and signed for."

Sean inhaled deeply. Opening the envelope, he pulled out the file and leafed through it. Some pretty important names flashed before his eyes.

"Why would Marissa murder James?" he asked, looking up.

"Because he caught her snooping in my bedroom looking for this…there's more to this story, and I want to provide you with details, but for now, my son has been kidnapped and is missing. If anything happens to him, I'll simply die!" Tears threatened again.

"We'll find him. Let me call the squad room and get Tom out here. We'll need a description of the suspect and everything the three of you know. Understood?" he asked, looking at all three women. Each nodded.

Once Tom arrived, Sean went out to talk with him before they both entered the house.

"Before you say anything, I have evidence that proves Michaela is innocent," Sean spoke up as soon as Tom opened the car door.

With his hand resting on the top of the door, Sean handed the envelope to Tom. "You need to look at this, but more importantly, we need to put a BOLO out for Michaela's son. He was kidnapped."

"What?" Tom took the envelope from Sean but didn't open it. "When?"

"About two hours ago from what I can surmise. Marissa and her boyfriend have taken him as leverage to get this package." Sean pointed to the envelope that Tom held. "They thought Michaela had it in her possession, but she didn't know it existed until this morning." Sean pulled the door open so Tom could exit.

As they walked up to the house, Sean continued, "I have a vague description of the boyfriend and the car. I've already sent officers over to Marissa's place to see if they are holed up there." Wiping his hand across his brow, he sighed heavily. "They weren't, but I really didn't expect it to be that easy."

Tom nodded. "Marissa…" He shook his head. "I'm getting too old for this crap!"

CHAPTER 31

And he that stealeth a man and selleth him or if he be found in his hand, he shall surely be put to death.

—Exodus 21:16

Chase was shoved into a small room with nothing more than a bed and nightstand. The place was dirty with smudge marks on the walls and dirty curtains that were torn and barely hanging on the rod above the window. As he stumbled forward, he could hear the door being locked behind him. Turning, he tried the knob, but it wouldn't budge, and he began pummeling the door with his fists, yelling to be released.

It didn't take long for his fists to hurt and his voice to become hoarse. And still no one opened the door, instead the volume on the TV was turned up to drown out the noise he made. In resignation, he flopped on the edge of the single wide bed where the rumpled and dirty cover was half off the bed, exposing dirty sheets and a grimy pillow. The room itself was awful and smelled of urine. Peering down at his swollen and reddened fists, he was more determined than ever to find a means of escape; beyond being scared, he was getting mad.

*****

Clara pulled up in front of Marissa's bungalow but didn't see her car parked in the driveway. That meant only one thing; she was at Michaela's. Putting the car into drive, she sped off in the direction of the B&B.

The more Clara thought about the affair, the angrier she got. Her lips thinned, her heart raced, and heat flooded her cheeks to think of the infidelity Marc and Marissa wreaked not only on her but that of the church family.

She eased up on the accelerator and parked in front of the house next to the bed-and-breakfast. Seeing Marissa's car parked in the lot, she unclasped her seat belt and reached for her purse when Marissa came out. Clara ducked down and spied on her over the dashboard.

Wiping tears from her cheeks, Marissa climbed into her car. Inserting the key into the ignition, she didn't turn it over but simply sat hunched over in the front seat. She didn't know if she could live without Marc in her life. But she had to; she'd confessed to Michaela that she not only had a hand in killing Brad but that she purposely murdered James. Damon had called to tell her that he had Michaela's son and he was headed to their undisclosed location, a small run-down house that no one knew anything about. Damon had rented the place a year earlier in as-is condition.

It hadn't been their plan to abduct Chase, but having him would force Michaela to exchange the package for her son. But then what? They couldn't let Michaela go. And what of Chase, take him with them? She put the car into reverse and backed out of the parking space and then shoved the gear into drive. Stopping at the entrance, she looked to the left and then pulled out onto the road.

Clara raised back up in her seat as Marissa pulled out. Turning the key in the ignition, she put the car into drive and followed her at a distance.

Parking a few houses away, Clara watched as Marissa turned into a driveway and pulled into a garage. When she got out, she closed the garage door before heading around front. The door was opened by a man.

Clara's eyes narrowed. Just like the whore; go from one man to the next and after Marc declared his love for her. She wanted to get out of the car immediately and shoot them both. Then she visualized the news broadcast. "A man and woman shot to death by an unknown perpetrator." Clara smiled, thinking how Marc would take the news. The smile slowly vanished. If he ever found out she was behind the shootings, he'd never forgive her, but did she even want his forgiveness?

*****

Chase recalled seeing the man who abducted him before, but where? And then he realized, he'd seen him with Aunt Marissa. One evening while staying with her, she had a knock on the door, and when she opened it, he caught a glimpse of the man on the other side. Aunt Marissa turned and said she'd be right back and stepped out on the stoop, closing the door behind her.

Piqued by his curiosity, he spied on them through the sheer curtains. They talked in low voices, and then they kissed. That was enough for him to stop spying.

The volume on the TV was suddenly turned down. Chase leaned toward the door and now could hear voices. Someone had come to the house. Jumping from the bed, he began pummeling the bedroom door with his fists again in hopes of being rescued. But whoever it was, they weren't here to rescue him.

Listening closely with his ear pushed against the door, he realized the other voice he heard was Aunt Marissa. His mom was right, she was not to be trusted, but why did they kidnap him?

The light coming through the small window behind the nightstand gave Chase another idea. Maybe, he could escape through the window. He picked up the lamp and set it on the floor and moved the stand being as quiet as possible. Once he had access to the window, he pushed the sheers aside…

*****

"Did he recognize you?"

"I think he did, but I put the fear of God in him." Damon pulled a beer from the fridge and tapped the bottle against the edge of the counter, popping the lid off, letting it fall to the floor. He pulled a long drink before turning to Marissa.

"I don't want him hurt," she said with determination. "He's simply leverage, and that's all."

"Yeah? And what about the fact the kid can identify me?"

"Get real, he probably only got a glimpse of you since, as you said, you put the fear of God in him."

"Well, you're not the one who's taking chances now, are you?" He smirked, raising a brow.

"And what does that mean?"

"It means you put the kid in jeopardy. Besides, Michaela can identify you…she hands over what we're looking for and you release the kid. She talks. It's obvious, both have to be dealt with."

"No! You can do what you want to Michaela, but you don't touch Chase!"

"What is the kid to you anyway? And why the hell are your eyes red. It looks like you've been crying…"

"Get real, Damon, I haven't been crying. It's merely allergies. Like I told you before, Chase has been in my life since he was born, and I've come to love him like he's my own." Marissa threw her long hair back over her shoulder.

Damon took his beer and headed to the living area, and he turned up the volume on the TV. Following him, she sat down heavily on the sofa. "We have to talk this through."

Damon took another swig and set the bottle down on the small wooden coffee table. He turned to Marissa and tilted her face up to meet his. He kissed her, and she found herself responding even though she was upset. Shifting back to look at her, he suggested they make use of the other bedroom.

Standing, he put out his hand and pulled her up off the sofa and turned toward the other bedroom. Once inside, he kicked the door shut and started pulling his clothes off, letting them land in a heap on the floor. Marissa wasn't in the mood. All she could think of was Marc and the intimacy they shared each week. For the past few months, their weekly rendezvous simply wasn't enough time together. She missed how Marc gently caressed her body and how he made love to her as if he revered her.

She tilted her head forward, and Damon kissed her nape, and she closed her eyes, pretending it was Marc. As Damon's hands came around to knead her soft flesh, she moaned, and before long, she was disrobed and lying beneath him.

CHAPTER 32

Two are better than one, because they have a good return for their labor.

—Ecclesiastes 4:9

Back at the precinct, Sean and Lana met with Darnell Madsen, a young graphic artist that was an ace in using the facial composition software to recreate the face of the boyfriend. Once they were through, Sean hoped the perp would be in the FBI database.

Thank God Sanders owed him a big favor. Resources at the precinct were slim, and they were lucky they could get Darnell to work with the police for the entire county. But having an ace up his sleeve, Sean knew he could call on Sanders who worked at Quantico to see if the boyfriend was in their database and hopefully obtain his address or last known address if it come to that.

Time was of the essence. He had no idea if Chase was in danger or not. Michaela told him that she didn't think Marissa would actually harm him. She had no idea that Marissa was even seeing anyone, but then she wasn't aware how much Marissa hated her either. It pained him to see Michaela so broken. She was under investigation for murder, arrested, interrogated for hours, tied up, threatened, her son taken, and now betrayed by someone she'd trusted. And yet she was resilient. He admired her all the more.

It took about an hour for Darnell to create a graphic composite of Marissa's boyfriend when Lana exclaimed, "It's him!"

Sean picked up the phone and called Sanders immediately. He'd known Sanders from high school when they were both on the football team. They'd hung out and upon graduation attended the same college. But Sean ended up meeting Sheila and fell in love, and the rest as they say was history. He decided to go into the police academy while Sanders went into the FBI. He still envied Sanders for his decision. Through the years, their communication with one another had grown further apart, mostly due to Sanders getting married and now having a family with three young daughters whom he adored.

"Ryan, I know this isn't a friendly call to ask about the weather or family, so what's up…and, yes, I think we're about caught up on favors!" Sanders laughed.

Sanders referred to a prior case. As a relatively new agent at the time, they had a suspect who practically ended up on Ryan's doorstep. In actuality, the suspect had been pulled over because his registration had expired. Running the plate indicated the car had been stolen, and the guy ended up in jail. It really wasn't a favor, but Sanders was elated that he'd been picked up and arrested but was appreciative that Ryan handed him over without making a big deal over jurisdiction.

"I hate to cut to the chase, but a boy has been kidnapped. I'm sending over a face composite and hope you can identify the perp for me. I know I'm asking a lot, but this case is personal."

Sitting up straighter at his desk, Sanders replied, "Send it over. Might I ask how personal?"

"Very…"

"I'll see what I can do and get back to you as soon as I have something!"

CHAPTER 33

Keep me from the snares which they have laid for me and the gins of the workers of iniquity.

—Psalm 141:9

Slowly easing the window up, it screeched, and Chase paled. Peering over his shoulder at the door, he waited, but nothing happened. Maybe, they didn't hear it. Pushing the window up further, it screeched again, and he held his breath. Perspiration dotted his forehead, and under his breath, he swore. Glad that his mom wasn't around to hear the profanity, he attempted to push the window up further. While it was still stiff, it made no further noise.

He punched against the screen, and it popped off easily, landing on its edge against the fence. He peered out looking both ways. Sitting on the window ledge, he swung his legs over and pushed himself off to land lightly on his feet.

He dropped to his haunches and looked around. Bent from the waist, he walked toward the front to see if he should make his escape that way. Seeing how open it was with little landscaping, he turned around to see what the backyard looked like. Lots of overgrown plants and trees would help shield him. Hunched over, he made a run for the back gate, hoping it led to an alley.

Unlatching the gate, it made the ringing sound of metal against metal that gave Chase pause. Looking over his shoulder, he didn't see anything and hoped the TV was loud enough from inside the house to drown out the sound of the gate. As he slid the gate latch home from the alley, he took one more glance at the back of the house.

While the back door was obscured with bushes, some of the windows were not. He hoped that neither Aunt Marissa nor her boyfriend saw him.

He didn't know where he was. The man didn't blindfold him, but he did tell Chase to get down in the seat and stay down until they reached their destination. But what part of town, Chase was clueless except that it did take some time before they got here. The house didn't belong to Aunt Marissa, so he assumed it might belong to that boyfriend of hers.

*****

Watching the house for about ten minutes, Clara decided it was time. She pulled the gun from her purse and started to open her car door when she saw a side window slide up on the side of the house, then the screen was pushed outward, and a boy crawled through the opening. She hesitated and then gasped. That was McCrea's kid. What was he doing here?

When he hunched over and ran toward the back of the house, she sat stunned. She didn't see Chase with Marissa when she left the B&B. Was he here alone? She couldn't fathom what was going on. But with Chase out of harm's way, she could make her move. Still, she hesitated. Her cell rang again, and Marc's photo came up.

"Hi," she answered after the fifth ring.

"Where are you, Clara? I tried the landline before trying your cell, but you never picked up."

Taking a long, shaky breath, she replied, "I'm getting ready to make atonement for your sins."

"What? What are you talking about?"

*****

Marissa slowly eased out of the bed and stood. Bending over, she retrieved her clothes and slipped them on. "I'm going to check on Chase…"

Damon plumped the pillow under his head and watched Marissa dress. "You do that…" he said, closing his eyes to take a nap.

Marissa sneered. Damon was good in bed, and she enjoyed having sex with him, but that's where it ended. For now, he was merely a means to an end.

Putting an ear up to the door, Marissa couldn't hear any sounds coming from within. She figured Chase would be exhausted and asleep after all the yelling to release him. But when she opened the door and peeked in, Chase wasn't in bed. Stepping further into the room, she peered behind the door before turning and seeing the lamp on the floor and the window opened. Looking out, she peered both ways. Chase was gone.

"Damon!" she yelled. "He's gone. The bedroom window is open, and he crawled out."

Damon jumped out of bed and slipped his pants on before joining Marissa. "That little bastard! I wonder how long he's been gone."

Marissa looked at him. "How long do you think we were in the bedroom?"

"Maybe, half an hour?"

"Then he couldn't have gotten far because I doubt that he's been gone long. You better board up this window so when we find him, he can't escape again."

"I saw some wood lying out back," Damon said, leaving the room.

Making quick work in nailing the board across the window at an angle, Damon was quickly losing his patience with the boy. The incessant shouting already pissed him off, but now having escaped, he was more than pissed. When he got his hands on the kid, he was going to smack him good. With the task completed, he threw down the makeshift hammer having used nails that were already in the board. He pulled out his keys and jumped into his car.

Marissa ran out. "Where are you going?" she yelled.

"To find the little bastard," he shot back.

"I'm sure he didn't get far. I'm going to take a look around the neighborhood."

"You do that!" Damon shouted, throwing the car into reverse and peeling out.

*****

"Marissa. I can guarantee you'll never see her again…" Clara hung up before Marc could reply.

Once again, as she was getting ready to exit the car, the man she'd seen open the door earlier came barreling out of the house and proceeded to nail up a board across the very window Chase crawled through.

Clara sat perplexed. She was more upset than ever that Marc would declare his love for this woman and then she would drive over to the other side of town to meet up with another man. Marissa came barging out of the house next when the man got into his car. Words were exchanged although she couldn't make out what was said.

As the man pulled out of the driveway, Marissa headed for the sidewalk in the opposite direction, passing by Clara's car. She quickly hunched over in the driver's seat, hoping Marissa wouldn't spot her.

*****

Running toward the end of the alley where it met the side street, dogs started barking with a few hitting the back fence of their respective yards, growling in displeasure. Chase kept stopping and diving into recesses along the way before proceeding to the end of the alley. Each time, he looked over his shoulder in fear of being caught. So far, the coast was clear.

He stopped to catch his breath, trying to see a street sign. Maybe, he could knock on someone's door and ask for help or better yet if he could use their phone so he could call his mom. He still couldn't believe that Aunt Marissa would do this! What was she hiding and why did he and his mom have to sneak out in the middle of the night? He gulped and fought back tears that threatened. No way was he going to cry.

Taking off down the side street, he continued until it connected to Peach Street. But he didn't know where Peach Street was either. He stopped and sunk down on his haunches, his heart pounding against his rib cage. He took a big gulp of air and then swallowed hard.

Hearing a car speeding by on the street behind him, he looked up to see a red Chevy Camaro shoot by. It was the same car that he was forced into. Terrified, he flew into some bushes to hide. A few minutes passed, but he didn't see the car returning. Maybe, they didn't even know he was gone yet.

"Just what do you think you're doing?" a voice behind him rang out.

Chase jumped at the sound and turned to look right into the eyes of a woman with curlers in her hair and arms resting upon her hips. She jutted out a foot and then raised a finger at him. "Get out of my bushes this instant!"

Standing, he stepped out onto the manicured lawn. "Where are your parents, young man? Didn't they teach you anything at all?" She hissed. "If you were my son, I'd be taking a good strap to your backside!"

"I need your help!" Chase interjected. "I was kidnapped and held in a room. I need to call my mom to let her know I'm all right and have her pick me up…"

"What? Don't give me a line like that!" She shook her head and eyed him menacingly.

"Really, please, can I just use your phone to call my mom, please!"

"Get out of here!" she yelled, pointing to the street.

Chase turned and ran; looking back over his shoulder, she continued to watch him, shaking her head.

He almost tripped over a rise in the sidewalk but caught himself. He needed to find someone to help him. Turning the corner, he pulled up to catch his breath, and before he realized what was happening, arms were wrapped around his shoulders. He looked up into the eyes of his aunt.

CHAPTER 34

Would not God discover this? For he knows the secrets of the heart.

—Psalm 44:21

Taking big gulps of breath herself, Marissa shook her head. "I can't let you go, sweetie."

"Don't call me sweetie!" Chase yelled, trying to throw her arms off his shoulders. "Why did you have your boyfriend kidnap me?"

"I'm sorry, Chase, but you have to come with me. And believe me, I'm much gentler than Damon. He's really pissed off and took the car to find you. I figured you couldn't have gotten far. I'm the only one that stands between you and him, so let's go and minimize the damages." She nudged Chase forward and took him by the upper arm.

Chase pulled his arm out of her grasp and gave her a dirty look. "Mom was right, you can't be trusted!" he shouted.

"Fuck your mom!"

"What? You can't say that. I hate you!"

"Chase, stop this instant. I've never taken a hand to you, but I will if I have to. Do you understand?"

"I hate you!" he shouted again.

"Yeah, that's a little redundant, don't you think?" Marissa reached out and grasped his upper arm again with more strength and pushed him forward.

He wanted to cry but wouldn't let Aunt Marissa take pleasure in knowing she was frightening him. As soon as they were back in the house, Marissa shoved him into the same room he was locked into before. The window he escaped from now had a board nailed across it. She pushed Chase onto the bed and then took out her cell phone.

"I got him."

"Where the hell was he?"

"He was in the neighborhood just as I figured. Maybe, next time you'll cool your heels and we'll be more alert, if you know what I mean."

"Don't give me shit, Marissa. I'm on my way back. When I get there, it's time to call Michaela..."

*****

When the cell rang, Marissa's photo and name came up. Having left her own device behind at the B&B, their only hope was that Marissa would call Heather's cell. Michaela looked up at Detective Hanson and held the cell up so he could see. He nodded, indicating she answer.

"Marissa..." She held Detective Hanson's eyes.

"I guess you know by now that I have your son. We want the package."

Michaela hedged as Tom had instructed which went against her instincts to just hand over the package immediately so she could have Chase. "What package? You still haven't told me what the hell you're talking about, Marissa!"

"Oh, give me a break. This is getting old even for you. Let me break this down. You hand over the package or I won't be able to stop Damon from hurting him. Got it?"

Michaela who had turned her cell to speaker peered over at Tom with worry etching her brows. He nodded again, indicating everything was going as expected. "I understand, and I would gladly hand over a package if I had it. But I don't. You have to believe me!"

The line went dead, and Michaela folded. "Oh god...oh god..."

Tom placed a hand on her shoulder. "They know that if they did anything to Chase, they would lose their leverage. They won't harm him!"

CHAPTER 34

"But what about the boyfriend? We don't know what he's capable of!" Michaela exclaimed.

Lana brought her a cup of hot tea and sat down beside her. "It's going to be all right. These detectives know what they're doing," she said gently, rubbing Michaela's upper arm.

"I have confidence in both Detective Hanson and especially Sean," Heather added. Looking over at Detective Hanson, she continued, "You're both fully capable, it's just that Sean would put himself in harm's way to see that nothing happens to Chase because he's in love with Michaela."

Tom nodded. "I know..."

The cell rang again, and they all stopped talking. She answered, putting it on speaker so Detective Hanson could hear. "Marissa..."

"Leave the package at the park, and you know to which park I'm referring. Place it in the receptacle near the bathrooms at one o'clock this afternoon. If it's not there, we'll be leaving the country and you'll never see Chase again. I hope I've made myself clear."

"Marissa..." But the line went dead again. She sagged against Lana before lifting tear-swollen eyes to Detective Hanson.

"It's okay. We expected a demand for an exchange. We're on target," he added, nodding his head. "It's going to be okay. You have to trust us. Where's the drop off?"

"It's at the community park I used to take Chase to when we lived on Sutton Road."

Tom punched in numbers on his cell. "We have a drop-off location for the exchange," he said without preamble.

"Good, I also have news. It looks like we have the address for the boyfriend. His name is Damon Young. I'll text the address. Right now, we're forming a SWAT team and making plans."

"That's even better!" Tom clicked off. "We know who the boyfriend is and we have his address. Do you recall a Damon Young?"

Michaela shook her head. "Like I say, I wasn't even aware that Marissa was seeing anyone."

Tom made a move to stand when Michaela cried out, "Where are you going?"

"I'm heading out to meet with Sean. They're putting a SWAT team in place, and we'll get your boy."

"I want to go!"

"I'm sorry, Mrs. McCrea, it's dangerous, and the fewer civilians, the better. Don't worry though, everything is under control, and we'll have your boy back before the day is out."

"I have to go, please, Detective Hanson…"

Lana placed an arm around Michaela's shoulders and slightly squeezed. Heather sat down on the other side of her and patted her leg.

"Michaela, I think Detective Hanson is right. If you're there, I think you'd be a distraction, certainly for Sean, and he'll need to focus on getting Chase back," Heather coaxed.

"What about the drop-off location?" Michaela asked.

"I think it's going to be a moot point, but don't worry. I have to go…"

CHAPTER 35

Do not repay evil with evil or insult with insult.

—1 Peter 3:9a

When Marc's photo showed up again on Clara's cell, she avoided answering. She'd deal with him next. She waited for Marissa to return to the house, figuring that she was looking for Chase. She was rewarded when fifteen minutes later, she saw Marissa return with her hand on Chase's upper arm. Both looked unhappy.

If she approached the house now, Chase would be in harm's way. As she was debating what to do, the man returned, turning into the driveway at break-neck speed, tires screeching. He got out and slammed the car door before making his way into the house.

And still Clara sat waiting. She hoped to catch Marissa alone, but obviously, that wasn't going to happen. Contemplating what to do next, she decided it might be best to simply wait. She had originally gone to Marissa's home to catch her alone and confront her before shooting the bitch. Now she was on a merry-goose chase following her to parts of town she'd rather not be in. And here she sat, wondering when Marissa would leave.

*****

With an address in hand of one Damon Young, Sean and Tom were on their way with a SWAT team. The last couple of hours had been harried with preparations in storming Young's property. They had to work swiftly and figure out exactly where Chase was within the home to ensure his safety.

The small house was rundown and in need of repair. The lawn was dead, and trash strewn about the place. Sean shook his head. If Marissa and the boyfriend were both involved in the black market, why was Damon living in a shack?

With men stationed and ready to fire, if need be, they sent a couple of SWAT team members to canvas the house. One of the officers crept along the back wall, peering into windows while the other went around to the side of the house.

Chase sat up on the edge of the bed when he heard shuffling on the other side of the boarded-up window. Peering out between the boards and the bottom of the window, he saw movement and jumped back.

*****

Clara was dumbfounded when police cars started showing up and angling their vehicles toward the house she was watching. She immediately hunkered down in the car to keep from being seen. Other patrol cars cordoned off the street to keep civilians out. What was going on? It wasn't long before one of the officers pulled out a bullhorn.

*****

"The next time that kid even attempts an escape, I might strangle the little bastard!" Damon said before taking a gulp of beer.

"He won't be escaping, you boarded up the window, and we have given Michaela a drop-off location to make the exchange."

"Except that's not what's going to happen. You'll be staying here with Chase, and I'll be meeting Michaela. How would you like it done?" he teased, running a finger down her cleavage. "If only you could watch, huh?"

Marissa closed her eyes. "I really don't care how. I just want her gone. But I am curious," she said, lifting her head to look into his eyes. "What's your favorite way?"

"I always fantasized tying the person up tightly and then…" He stopped short. "Before meeting you, I always thought it'd be fun to have my way with them before finally strangling them in the midst of the act while I'm still inside."

"That's disgusting, Damon, even for you!" Marissa turned away from him and walked over to the front window. "What the…" Turning, she looked over at Damon. "The police…"

"What?" Damon looked up from the TV and dropped the remote he'd picked up onto the coffee table. Peering out the front window, he spat; "shit!"

"There are police out front. How'd they find out where we were? What are we going to do?" she screamed, losing complete composure as she turned from the window and sat down heavily on the couch.

Sean and Tom stood behind one of the police cars, talking with the hostage negotiator. Sean was sweating bullets, and though both had donned bullet proof vests, he still was worried they might not get Chase out of harm's way. It would kill Michaela if anything happened to Chase, and he felt directly responsible for his welfare.

The hostage negotiator pulled out a bullhorn. "This is the police. Release your hostage and come out with your hands raised. You are surrounded!"

"No way," Damon announced, looking over his shoulder at Marissa. "We have the kid for leverage, they won't be coming in with guns blasting for fear the kid will get hit."

"Damon, this can't be happening. I won't have Chase in the line of fire!" Marissa wrung her hands and for the first time wondered how solid their plans were.

"Get the kid," he ordered.

"No!" Marissa stood with hands fisted.

"This is the police. Release Chase McCrea and come out with your hands up."

"If you don't get him, I will!" Damon turned from the window and pulled a revolver from the waistband of his pants.

"No, you won't harm him!" Marissa screamed.

Damon pushed her out of his way, and Marissa stumbled back onto the couch. She reached out and grabbed his leg. "No!"

Damon slapped her hand away. "Look, it's either us or the kid! Be reasonable, and don't let your feelings for the kid cloud your judgement."

Marissa jumped up from the couch and grabbed her purse that was lying on the coffee table. She pulled out a handgun and aimed it at Damon.

"Stop," she ordered.

He partially turned to look at her. "You won't shoot me, Marissa. We have plans. We'll be rich, and the original files will be recovered. It's simple. We get rid of Michaela, and there will be no one to testify against us."

"You fool!" she spat. "We'll be running from the police for the rest of our lives after kidnapping Chase. Even if we use him for leverage to get out of this mess, it won't end well for us. Besides, Michaela isn't the only witness, what of Heather and her mother for Christ's sake!"

*****

Chase stood back with his heart pounding when he saw a man peering in. He jumped and almost yelled. The officer saw movement and hastily stepped to the side and hunkered down. Holding his weapon, he quickly stood, stepped in front of the window, ready to fire.

*****

"Damon, I told you from the beginning that Chase is not to be hurt. The circumstances have changed. We never bargained for the police to find us. We were supposed to use him to get Michaela to hand over the files. That's all!"

"And before we do that, we'll also use him to get out of this mess. They either leave or we slit his damn throat. They won't take any chances of that happening."

"Not happening…" She pulled back the trigger.

*****

Instantly, the officer saw it was child, the boy they were trying to rescue, and not one of the suspects. He lowered his weapon, and stepping closer to the window, he pointed to his badge. Chase sagged with relief and stepped up to the window.

The officer motioned for him to step away and then, reaching up, pulled at the board covering the window. It wasn't nailed well and was haphazardly put in place to keep the kid inside. It wouldn't take much effort to pry it off with a good yank.

It came off swiftly. Pushing up on the pane, the window didn't budge. The officer motioned Chase closer, and he pointed to the top of the pane. Chase looked up and saw it was locked, so he reached up to unlocked it. Together, they pushed the window upward so Chase could escape.

*****

Angered now, Damon made a lunge for the gun, and the two scuffled before falling to the floor. The gun went off, and blew a hole through the door to the bedroom where Chase was being held. They both froze.

Damon jumped up and threw open the door. Marissa reached over and grabbed the gun that had fallen to the floor and aimed it at Damon. "Is he all right?" she asked calmly.

He turned swiftly back to Marissa. "He's not—"

She fired, and Damon went down like a sack of potatoes, clutching his chest. He looked up at Marissa in shock. She dropped the weapon and started to step over him to check on Chase for herself, but he grabbed her ankle with more strength than she expected. Looking down, she kicked at him, and his hand fell away. "You shot me!"

"Damn straight!"

*****

Pushing open her car door, Clara got out but left the door ajar so as not to bring attention to herself. After hearing gunfire, everyone's attention was diverted to the house, and Clara made her way to the other side, walking behind patrol cars.

Everyone was focused on the front door, making it easy for Clara to slide through without being noticed.

*****

Marissa opened the door, hoping to God that Chase wasn't hurt when the gun went off. Stepping into the room, she saw the window open and the board missing. She almost collapsed in relief but also despair. With no bargaining power, no hostage, and no partner, there was nothing else to do but surrender, but she wasn't going to go down easy.

*****

Hearing gunfire, the police stilled, turning their attention to the front of the house. Sean whispered, "Oh god, no!"

And then one of the SWAT officers appeared at the corner of the house escorting Chase. They motioned for him to get down, and both the officer and Chase hunkered down in place.

Sean started toward them when Marissa opened the front door with her hands held up. Sean hit the ground for cover.

"Shooter!" someone rang out. And from the corner of his eye, Sean saw another woman approaching the front of the house with a weapon drawn and aimed at Marissa.

Fire broke out, and the woman hit the ground hard with the revolver going off as she fell forward. The gun flew out of her grasp, coming to land about 3 feet away from where she laid.

CHAPTER 35

Marissa fell back against the doorjamb, blood seeping from her left shoulder.

Several police ran toward the other woman, and kneeling beside her, one shook his head after placing fingers to her neck. Seeing the woman down and Marissa hit, Sean jumped up and ran toward Chase and the officer waiting at the corner of the house.

While everyone's attention was still drawn to the woman who open fired, another crack of gun fire echoed, and Marissa dropped the gun that she held in her hand.

For a mere second, time held suspended, and Tom saw Sean go down, hitting the ground hard. He ran toward his partner.

Tom was the first to reach him while other officers ran to apprehend Marissa and kick the weapon away from her reach. Sean peered up at Tom in pain and whispered, "How?"

Everything happened so fast, but Tom managed to see Marissa fire on Sean while everyone's attention was momentarily diverted to the other woman. He wasn't able to react fast enough but was glad that he didn't have to fire down on Marissa. At least the bullet she'd taken came from the other woman and not the police.

Chase wiggled away from the officer and ran to Sean's side. "Sean, Sean," he cried, getting down on his knees beside him, tears pouring down his cheeks.

Tom wrapped his arms around Chase. "He'll be fine, don't worry. It looks like it's a clean shot."

Marissa was handcuffed though she was shot in the shoulder, and an ambulance team put her on a gurney and rolled her to a waiting ambulance. Other paramedics ran to Sean and started administering first aid before placing him on a gurney.

"It looks like he'll make a full recovery," one of the paramedics said, looking at Tom.

Tom nodded as he and Chase stood. The paramedic placed his hand on Chase's shoulder. "He'll be okay, son."

After getting Sean into the ambulance, they fired up the sirens and took off.

CHAPTER 36

For I will restore health unto thee, and I will heal thee of thy wounds, saith the Lord;

—Jeremiah 30:17a

The beeping noise was constant. It was grating on his nerves, the constant beep.

Beep. Beep. Beep.

Sean stirred and slowly opened his eyes as the noise penetrated into the very fiber of his being. His eyes swept the ceiling, and he turned his head to see the beeping noise was coming from a machine next to his bed, monitoring his heartbeat. He was in the hospital?

He turned his head, and his eyes landed on Michaela curled up in a chair beside the bed. She was asleep. What was she doing here? Then thoughts came flooding back as he recalled what happened.

A nurse walked by the open door but didn't stop. He felt lethargic. He tried lifting an arm but felt the confines of the tubes taped to his arm. Michaela stirred, but she didn't wake.

Sean's eyes traveled back to her, admiring her soft curls that were tousled from sleeping. Her full lips were slightly parted, and she breathed deeply. A crash out in the corridor jarred her awake instantly. She sat up and then looked over at Sean, and seeing him awake, she smiled and stood.

"Hey, there...how are you feeling? How long have you been awake?" She rubbed the back of his hand with her palm.

"I'm groggy and feeling out of sorts. When can I leave?" he asked gruffly.

"Leave? I don't think that will be happening today."

"Hell, how long have I been here?"

"Three days…"

"Three!"

"I'm afraid so. Are you in pain?"

"No…yes… I don't know!" He looked around the room with furrowed brows before his eyes came back and connected with hers. "How long have you been here?"

"I've been back and forth trying to spend as much time here as possible. Chase is worried sick about you." Her eyes took on a shimmer, and her bottom lip trembled.

He felt like an ass. He tried raising his arm up again, making it further this time. She took his hand in hers and brought it up to caress the back with soft, full lips.

"Michaela…"

"Shhh, you need to rest. We have time to talk once you're released," she said softly.

The nurse walked in. "I see you're finally awake. We thought you were going to sleep right straight through Halloween." She pulled the covers down far enough to expose his arm. She placed two fingers to the inside of his wrist to take his pulse and raised her arm up to watch the time. He started to say something, but she quickly shushed him.

That irritated him even more. "Okay, big guy, let's take your vitals, and I'll call the doctor in."

Michaela smiled softly at him. "I'll be back…" she promised and turned to leave.

He wanted to tell her to wait. Instead, he turned to the nurse. "I'd like my fiancée to stay."

The nurse merely eyed him and nodded. "As soon as I take your vitals and the doctor sees you."

As Michaela turned into the hospital corridor, she overheard Sean and halted. Leaning against the wall, she finally let the tears fall. Was it true? Did he really want to marry her? She sat down heavily on the bench nearby and watched as doctors and nurses rushed past. She closed her eyes and leaned back against the wall when someone tapped her on the shoulder. Looking up, one of the nurses asked her if she was okay.

She nodded. "I'm more than okay… I'm engaged!"

The nurse laughed and congratulated her before rushing off.

An elderly couple rushed down the corridor and stopped by the door to Sean's room. The woman entered only to be asked to leave by the nurse tending Sean.

"Mom!" Sean's baritone voice sounded from within the room, and Michaela's head snapped back to the older couple.

This was Sean's parents? She could see Sean's eyes in the older woman, and he resembled his dad a great deal. She hoped she would get to meet them, and the joy that filled her moments ago subsided. What if they didn't like her?

"Mom!" Michaela's head whipped back in the opposite direction, seeing Heather trying to hold onto Chase. She jumped up, and Chase ran into her arms.

"Is Sean going to be all right?" he asked.

"Yes, yes he is!" Michaela assured him.

"I'm sorry, do you know our son?" The older woman approached Michaela while studying Chase.

"Yes…"

"Oh yeah, we were worried sick about him, but he came to my rescue when I was kidnapped. I hope he's not mad at me for getting shot!" Chase interrupted with his thoughts pouring out.

"Oh…" The older woman's eyes snapped back to Michaela, and she studied her for a moment before speaking again. "It must have been awful for you having your son abducted!"

"Emma, the nurse said we can go in now." Sean's dad had approached, placing his hand at her waist to steer her back to Sean's room, and they both disappeared inside.

"Mom, I want to see Sean."

"Maybe, tomorrow, sweetie. For now, I think we need to head home, and I promise that you'll get to see him soon."

Heather watched the older couple as they entered the hospital room and then turning to Michaela raised her brows before saying, "Come on, you two. I promised Chase we'd go get ice cream…"

CHAPTER 37

Come, let us take our fill of love until the morning.
Let us solace ourselves with loves.

—Proverbs 7:18

"You look awful, dear," Emma spoke up upon entering Sean's room. "I was so worried when I got the phone call that you'd been shot and was in the hospital." Leaning over the bed, she gave Sean a warm kiss upon his brow and patted his cheek.

He felt just like a kid again but was glad to see his parents. They were constantly traveling these days, and he knew they were vacationing in Europe and hearing word of his hospitalization canceled their plans to come straight home.

"The nurse said something about I should be released tomorrow or the next day. Did you see a woman in the corridor?" he anxiously asked.

"You mean the one with the little boy?"

"Yes, I'd like for you both to meet her."

"She left son," his dad spoke up. "From what we can deduce, you were shot rescuing her little boy. What kind of mother isn't watching over her child so that he's abducted anyway?" He harrumphed.

"She didn't let him get abducted, Dad. He was taken from her, and there's a lot more to the story." Sean shot back.

His dad paused and looked earnestly at him before responding, "You've fallen for her?"

"Oh, honey, remember Sheila..." His mom warned before sitting in the chair that Michaela vacated just moments ago.

"Mom, I think I recall Sheila. I was married to her after all." Sean tried sitting up in bed, and his mom jumped up, placing her hand upon his shoulder.

"Please, lay back, dear. You've been shot and need your rest."

"I've been resting, and according to Michaela, I've already been in the hospital for three days. I've rested enough, and I want to leave. The little boy with Michaela, how was he?" He looked at his dad with intensity.

"The boy seemed fine enough."

Sean eased back down in the bed and sighed.

"When is Halloween?" he asked impulsively.

"Halloween...aren't you a little too old to think about trick-or-treating?" His mom smiled and winked at him.

"Day after tomorrow;" his dad piped up.

*****

The next few days went by in a flurry with Sean being released from the hospital. His parents took his convalescence as a means to get him to temporarily move back home with them. Sean, still weak and tired, gave in to their demands though he would have preferred to go home to his condo.

The second of November, he managed to finally put in a call to Michaela. He was disappointed that she never returned to the hospital or tried to find out where he was, but then she had her hands full. Chase was no doubt still reeling from the ordeal of being kidnapped by his aunt and her boyfriend. Michaela would still have guests checking in that had reservations and trying to keep all the balls in the air. Not to mention, she herself had gone through a lot. And today was Marissa's arraignment hearing. He didn't know if Michaela planned to be in court or not. He hoped to hell that Marissa wouldn't be dismissed on bail.

With cell in hand, he called Michaela with his heart pounding. He didn't want her to think he up and abandoned them.

"Hello..."

CHAPTER 37

"Hi!" He hesitated and felt like a teenager again; he didn't know what to say so he asked about Chase. "How's Chase?"

"He's as fine as can be expected. He hasn't let me out of his sight."

"It will take time. He went through an ordeal."

Silence.

Sean was about to ask if she was still on the line when she finally spoke up. "Sean, I'm so sorry you were shot."

"Sweetheart, that wasn't your fault, and besides, I'm fine now." He quickly added, "In fact, my parents persuaded me to stay with them while I mend. Being tired and on the puny side, I let them have their way."

More silence.

"How are you holding up?" he asked.

"You should be resting from what I understand." He loved hearing her soft voice on the other end. "I'm holding. Marissa's arraignment is today..."

"I heard. Will you be going?"

"No, I can't bear to see her just yet. It's still hard to believe that Clara would shoot Marissa. I thought I was the one she disliked. I simply don't understand what brought her to shoot Marissa. It makes no sense."

"When the trial starts, everything will be revealed so you can get the closure you need. But Clara was killed by the SWAT team when she drew a weapon on Marissa, so we won't ever know her side of the story, or for that matter, the boyfriend's story since he died on the way to the hospital. I wished I could see you. I miss you and was hoping you'd return to the hospital before I was released."

"Your parents arrived, and I didn't want to intrude."

"When I leave here, which will be sooner than my parents would like, I want to see you. And besides, I wanted to take you out on a real date now that this case is solved." After a short pause, he added, "And I was hoping that you'd wear that little black number..." he said hopefully.

Michaela laughed. "The one you thought was inappropriate?"

"Mmmmm, that one!"

"What do I get in return?" she asked daringly.

"My heart…"

"And what about your ex-wife? Are you still in love with her?" Michaela took a deep breath and then held it, waiting for his reply.

"I don't think I ever truly loved her," he said hesitantly. "We were married at a very early age, and she was more instrumental in having me go into the police academy instead of the FBI. She wanted me home more and was afraid if I went into the FBI, she'd rarely see me. As it turns out, the police department was no better."

After a pause, he continued, "We fought constantly, and I had her laying down demands and alternatives. Finally, we both had enough and got a divorce."

"Do you have any children?"

"No, thank goodness. She was adamant that if I couldn't be home every night, we wouldn't start a family. The real kicker is she did get pregnant, but when she found out, she got an abortion without telling me. I didn't know about it until afterward. The catalyst that brought our charade of a marriage to an end."

"I'm so sorry… I can't imagine how much that must have hurt…"

"I wanted a family and still wonder how life could be different had she not aborted the baby. But I guess it wasn't met to be."

"Where is she now?"

"She lives in New York with her new husband and three children. And though we ended on bad terms, we eventually came to like one another as mere friends. We rarely speak these days because I'm busy and so is she."

*****

The first week of November found the B&B busy, and Michaela wished more than ever that she had the extra help needed to make it run smoothly. Chase was still reeling and coming to terms with his recent adduction and betrayal by an aunt he dearly loved.

That evening while bent over the desk catching up on paperwork, she felt she was being watched. Glancing up, she spotted one of her guests, a woman that was probably around her age, perusing the gifts adjacent from the office. The woman smiled and resumed picking up items before replacing them.

Finally, Michaela asked if she could be of some help.

"No, thank you," she said. "I'm just looking. Do you make some of the jams you sell?"

"Some but not all," Michaela answered.

"I love how you have things displayed, it's very nice. By the way, I really enjoyed the appetizers you served during the social hour. Do you give away the recipes by chance?"

"I don't mind sharing the recipes, but I haven't had the time to print any to be available for guests. Was there one in particular you'd like to have?"

The woman laughed. "All of them!"

Michaela smiled. "I'll see what I can do for you. You're scheduled to leave day after tomorrow?" She glanced down at her computer and brought up a screen, but before she could look up the information, the woman answered.

"Yes, day after tomorrow. I'd be so grateful, but you could also just email me the recipes if that would be easier than printing them."

Michaela looked up from the screen. "That's even better. Can I use the email provided when you made reservations?"

"Sure!"

Once in the guest room, the woman used her cell to call Sean. "Hey, before you get upset with me, I want you to know that I'm merely performing a request that Mom made and that I have nothing but positive reviews..."

"Karen, where are you and what are you talking about?" Sean asked, clearly puzzled.

"First, mom wanted to know more about Michaela McCrea..." she begun.

Sean exploded. "Where the hell are you and what'd Mom ask you to do?"

"Hold your horses. I'm actually booked at the bed-and-breakfast at Mom's request. Look, John and I wanted to see you anyway, and because you're staying with Mom and Dad, she suggested we book a room at this wonderful little bed-and-breakfast. It wasn't until later we realized exactly what Mom was up to."

"Damn it!" Sean yelled.

"Look, we love the place, it's well-maintained, and for your information, we found Michaela to be quite charming. You have our vote!"

"Your vote? What exactly are you voting for?"

Karen cleared her throat. "After Sheila, you deserve to be happy again, Sean. Michaela is a lovely person, and if you have feelings for her, need I say more?"

"So this little episode was merely to give Mom the skinny on a woman I've fallen for. All of a sudden, I need Mom's approval or blessing? To hell with that…"

"Don't shoot the messenger. We'll be there tomorrow for a family dinner Mom's cooked up. You know Mom. It's not that she's trying to cause problems, she's just worried. You could have been killed, Sean!"

Hanging up, he glared at the cell when there was a soft knock on his old bedroom door. "Sean, are you hungry, dear?" Emma opened the door and peered in. "I heard you yelling. Is everything okay?"

Sean looked up at his mom in exasperation. "It was Karen calling to tell me where she and John are staying at your request to spy on Michaela. Whom I see, who I date, and who I decide to marry is strictly up to me. I appreciate your concern, but I'll have you know. I plan to ask her to marry me."

Emma smiled. "All righty then…"

*****

True to his word, Sean stopped by on a Thursday evening with flowers in hand to take Michaela out for dinner. As requested, she wore the black dress he previously thought revealed far too much. Upon seeing her, his eyes lit up, and his focus lingered on her cleavage, ravaging her with his eyes.

She was embarrassed by the outright display, but it also left her feeling weak with heat flooding her lower parts. When Sean finally raised his eyes to meet hers, she could see the hunger in them. He advanced on her, and raising her chin, he kissed her soundly on the lips, and then his tongue explored, and she parted her lips for him. His tongue was warm and sensual, and when his tongue retreated, she used hers to advance, exploring and delighting in the feel. When they pulled apart, both were breathless.

Michaela turned to grab her wrap when Sean's arms encircled her waist from behind, and she leaned back against his solid frame and sighed. He dipped his head and nuzzled her neck. His hands inched upward until they cupped both of her breasts. Her breathing hitched, enjoying his lovemaking. He gently turned her around in his arms, and cupping her face, he lowered his head. At first, his kiss was gentle, but as the kiss grew, his pressure increased, and his need for her grew.

Michaela pulled away and said, "I guess we're not going to dinner."

When Sean started to protest, she took his hand to lead him up to her bedroom. As they ascended the stairs, Michaela kicked off her heels upon reaching the landing.

"We should wait," Sean whispered. "Do this right…"

"I don't want right, I want you," she whispered back. "Make love to me…"

CHAPTER 38

Riches profit not in the day of wrath.

—Provers 11:4a

The days flew past since Sean's hospitalization and subsequent release into his parents' care. Halloween seemed like a distant memory, and now Thanksgiving was just a couple of weeks away. Usually, this was the time of year Michaela loved most—upcoming holidays, cooler days, leaves falling from the trees creating a colorful display upon the ground. But the festivities this year were marred with Marissa's trial, which lasted but a few days. She should have gotten at least two life sentences. She murdered two men and was responsible for Brad's murder, not to mention kidnapping. Michaela wondered if the people she dealt with would have her murdered while in prison and worried over her fate. Another trial started with the people involved in the black-market trade. Michaela was not called as a witness, for which she was grateful.

Marissa was handed a sentence of twenty-five years. But knowing the judicial system, it meant she'd get out after ten and most likely sooner for good behavior.

Sean and Michaela laid in bed after making love. Satiated, Michaela rested her head in the hollow of Sean's shoulder. She reached up and traced his five-o'clock shadow, confessing she loved his dark whiskers. He in turn touched her dimples and told her how cute they were. She blushed.

"And that too. I love how easy you blush." He laughed.

She in turn ran her palms up and down his bicep and told him she loved the way his muscles bulged in doing simple chores. He smiled and flexed his arm for her, causing them both to laugh.

"I love your petite nose, green eyes, and soft curls," he added, running his fingers through her hair. Pulling a strand closer, he sniffed the fragrance of the tendrils he held in his palm.

Over the course of the last two weeks, they made love several times. While Michaela wrestled with her faith and belief that sex was meant for the marriage bed, her body won over. Her feelings and love for Sean were so great that she doubted she would have kept her resolve to abstain.

She looked over at him now and reached up to rub his five-o'clock shadow with her fingertips. "I still can't believe that Marissa was behind all this," Michaela said, shaking her head. "I thought she was a friend, a sister-in-law who supported me through thick and thin. I must not be a good judge of character. And all this time, she despised me."

Sean reached up and tucked an errant curl behind her ear. "I think you're doing fine on the character assessment. Look at Heather. And don't forget, you were drawn to me…" Sean's smile broadened into a grin when Michaela looked up at him. She smiled and dipped her head, his breath tickling her ear.

"And don't be feeling sorry for Marissa either. Word has it that she's already asked for conjugal visits while in prison."

"What? Who?" Michaela reared back to look Sean square in the eye, clearly surprised by the news.

"Marc Hodges, your pastor. Apparently, they've been having an affair for a couple of years. And one of their weekly rendezvous points is one of the church member's homes in disguise of doing church business." Sean air-quoted.

Michaela let out a gasp. "Pastor Hodges? I just can't believe it. He's married, and he's a preacher!" she added.

Sean laughed. "Was married. According to him, Mrs. Hodges indicated she was going to do something extreme when he talked to her that day. He felt things off and went home to discover the gun safe open and the firearm missing. He thought that Clara was planning to commit suicide. And as for Marissa, after questioning her extensively, she actually is in love with the man, if you can believe that. I mean, how much in love can a person be if they're screwing everyone…" Sean winced and sharply turned his head in Michaela's direction.

"Including my late husband. I just have to believe it really was only the one time, but even that hurts." She clasped her hands together.

Placing his hand over hers, he gently squeezed. "She used everyone including Damon. If she did one thing right and one thing only, it was that she did love Chase and was willing to murder to protect him, and that's exactly what she did," he reminded her.

Tears brimmed and Michaela nodded. "She did. She protected my son with her own life. Do you think I should try to see her?"

"No. And don't get all emotional on her account. I doubt she'd receive you as a visitor. And I doubt Chase has forgiven her for kidnapping him. And quite understandably, I agree with him. He needs time to heal. It was as much a betrayal to him as it was for you."

Michaela nodded. "I guess I should find a new church. I still can't believe that Pastor Hodges was having an affair with Marissa!" She rolled her eyes. "I trusted him too!"

"Love does funny things to a person," he said, thinking back to how many times he could have gotten kicked off this assignment because he fell head over heels, as they say, in love with Michaela. He was attracted to her from the get-go.

"So Marissa admitted she was the one behind the break-in at the bed-and-breakfast as well as the man who chased me the night after I left the restaurant?"

"Yes, and it was Damon who actually chased you. He never intended to catch you, just scare you so badly you'd hand over the package. She even admitted they were so desperate to find that package they ransacked Collins's home, thinking he might have found it first." Sean shook his head. "They were getting pretty desperate toward the end."

"And the car that tailed Heather and I, who was that?" she asked, perplexed.

"Marissa claimed she had nothing to do with that. Our best guess is that it might have been the people whose names were in the file. The mere fact that the car had a tracking device was beyond Marissa and Damon's capabilities. But I have been meaning to ask, how'd Heather realize the car might have a tracking device?"

Michaela laughed. "Don't ask. She watches way too many crime dramas and loves to read."

"She's a good friend and a sweet person. Why isn't she married?"

"Heather? She was married for a while, but her husband's work was moved overseas, and he went unaccompanied. It wasn't long before he found someone else and asked Heather for a divorce. It wasn't pretty! She went back to using her maiden name."

Sean reached out and traced her collarbone with his finger. "You have such soft skin…the type of skin that begs to be kissed." Leaning over, he nibbled at her neck and throat, causing Michaela to moan, letting her head fall back. He nibbled around to the front and then proceeded to kiss downward, covering the swell of her breasts.

"What about the phone calls?" she whispered.

Raising his head, Sean replied, "She admitted that between her and Damon, they wanted to keep you on your toes. Together, they had a schedule so you wouldn't suspect Marissa. They had things pretty well-timed except for taking their dear sweet time in trying to find the missing files. I still don't understand why they didn't try harder in finding them from the beginning." Sean nibbled her at her throat again before pulling her closer. He wanted to feel her and couldn't seem to get enough.

"She told me they made copies. What I don't get is why they destroyed the copies Brad made unless it was pretty obvious that they were copies and not the original files," Michaela speculated.

"I guess we'll never know for sure, but I figure they had someone else they were using to make better copies so they looked authentic. Not being privy to the ongoing trial for those involved in the black-market scam, I have to wonder what caused them to question the copies."

*****

Sean made a date with Michaela for an afternoon, planning to surprise her with a picnic on the beach. Though the weather had turned cool, the days were still sunny, and if need be, they could cuddle up under a blanket.

"Where are we going?" Michaela asked as they walked to Sean's car.

"It's a surprise…" He lifted his brows and smiled mysteriously.

"You're teasing!"

When Sean parked the car on the side of the road giving them beach access, Michaela exclaimed she hadn't been to the beach in a long time.

Sean only smiled and helped her out of the car before opening the trunk to pull out a basket and two blankets, one to recline on and the other to cover up if they needed it.

"A picnic! Oh, Sean, that's so sweet!" Michaela smiled, showing the dimples he hoped to see for a lifetime.

After settling, Sean opened the basket and pulled out two glasses and a bottle of cold champagne.

"Champagne? I haven't had that in years," she confessed. "What's the special occasion? That the case is solved, I'm innocent, and the trial is behind us?" She guessed, laughing as she turned to watch a toddler wander up the beach with his mom in tow.

"Nope." Sean pulled the cork, and the bubble spilled out.

He poured the glasses and handed Michaela one of them. They each took a sip. And then he was reaching for her, pulling her close so they could kiss. His tongue found hers, and the kiss lingered and their breathing grew more labored. When they parted, Sean traced her lips with this forefinger. "I love you…"

Michaela leaned in to him and placed her head on his shoulder. "I love you too!"

They both took another sip of champagne and looked at one another with hunger in their eyes. "Maybe, we should have just gone upstairs at the B&B," she suggested breathlessly.

"I think you make too much noise for that," he ground out, teasing her. "I think the entire neighborhood can hear you," he carried on.

Michaela laughed and slapped him on the upper arm. "I do not!"

CHAPTER 38

"I guess the only thing to do with you is propose and make a decent woman out of you. I mean, Mrs. Hensley asked if you were okay because she heard screaming!"

"Sean! She did not!" Michaela exclaimed, her face turning red with the thought of being overheard.

Sean stood, and when she looked up, he held a small box in his hand and knelt down on one knee in front of her. "Will you marry me?"

Opening the lid of the box, a beautiful diamond set sparkled inside. Michaela put down her glass and turned shimmering eyes to Sean. She threw her arms around his shoulders and was laughing.

"Yes! It sure took you long enough," she added.

Sean removed the engagement ring, and holding up her left hand, he slid the ring onto her finger. "I love you," he said. Picking up their glasses, he refilled both to the top. Holding hers out, she took it, and he toasted to their happiness.

"It's beautiful!" she said, admiring the ring, turning her hand one way and then the other so that the diamond sparkled.

"By the way, I asked Chase for his permission for your hand," Sean said, looking away slightly embarrassed.

"So that's why he's been acting a little strange." She looked up at Sean. "I think my chest is going to explode from the happiness I feel. Oh, Sean!" Tears slipped down her cheeks as she hugged him tightly about the neck.

Pulling away, she asked, "When should we set the date?"

"I was thinking Easter would be ideal, not on Easter itself but spring when new life begins…"

"That's a beautiful thought!"

"And then later, I want to make slow, passionate love to you," he murmured before leaning in to kiss her.

"And I thought this afternoon might be a great time, too, before Chase comes home," she said with a gleam in her eye.

Sean definitely loved this woman!

*****

Michaela just finished checking in guests when Chase walked into the office. "I'm hungry…"

"What sounds good? We have apples and bananas in the fruit bowl, sweetie."

"I'd rather have chips." Looking up at his mom with a troubled gaze, Michaela knew exactly what he needed: time with her.

"Let's fix some hot chocolate and grab some of those cookies I baked yesterday. We can sit down at the kitchen table, just you and me. Sound good?"

His eyes lit up, and he nodded. Picking up Snickers who had followed him into the office, all three filed into the kitchen, and while Michaela made hot chocolate, Chase got the cookies and some napkins.

"So what's on your mind, sweetie?" Michaela asked after they both settled into the kitchen chairs.

"I'm confused. If God is good, why was I kidnapped? I thought he would protect me."

"Free will. God isn't a puppeteer, and he lets everyone have free will to do what they want, be it for good or bad," Michaela answered, taking a sip of hot chocolate.

"But I didn't do anything bad or make a bad choice, Mom, so why did he let Aunt Marissa's decision hurt me?"

"That's a good question, sweetie, but you have to remember that as God allows good and bad things happen to good people, he also allows good and bad things happen to bad people too. And in the Bible, it never says in his word that he will protect his children from bad things. But it does say he'll be with us through those trials."

"Why do you think Aunt Marissa did what she did?" Chase popped a piece of the cookie into his mouth, chewing thoughtfully.

"I wished I knew, but if you recall the Egyptians and how Pharaoh refused to let God's people go and the ten plagues that followed… God used Pharaoh's hardened heart for his ultimate purpose, to free his people. God uses the bad and the good for his purpose. I think he used Marissa's hardened heart to bring about the things that happened, like meeting Detective Ryan and putting bad people behind bars, punishing them for their crimes."

"But if she killed Dad, how's that in God's will?"

"So much has happened in our lives, and while I loved your father very much, I think it was his time." She sighed heavily. This was a deep subject and one not to be treaded lightly.

"If Aunt Marissa asked God for forgiveness, do you think he would forgive her?" he asked with furrowed brows.

"Yes, he would forgive her…"

"How's that fair!" Chase yelled.

"It does seem unfair to us, but while God would forgive her, it doesn't mean she wouldn't be punished for her crimes. It simply means while she must pay for that, God would still forgive her. It doesn't erase what she's done."

"I don't get it. I would really like to give her a piece of my mind, and I wouldn't be using nice words, Mom. Sorry!"

Michaela reached over and tousled her son's hair. He dropped his head and pushed her arm away. "I really am too old for that, Mom."

She laughed. "Indeed you are, and I'm so very proud of you and how you stood up for yourself when you were held hostage. You're becoming a young man."

Chase smiled and dropped his eyes. "Maybe, instead of hot chocolate, I could try some of that wine you serve guests every afternoon."

"I don't think so. You're a long way from that happening!"

"So why are we changing churches?"

"It's time to find a church where the pastor is an upright man to lead the congregation. Pastor Hodges has been led astray, and his focus is no longer on the church I'm afraid."

"What happened?"

"That's a story for when you're older, much older!"

"Oh, Mom, I know a lot more about things than you think. I'm old enough!"

"I'm not!"

Chase's eyes connected with hers, and then he laughed.

"You look grown up…"

EPILOGUE

Standing deep in snow, Michaela peered up at the tall pine as she walked around its circumference. Bundled against the cold, she wore a brown overcoat, mittens, a beanie, and a long scarf to keep her neck warm. She started to call for Sean to tell him she found the perfect tree but knew he probably wouldn't hear her.

Sean had wandered downhill eyeing tree after tree only to discard each for one reason or another. This was their first Christmas together, and he wanted it to be perfect. They set their wedding for April and then changed it to February around Valentine's and then finally January. Between Thanksgiving and Christmas, they found they couldn't keep their hands off each other, and they made love several times. The stolen moments were precious and exciting. He smiled, remembering how Michaela melted in his arms, her soft kisses, passionate nature, and loving embraces.

Once they were married, they made love every chance they were given. Stolen moments in the upstairs office, the shower, and even outside. One night, they even booked themselves into one of the guest rooms and made love throughout the night. Nodding his head, he was enjoying every single moment of married life. They now had the luxury of spending time with one another and finding ways to please each other. And that little number he saw in her closet, she wore it for him, doing a strip tease that left him ready to pounce on her. His smile broadened, thinking that maybe tonight, after decorating the tree, they could make love in front of the fireplace. He could imagine a roaring fire popping and crackling in the hearth, some music, wine, candles, and Michaela stripped naked lying beneath him.

As he peered up at another tree, something hard hit him in the back of the neck. Turning, he saw Michaela laughing. Rubbing the back of his neck, he looked down at the offending snowball. Well, hell, she couldn't have thrown it that far, at least from 90 feet away. He picked it up and found a rock in the middle. Looking up, his brow furrowed, rubbing the back of his neck.

He started toward her with purpose in his stride. Michaela's laughter died upon her lips. Had she actually hurt him? He seemed upset by the scowl on his face. Her upturned lips dipped downward, and worry started to rear its ugly head.

Eighty feet away, and he was bearing down on her. She blanched.

Sixty feet away…

He was definitely mad. She dropped her hands to her sides and wanted to shout that she was sorry, but he looked mad, really mad!

Forty feet away, and he was picking up speed.

Twenty feet away! Michaela didn't hesitate now but turned to run. The snow was thick, and just trying to put one foot in front of the other was a challenge. She could hear the crunch of the snow behind her, and looking over her shoulder, her eyes widened at how close he was.

Ten feet away, and he was gaining ground.

Five feet away, and she could feel his breath on the back of her neck.

Barreling into her with impact, his arms wrapped around her to support her from falling forward, and then soft lips grazed her neck. "You're going to pay for this?" Sean threatened with a laugh.

"Let me go!"

"Never!"

Sean turned her around to face him. His voice softened, and he whispered, "Never!"

Dipping his head, he kissed her lightly upon the lips and repeated. "Never…for as long as I live on the face of the earth."

His kiss warmed her heart and her body. "I have something to tell you," she whispered into his shoulder.

"What?"

Lifting her head, she looked into his gray eyes and reached up to rub his chin with her gloved hand. "We're going to have company come spring."

"What?" He furrowed his brow, looking perplexed. "What do you mean we're having company? Who's coming?"

She laughed. "I mean we're going to have company around the end of May. I think the office space in our private quarters will have to be turned into a nursery." She glanced up at him to gauge his reaction.

At first, he felt dumbstruck. Then as her words sank in, he laughed. "We're going to have a baby?"

She nodded her head. "Are you happy?"

"Am I happy? You've made me the happiest man ever. A baby! We'll have to get a crib, and diapers, and what else do you need for a baby?"

"I have stuff in storage from when Chase was a baby."

"Chase, how do you think he'll handle the news?"

"I think he'll be truly excited."

"In May, that means you're three months along," he calculated. "How long have you known?"

"About a couple weeks. I was trying to figure out the best way to tell you."

Looking down at her in alarm, he said, "You shouldn't be out in this cold, and here I came barreling into you. I didn't hurt you, did I?" he asked in concern as his hands started to feel her stomach and then her arms and torso.

She laughed. "No, you didn't hurt me, and I'm perfectly fine in the cold. Besides, I have a heavy coat on."

"A baby…" he whispered. "Do you already know if it's a boy or girl?"

"Nope, and I don't want to know. Do you?" she asked with a lift of her brows.

"I just want a healthy baby and a happy family. Hell, I want more children. We talked about it but felt we needed time after all that happened. But given our ages, we don't have a lot of time if we plan to add to our family."

"Hey, we're not that old, and who's to say? Maybe, I'll have twins…" she mused with a sly smile on her face.

ABOUT THE AUTHOR

Realizing her lifelong dream of becoming a novelist, Cylinda Mathews is currently traveling the US with her husband, Ron, and two dogs, Marley and Ramsey, in their fifth wheel. They have two grown children and three grandchildren. During their military career, they moved seventeen times in twenty-five years, which is why being a military wife is considered the toughest job in the Navy. With a career in crochet pattern design spanning thirty-five years, she has thousands of published patterns at CrochetMemories.com. Other interests include cooking, gardening, reading, blogging, and crafting.

CPSIA information can be obtained
at www.ICGtesting.com
Printed in the USA
LVHW041327310522
720087LV00003B/93